Evelyn James has always loved the work of writers such as Agatha Christie. She began writing the Clara Fitzgerald series one hot summer, when a friend challenged her to write her own historical murder mystery. Clara Fitzgerald has gone on to feature in over thirteen novels, with many more in the pipeline. Evelyn enjoys conjuring up new plots, dastardly villains and horrible crimes to keep her readers entertained and plans on doing so for as long as possible.

Other Books in The Clara Fitzgerald Series

Memories of the Dead

Flight of Fancy

Murder in Mink

Carnival of Criminals

Mistletoe and Murder

The Poison Pen

Grave Suspicions of Murder

The Woman Died Thrice

Murder and Mascara

The Green Jade Dragon

The Monster at the Window

Murder Aboard Mary Jane

The Missing Wife

The Missing Wife
by
Evelyn James

A Clara Fitzgerald Mystery
Book 13

Red Raven Publications
2018

© Evelyn James 2018

First published as ebook 2018
Paperback edition 2018
Red Raven Publications

The right of Evelyn James to be identified as the Author of this work has been asserted in accordance with the Copyrights, Designs and Patents Act 1988.

All rights reserved. No part of this book may be reprinted or reproduced or utilised in any form or by any electronic, mechanical or other means, now known or hereafter invented, including photocopying and recording, or in any information storage or retrieval system without the permission in writing from the author

Chapter One

Clara sat in her office. It was early March and a fire still burned in the hearth to take off the slight chill that crept into the room. Spring had arrived, but that did not mean they had dispensed with the cold weather just yet.

Clara prided herself on being Brighton's first female private detective, quite an achievement for a young woman, (Clara was only in her twenties) who had to confront male prejudice around every corner. What had begun with humble origins – locating lost pets or investigating stolen flower pots and garden ornaments – had bloomed into a thriving business that enabled Clara to live quite comfortably. That didn't mean it was all peaches and cream, however. The more famous Clara had become and the greater her reputation for solving crimes the police could not, the more she found herself being asked to solve murders and other acts of violence. Tracking down lost cats might have been a little dull, but it rarely involved blood and gore, nor did it present a risk to Clara's own wellbeing.

Not that Clara resented her work; she actually rather enjoyed it, but she was fully aware of its disadvantages. As much as anything, Clara persisted in her line of work to help people. Some inner sense of duty made her agitated at the sight of an injustice.

She was feeling agitated right at that moment as she listened to the tale being told by the good-looking young gentleman, in a dark grey suit, sitting before her desk. He was darkly handsome – brooding, some might say – he had very deeply set brown eyes that glimmered with all manner of secret emotions. He talked well, with a soft Irish accent. He had dressed smartly for his appointment with Clara, imagining he needed to make a good first impression to get her to take the case. Clara rarely turned anyone away, even those who she felt could not afford to pay her. She always moderated her bill in those instances.

The gentleman's name was Dylan Chase. He was a regular in the army and had worked his way up to captain during the last war. He continued to serve after the close of hostilities, explaining to Clara that his male family line were all military men, and someone had to stick around to make sure peace continued. He did not begrudge his career choice, even when it meant spending a great deal of time away from home and his wife.

"We married in 1916," he explained. "Elaine lived with her parents until the war was over, just in case. I have always been a realist and I wasn't sure I would survive the war. I was one of the lucky ones. Nearly five years of conflict and not a scratch, except for the time I fell into a trench and bashed my knee. I sometimes found it unbelievable. Elaine always said I had a guardian angel looking over my shoulder."

Captain Chase paused.

"In all that time, it never occurred to me that it might actually be Elaine who needed a guardian angel."

Captain Chase had been serving at Dublin Castle in Ireland. The British army had stationed men there due to the 'troubles' which had surfaced dangerously during the war. There were those in Ireland who desired for the country to be independent of the rest of Great Britain, self-governing and self-sustaining. However, there were also a lot of people who believed independence would be detrimental to the country and wanted to stay part of the Empire. The whole affair had been complicated by German involvement during the early part of the war. The Germans had tried to send guns to the Irish insurgents, hoping to stir up enough trouble to distract the British from the conflict in Europe. It had almost worked too and, throughout the war, British military units had had to be stationed in the country. A waste of manpower, but there was nothing else for it.

Captain Chase considered himself Anglo-Irish; his mother had been English. He had no qualms fighting his own countrymen to keep Ireland part of Britain. If he felt fractionally betrayed at the government's decision to allow Southern Ireland to become independent, while Northern Ireland remained part of the Empire, he did not make any hint of it. With the signing of the Anglo-Irish Treaty, the British forces in Ireland were slowly being withdrawn. Captain Chase had finished his last tour of duty in Dublin and had returned home on leave, only to discover a new drama in his own front room.

"Elaine had not written any letters for a while, or so it seemed," Chase explained. "I wondered if it was just a case of the letters not reaching me, what with me being in the process of going from Dublin to Bristol. The letters might have been sent to Ireland first and would have to be forwarded to me. It has happened before. I was not perturbed. I wrote Elaine to let her know I would be home soon.

"Since 1919, Elaine and I have lived in a little house on the coast. It is on the outskirts of town and I suppose you might call it remote. Elaine's parents moved to Market Harborough last summer to be nearer to her sister, Julia. Julia lost her husband in the war and has three young children to raise. She also keeps an eye on her mother-in-law who has been very unwell since the death of her son. She lost her own husband to the flu epidemic.

"Elaine and I have no children, not as yet, at least. Elaine's parents thought it best to move nearer to their daughter Julia and assist her, as Elaine and I really don't need any help from them."

Captain Chase came to a halt again. He seemed to become overwhelmed by emotion at points in his story and would have to stop for a while and regroup. Clara was certain that he was a man genuinely in grief, despite what the newspapers had muttered. She knew why Captain Chase was there, she had read about his story, and the speculation that went with it, in the local paper. She had determined, when he first made the appointment to speak to her, to listen to him with an open-mind and not to allow the nasty rumours in the papers to cloud her judgement.

"Elaine sometimes becomes lonely," Captain Chase managed to continue at last. "I encouraged her to become involved in local groups, to make friends. She did. I was certain she was a lot happier, a lot more content. Which made it a terrible shock to walk into my home and find it empty.

"Sitting on the doormat were my last two letters, dated from the previous Friday and Sunday. They had never been opened, never been noticed as far as I could tell. There was no sign of anything sinister. Elaine's clothes were in the wardrobe, her best hat and coat hung on the hall stand. Our old suitcase, the one I inherited from my parents and we used for holidays, was still under the bed. On the kitchen table was a half-written shopping list and the previous Friday's newspaper was sitting beside it. Elaine had circled an advertisement for a fabric sale at the local department store. She had been thinking of making up some new curtains for the front room, she had written to me about it in a letter and asked if I was happy with her spending the money. I had written back to say she should go ahead.

"At the kitchen sink, the dishes had been washed and were sitting on the draining board waiting to be dried and put away. Only they were all bone dry and had clearly been there for some time. The chickens in the back garden had been let out of their little house and never put away for the night. Sadly, a fox had killed most of them. The more I looked about our house, the more I saw signs that made me feel that Elaine had just popped out for a moment. Yet, for some reason, she had failed to return."

Captain Chase pinned Clara with his intense dark eyes. They glistened with emotion, as if at any point this stoic army man might breakdown and cry.

"You must have seen what the newspapers have been saying about all this?" He queried.

"I have," Clara admitted.

"I went to the police about an hour after I arrived home. It was the letters on the doormat that convinced me something was wrong. If Elaine had popped out that morning, why would the letters from Friday and Sunday still be sitting on the doormat? And the chickens, they made me stop and think. Elaine adored those birds. She would not have left them out for the night, to be picked off by a fox, unless she had been completely unable to get to them.

"I told the police all this and they came to my home. They poked around and said there was no sign of any crime having been committed. Then they asked me if Elaine's handbag was missing. I said I thought it was, along with her everyday coat and hat. They seemed to decide then and there that Elaine had merely walked out on me. There was no evidence of her being attacked and they didn't believe me when I said our marriage was solid. Of course, it was not long after that, the newspapers picked up on the story."

Chase grimaced bleakly and Clara could understand why. The Brighton newspapers had not only picked up the story of his wife's disappearance but had run away with it. They ran articles on Elaine Chase, discussing her last known movements and talking to those who knew her. At first, they merely supposed she had deserted her husband. A few spurious letters from 'Elaine' claiming she was in various parts of the country (and one even purporting she was in India) were sent to the media and reprinted. Adding to the speculation. Each of these 'Elaines' proved no more than someone with more time than sense on their hands. As the mystery deepened and no genuine sightings of Elaine could be discovered, the press began to turn its attention to a darker possibility. It was not long before the papers were printing speculative articles concerning the idea that Elaine had been murdered. The natural next step was to point an accusing finger at Captain Chase. Despite the fact Elaine had vanished while he was in Ireland, the rumour began to spread that Chase was a killer. People thought he had perhaps arrived in Brighton a day sooner than he claimed, had done away with his wife, and then made up the story about her disappearance.

It was all beginning to verge on the precipice of slander; one woman even came forward and claimed to be Captain Chase's long-term mistress. Until it was proved that the woman was actually a middle-aged housewife in Yorkshire, who could not identify Chase from a selection of pictures, the local gossip was that Chase had murdered his wife so he could marry this mistress.

All of this Chase had endured with fortitude. He had not made a fuss, hoping that the attention to his case might at least reveal fresh information about where his wife was. The days had ticked by; no explanation for Elaine's disappearance was forthcoming. Captain Chase had begun to give up hope, and then he had remembered an advertisement he had seen in the back of one of those newspapers that discreetly called him a murderer. It was an advertisement for Clara Fitzgerald, private detective.

"The newspapers have labelled me a killer," Chase said. "I do not even care about that. All I care about is finding Elaine. She did not desert me, and I certainly did not harm her. I am at the end of my tether with all this. The police seem to have lost interest. I fear I will never find her at this rate."

Captain Chase fumbled in his pocket and produced a

letter. It had been folded and unfolded a number of times and was disintegrating at the creases. He held it tentatively out to Clara.

"This is the last letter Elaine sent me. There is a subtle reference to being uneasy about something. I thought maybe it was important?"

Clara took the letter and read it. Largely it contained mundane news that was only of interest to the recipient, however, just at the bottom, before a paragraph on cleaning the range, Elaine had written a cryptic few sentences.

All is going well at rehearsals, but I have this strange feeling, so hard to describe it. Foreboding sounds too dramatic, and yet it is rather like that. Maybe it is because we are working on the Scottish Play and everyone is talking superstitious rot, but I keep feeling that something might happen. Something bad. But, you know how I talk such nonsense sometimes! I should not have even written that, it is probably pre-performance nerves. I hope you will be back for the first night. I am very excited.

"Elaine had joined an amateur dramatics group to make new friends. They are performing Macbeth and Elaine will play Lady Macbeth. If she comes back..." Chase drifted away for a moment, his mind elsewhere. Then he glanced back. "It is Elaine's first big part. She was nervous and I put down her talk of foreboding to that. But what if it was something else? This letter is the only tangible clue I have to what happened to my wife, and even then it is really nothing at all. The police are not interested."

"The police have a lot of cases on their plate and limited manpower," Clara said, feeling the need to defend them. "They have a tendency to put cases that look challenging to solve to one side rapidly."

"I am convinced my wife is alive," Chase added. "And I think she is in trouble. She was last seen at a rehearsal for the play. She said she was going to buy some bread before walking home. Something happened to her during that time."

Captain Chase hesitated.

"I can understand if you do not care to take on this case. The police have already explained to me that there is nothing to work with, no clues, no motive, nothing. If you feel the same…" Chase tailed off.

"Captain Chase," Clara said gently. "I am not the police. I have a great respect for those who bring law and order to our country, but I am aware of their shortcomings. I shall investigate this matter for you, but I cannot promise anything. Your wife may be dead, I have to make plain this possibility. But I will do all in my power to provide you with an answer."

"Thank you, Miss Fitzgerald," Captain Chase sighed. "I know my wife is alive, and I know you will find her!"

Clara said no more. She did not make hopeless promises.

Chapter Two

Annie came to know the Fitzgeralds during the war. She had been in the hospital where Clara was serving as a volunteer nurse. Annie had lost her family when a zeppelin dropped incendiary bombs on their home. She had never known such devastation; the emotional trauma had nearly been the end for her. A chance friendship with Clara had led to new things, a lucky circumstance for them both. Clara's brother Tommy had been due to come home from the front. He had been severely injured and was crippled, at least temporarily. Clara needed help looking after him and it had been agreed that Annie would join the Fitzgeralds as a nurse for Tommy.

Before long Annie realised that Clara needed more than just a nurse for her brother. Clara was an intelligent and resourceful woman, but a hopeless cook and even worse at organising the mundane running of a household – such as getting the washing done and making sure the rugs were beaten. Annie, who admitted to herself freely that she liked a home spick and span, could not resist slowly taking over each task Clara was clearly struggling with. Eventually Annie had slipped into the role of housekeeper with no one really noticing. She cooked, she cleaned and, above all, she kept an eye on the Fitzgerald siblings who seemed (to her at least) hopelessly prone to getting themselves into trouble.

The years had merged. Annie loved the house and enjoyed her role within it. With all the talk of women's independence and taking over men's work, Annie sometimes felt she was old-fashioned for liking a spot of housework, but she could not help herself. There was something intrinsically satisfying about the sunshine glowing through a newly cleaned window, or a freshly blackened fire grate that looked as good as new. She would rather be cleaning than doing Clara's work, anyway. She could see nothing pleasurable or satisfying in tracking down thieves and murderers. In fact, she thought it rather grim and was rather disapproving of Clara's career choice. Not least because it often meant Clara was late for dinner.

Annie considered herself a very fine cook. She could whip up a steak and kidney suet pudding that would make a man's eyes water. There was a power in that pudding. Annie could have cooked for bigger households, wealthier ones where her work would be similarly rewarded, but she would not leave Clara and Tommy. One of the things that made her happiest was ensuring they were well fed. Clara sometimes griped that she was getting too stocky and would have to cut back; Annie ignored her. A woman shouldn't be too skinny, in Annie's opinion, it was unhealthy.

The war had put a slight cramp on her style. Food was rationed, especially goods such as sugar and butter. Anything exotic, such as dried fruit, was virtually impossible to purchase. Annie had felt the restrictions the most when she thought about making a cake. Annie loved cake and she could make a sponge so light it seemed to float off the plate. Annie had felt bereft during the hard years of conflict, when she could not whip up a stunning fruit cake for a birthday or Christmas, at least not without a lot of effort in sourcing and stockpiling ingredients. Annie considered this one of Germany's worst crimes – to deprive the nation of cake. She had been known to curse their name when considering her sugar supply.

Fortunately, that was all in the past. The war had ended, though for a couple of years certain goods were either still rationed or so expensive they were only affordable to the rich. Slowly prices were falling and it was now possible to buy dry fruit at a reasonable price, and Annie could have as much sugar and butter as she liked. For the dedicated cook, this was paradise.

Annie's only slight niggle, (and it was truly slight) was that her cakes were largely indulged in by only Clara and Tommy, and of course Clara's friend Captain O'Harris. While they were appreciative of her work, Annie had a desire to share her talents further. She wanted more people to taste her cakes and to be delighted. Annie's mother would have called it pride. Annie didn't care, she wanted people to know she was capable of making the best cake in Brighton.

Especially that Jane Jenkins who worked three doors down and had a habit of reminding everyone that she had won the best fruit scone prize for three years running before the war.

Annie had never won a prize for her cooking. She had never even entered a competition and Jane had a knack for bringing that up in most of their conversations.

It was a minor blip in the scheme of things, but it gave Annie the odd restless night. Which was why she had been truly jubilant when she read in the Brighton Gazette that the town's spring gala would include a cookery competition. Prizes would be awarded to the best bread loaf, best meat pasty, best fruit cake and best Victoria sponge. Annie felt her eyes widen as she realised this was her chance to shove Jane Jenkins best scones, metaphorically, down her throat. Annie wanted to enter all the classes, sweep the board, but after the first flush of enthusiasm passed, she realised she ought to concentrate on one category and make the best effort she could on one single cake, rather than spread her talents over too many baked goods. She opted for best Victoria sponge, knowing that was her speciality.

The rules for the competition, as outlined in the newspaper, were stringent. Everything must be homemade, including the jam for the sponge. Annie thought that obvious; shop-bought jam was simply inedible, as far as she was concerned, and you could not possibly make a prize-winning cake with it. Annie had nurtured some strawberries in the Fitzgeralds' garden and towards the end of the summer she had gathered them in great quantities to make a large batch of jam. She hastened to the larder after reading the newspaper announcement and confirmed to herself that two jars of that jam remained. Tommy loved jam on his toast in the morning and he went through Annie's hoard like there was no tomorrow. She hid one of the remaining jars behind a large sack of flour. She knew Tommy raided her larder when he thought she was not looking – as if Annie did not have a full inventory in her head of everything on the shelves!

The jam secured, Annie went through all her other supplies. She had a great deal of flour, but she could run through that at surprising speed; pastry, bread and, of course, cakes, all required the staple and she used it up on a weekly basis. She decided she ought to buy another bag just to be on the safe side. The cake competition was in a couple of weekends, she would want to practice beforehand, just to make sure she was at her finest. Her sugar stock was running low and she made a mental note to shop for more. Eggs were supplied by the hens she had also introduced to the Fitzgerald garden, however, they could be fickle layers in the unpredictable spring weather. Annie decided to save their beautiful, golden yolk eggs for her cake, and buy in a supply of eggs for the household. That left butter, which Annie always sourced from a local farm.

Satisfied that she would have the very best ingredients for her cake, Annie went to work on a practice sponge.

She had a stock of blackberry jam (the blackberries gathered from the bushes down by the railway embankment) which she would use for the filling. Deciding to be creative, she took an old apple from her store and cut it into slices. These she gently poached before laying them into the base of her sponge tin. When the cake was baked and turned over, the apples would be decorating the top. Apple and blackberry sponge sounded delightful.

Annie set to work creaming together her butter and sugar. It was a tough job that required a good deal of vigorous beating of the ingredients with a wooden spoon. Annie paced the kitchen back and forth as she worked, glancing out of the window at the sunlight in the garden. Spring always made her feel renewed and she took a deep breath and smiled.

The very next moment she came to a halt, let go of the spoon and pressed a hand to her side. She had a pain jabbing her, rather like a stitch from running too hard. She pressed her fingers deep into her side, forcing the pain to retreat. Slowly it eased. Annie shook her head. She must have pulled something, perhaps when she was cleaning out the chicken house yesterday. Going back to the satisfying work of creaming butter and sugar, she set to with her wooden spoon once more.

She was thinking of the look on Jane Jenkins' face when she won best Victoria sponge. Her smile had returned. A second later so did the stabbing pain in her side. This time it was worse, forcing Annie to put down her mixing bowl and to stand with one hand clutching the edge of the stone sink, while the other pressed into her side. She tried to take a deep breath, but the griping pain wouldn't let her. She closed her eyes and counted to ten.

Annie had had similar pains before. Once or twice as a girl she had been laid up in bed for a couple of days with an ache that felt like someone was stabbing her with a knife in the side. The pains had always passed and it was years since she had last experienced them. Now her biggest concern was that she might be forced to rest up, as she had been instructed by the doctor as a child. Annie was too busy to rest.

The pain retreated once more, but her side felt tender, as if it had left a bruise. Annie took a few moments after the pain had gone to restore herself. For the moment she felt unable to carry on with her cake making. She needed some fresh air.

Annie stepped outside into the back garden. The sun was warming this side of the house. She enjoyed the warmth falling onto her and relaxed further. The chickens clucked at her optimistically, they each had a name and Annie was convinced they all had unique personalities. She smiled at them and the pain seemed to drift into memory.

"Scared myself for a second there," she told the chickens with a laugh.

Annie fingered her side, poking at the formerly sore spot to see if anything would happen. Nothing did. The mysterious pain had disappeared as fast as it had come. Annie was about to go inside when she heard her name being called.

Looking over the low fence that separated the Fitzgerald garden from the one next door was Mrs McGree. She was an older woman with grown children whose renown for knowing all the local gossip had ensured she and Annie were firm friends. Annie felt it was wrong to gossip about other people, so she never did it herself. But that didn't mean she couldn't listen to what Mrs McGree was saying. Listening to gossip and spreading it were two very different things. Besides, Annie could not be rude and ignore the woman, could she?

Annie strolled over to the fence.

"Good morning."

"Fine morning," Mrs McGree agreed merrily. "Have you had the paper yet?"

"I was just reading it," Annie nodded.

"Did you see the notice about the cooking competition?"

"I did."

Mrs McGree's face burst into a big grin.

"Now there is a fine thing! I am entering the meat pasty class, I make a wicked beef and potato pasty. My husband says he could eat nothing but and be a happy man. Which class are you entering?"

There was clearly no doubt in Mrs McGree's mind that Annie would be entering the competition.

"I was going to enter the Victoria sponge category," Annie said promptly.

Mrs McGree rolled her eyes and tutted.

"Ach, you have entered the toughest class! You know, gal, everyone enters the Victoria sponge section."

"I don't mind competition," Annie said, priding herself that she could outclass anyone else's sponge making skills.

"That may be, but you know who else is entering that class?" Mrs McGree said.

Annie hesitated before saying;

"Who?"

"Only Miss 'best scones of 1911, 1912 and 1913' Jane Jenkins herself."

Annie hesitated for only a moment.

"That doesn't worry me, no one can beat my sponge."

Mrs McGree smiled broadly again.

"That there is fighting talk, and I like to hear it! Me, I don't care for such stiff competition. The meat pasty category will be under represented, I say, and most will opt for a standard Cornish pasty as their entry. I shall cook the finest beef and potatoes anyone has ever laid their gums upon, and the gentlest, tastiest of water pastries to encase them in. But you, my gal, you are setting yourself up for a big challenge."

Annie was undeterred. The more people she had to go up against, the more satisfying would be the accomplishment of winning.

"Here, will you try one of my pasties when I have made them and give your honest opinion?" Mrs McGree said, a sudden look of uncertainty crossing her face. "Normally only Mr McGree eats them. You might spot something he won't."

"I can do that," Annie said. "We can do an exchange. I'll try your pasties, you try my sponge."

"Sounds perfect, now, I must get back to my washing. I have far too much to do, as always."

They exchanged farewells and Annie headed back to the house, feeling revived and ready for action. If Jane Jenkins thought she could produce a better sponge than Annie, she was soon to discover she was sorely mistaken. Jane might have the way with scones – Annie would give her that, as she was not a fan of fruit scones – but she could not possibly have the 'touch' with sponge as well. No, Annie was certain she would win that category hands down.

Grabbing up her mixing bowl, she became to beat vigorously again. She only paused once, just to prod her side once more and see if anything happened. Nothing did. Whatever had caused the pain was gone. Relieved, Annie pounded the butter and sugar, humming to herself as she went.

In two weekends, she was going to show all of Brighton what her cakes were made of. She could hardly wait.

Chapter Three

Captain Chase had given Clara the name of the theatre group his wife had been rehearsing with. As far as he knew, they were the last people to have seen her before she disappeared. Chase could offer no clue as to why his wife might have voluntarily vanished; their marriage was happy and she seemed content. Clara knew, however, that what one person perceived as happy and content, could be a sign of misery and discontent in another. She was not ruling out the possibility that Mrs Chase had departed of her own accord, despite appearances suggesting to the contrary.

The theatre group was known as the Brighton Players and they had the use, as a theatre, of an old Methodist chapel. The seating for the congregation provided space for an audience and a specially constructed stage with wings at the head of the chapel gave the actors room to perform whatever they wished. Currently they were working on Macbeth. Captain Chase had been slightly dismissive of what he had seen when he went to the chapel to look for his wife.

"They have 'updated' it. Elaine said as much in a letter to me. It is no longer set in Glamis castle, but in a modern luxury mansion. I felt it had lost some of the atmosphere of the piece when I watched them. The stage was set with armchairs and a gramophone. Macbeth was wandering about in a dinner jacket and with a cocktail in his hand. It all seemed to be making a mockery of Shakespeare."

Clara reserved judgement. She knew that actors, amateur or otherwise, liked to place their mark upon their work, and with a piece like Macbeth that could be difficult. She supposed that bringing it up-to-date was the way the Brighton Players were trying to make this rendition of the Scottish play different from all the rest. Whether it would work or not was another matter.

Captain Chase informed Clara that the players had only two weeks before their first night and were putting in extra rehearsal time. The disappearance of Lady Macbeth at such a crucial moment was causing a good deal of consternation. Her under-study had stepped in, but was proving forgetful in her lines and there was a slight panic she would not be ready for opening night. The group had been coming together in the late afternoon for further practice. Clara was hopeful she would be able to catch most of the group together at one of these.

She arrived at the chapel and pressed down the handle of the big wooden double-doors. They had been painted a bold blue with two theatrical masks – one sad, one happy – outlined in black. The door opened without protest and Clara stepped into the chapel. To accommodate a reasonable audience, the seating swept nearly to the doors. On a busy evening, with patrons trying to hurry to get in, Clara could imagine things getting rather tight. Directly in front of her was a central aisle that ran straight as an arrow down to the stage. People were on the stage going through lines. Others were sat in chairs near the front. Several looked around as she entered. Clara could see their puzzled looks; she was unexpected and unrecognised.

However, no one bothered to get up and see what she

wanted, so Clara started down the aisle. She passed a woman who had a dress spread out on some chairs and a mouthful of pins. She glanced up at Clara without really seeing her, too busy with whatever alteration she was in the middle of. Clara gave her a polite smile nonetheless.

As she reached the front row of seats, a woman, who had been watching her progress, spoke up.

"This is a private rehearsal. The chapel is no longer open for worship."

Her tone was snide. Clara ignored it and slipped into the seat directly behind her.

"I am not a Methodist," she informed her politely. "I was hoping to have a chat with your group about Elaine Chase."

The name caused several others, who had been concentrating on the stage, to now turn around. Clara counted fifteen people sitting in the front seats, on the stage were three others. The dresser further back up the aisle brought the total to nineteen.

"My name is Clara Fitzgerald. I have been asked to look into Mrs Chase's disappearance."

"Why would you do that?" The stern woman who had first confronted her demanded. She glowered at Clara like some sort of incensed watch-dog.

"I am a private detective," Clara explained.

There were looks of uncertainty and surprise on the faces of the others. Some started to whisper to each other.

"Who are you?" Clara asked the woman before her. She had taken a dislike to her, but that did not alter the pleasantness of her tone.

"Wendy Cropper," the woman declared. "Stage manager."

"Were you around the last time Mrs Chase visited the players?"

"I was," Wendy informed her. "It was one of our Saturday morning rehearsals. I can't say we spoke. Her disappearing has made life very difficult."

"For her husband, yes," Clara replied, still polite but

wanting to remind the woman that there was more to this drama than a play.

"Did you say you are investigating her disappearance?" An older man, sitting on the other side of the aisle, asked Clara.

"I am," Clara told him. "I hope to discover where Mrs Chase is. Her husband hopes she is safe."

"She has left him, of course," Wendy Cropper snorted. "Could have waited until after the performance though. I protested her choice as Lady Macbeth, I said she was unreliable."

Wendy Cropper appeared to be the spokesperson for the small band, for better or worse. No one else was countering her unpleasant opinions, though some looked grim.

"What mood was Mrs Chase in when you all last saw her?" Clara asked the group.

Wendy, of course, was the first to speak.

"Not a sign of anything. Quite the cold fish that one. Secretive, that's it. She made no indication that she was going to run off. I find it disgraceful, she has left us in a dreadful position."

Clara did not even respond, she glanced around at the others, hoping someone else would offer something more useful. They were all silent.

"Dear me!" Clara declared. "For a lot of actors you are very quiet! One of your number goes missing directly after a rehearsal and none of you have anything to say."

"I…" Wendy started to bleat.

Clara interrupted her, smiling politely.

"I was not referring to you, you have been most forthcoming," she said. "It appears no one else in your group has a voice, however."

Wendy Cropper frowned, but she was too dense to take any offence at Clara's words. She didn't realise that Clara had been slyly inferring that her outspoken nature was overshadowing everyone else.

"Perhaps you do not want to speak up in public?" Clara

suggested to the actors. "I tell you what. I shall go sit quietly at the back of the chapel, you carry on with your rehearsal, and if any of you want to have a private word with me you can come over."

"I..." Wendy began again.

"Oh, my dear, I know you have no issue talking publicly and have already been most informative. Please do not feel you must depart from your work here to speak with me," Clara said firmly.

Wendy Cropper took this as a compliment.

"I have no problem speaking my mind. People are far too shy about such things, you know."

"I know," Clara told her, before walking away, trying not to laugh.

She sat at the back of the chapel and waited. The three actors on stage went back to rehearsing. They seemed on edge, but Clara was not sure if that was due to her presence or recent events. They had their scripts in their hands and kept stumbling over their lines. Clara thought they seemed ill-prepared for their fast approaching opening night. She had always enjoyed the theatre and had attended a number of performances of Shakespeare's better-known plays. She had watched Macbeth twice at the theatre – once in London, once in Brighton. She had also been present at an outdoor performance in the gardens of the Brighton Pavilion. It reminded her to bring up at the next Brighton Pavilion Committee meeting that they should do something similar in the summer. The committee was always trying to raise funds to enable them to keep up the repairs to the old building – it was a constant chore.

Clara was mulling over just what play would bring in a suitable crowd, when the dresser wandered over. She had a cup of tea in her hands.

"Thought you might like this," she offered it to Clara.

"Thank you," Clara was delighted to see there was someone friendly in the group. "You deal with the costumes here?"

"Someone has to," the woman chuckled. "Maureen Brown. I don't act, but I am good with a needle."

Having introduced herself, Maureen sat down beside Clara.

"Wendy is a thick-headed, mean-hearted hag," she said. "And that is putting things nicely."

"I rather got that impression when I spoke to her."

"She has to be the worst addition to this group we have ever had," Maureen continued. "She joined about a year ago and somehow managed to get the position of stage manager. She harangued the last stage manager until he resigned and she jumped into his post. I fear she will be the end of our little group."

"That would be a shame," Clara said honestly. "You should not allow one person to spoil things for everyone else."

"The trouble is, no one will speak up to her," Maureen sighed. "At least no one with any clout. I am just the dresser, no one listens to me. But if Mr Mitchell, our director, was to say something, I am sure everyone would side with him. But he is looking for an easy life and that is that."

"I am sorry to hear that," Clara said genuinely. She had joined the Brighton Pavilion Committee at a time of similar turbulence. Two of the members had begun to dominate the committee, preventing others from speaking up by belittling their opinions and making their own crass decisions whether the rest of the committee agreed with them or not. They were in serious danger of breaking up the committee and putting the pavilion back under threat of being sold and demolished. Clara had stepped in at just the right moment and dealt with them firmly. They had both resigned within a month and the committee was functioning efficiently and productively once again.

"I thought it might have been because of Wendy that Elaine upped and left," Maureen continued, she was watching the others on the stage with a sad glint to her eyes. "Elaine and Wendy clashed a lot."

"What about?" Clara asked.

"Simply everything," Maureen explained. "From what play the group should put on next, to set and costume design. Even the price of seat tickets once. Whatever Elaine said, no matter how sensible or rational, Wendy instantly countered it. She is that sort of person."

"How did Elaine take all this?"

"With grace at first. She was not the sort to storm into a full-blown argument, but you could see it was wearing her down. The last straw was when she was cast as Lady Macbeth. Wendy was away at the time, sick with a nasty cough. Dare I say, some of us hoped for her not to recover?"

Maureen snorted in amusement at the callousness of the statement.

"Anyway, when she did return she was irate Elaine had the part. She wanted Sarah to play Macbeth. Sarah is her little lapdog, you see."

Maureen nodded to the stage where a young girl was stumbling over her lines. This was the aforementioned Sarah. She presented her dialogue in a flat tone with no apparent attempt to imbue the words with emotion.

"Sarah is Wendy's niece and she can do no wrong," Maureen said with deep disapproval. "Wendy insisted she be made Elaine's under-study. The others agreed for an easy life. None of us imagined she would ever actually get on that stage."

"Did you see Elaine at that very last rehearsal?" Clara asked.

"I did," Maureen gave a strange smile. "I wish now I had spoken to her properly. Maybe I could have prevented her from disappearing, I don't know. I was so busy with my work. We are going to have a number of costume changes during the performance and there are so many alterations to be made."

"How did Elaine seem?"

"Just the same as always," Maureen shrugged. "I have

been thinking about things ever since she vanished, asking myself if there was some sign in her demeanour that day. But, she seemed perfectly fine. She came in, said hello, and went straight onto the stage to begin practice."

"Was there tension between her and Wendy?"

"No more than usual," Maureen replied. "I know Elaine was feeling pleased at being chosen for Lady Macbeth. She was intending to make it the best performance she had ever done, so as to rub Wendy's nose in it. She wanted people talking about her Lady Macbeth."

Maureen was quiet a moment, watching Sarah strut about on stage with her wooden acting and hopeless ability to remember her lines.

"Elaine, if anything, was feeling triumphant. She is tough, she was not one to be cowed by Wendy. That was why they were at loggerheads."

"Then, from your perspective, there seemed no reason for Elaine to simply vanish?"

Maureen shook her head sadly.

"Elaine never said a word to me."

"Did she ever talk about her husband?"

"Yes. She often mentioned him. She was looking forward to him being home soon," Maureen clamped her lips together. "The papers insinuate he killed her."

"Yes," Clara said noncommittally.

"He wouldn't have asked you to investigate her disappearance if that was the case," Maureen added.

Clara kept mute. Stranger things had happened, though her instinct was that Captain Chase was not a killer, at least not of his wife.

"Wendy has enjoyed sneering about Elaine going missing. It made her day."

"Was there anything worrying Elaine?"

"Not that I know of," Maureen sighed. "I am really being most unhelpful. But, honestly, she walked in here right as rain that morning, and walked out with a smile on her face. She had just put on one of the best performances of Lady Macbeth I have seen in a long time. I think she would have made this play. Now…"

They both looked up as Sarah tripped over her lines once again.

Chapter Four

Maureen's commentary on Elaine's disappearance, while not obviously insightful, did tell Clara one thing – it seemed highly unlikely that Elaine was planning on disappearing. When people intend to vanish, they imply it in their looks and gestures, in their words and their actions. They might start to distance themselves from activities or to take less interest in the things they normally enjoyed. There was always some indication, even if it was only really recognised after the person had departed.

People did not runaway when they were happy in their life, that was obvious. If Elaine had been depressed or unhappy then her disappearance might be explained by her suddenly tiring of her life. That had not been the case. Elaine had, as far as Maureen could see, been content with her lot. In fact, she had been on top of the world the day she left the theatre for the final time. Elaine had every reason to remain in Brighton, and apparently none to leave.

That left a handful of possibilities; something occurred so suddenly that she was forced to vanish on the spur of the moment with no planning or forethought; some unexpected accident befell her; or someone decided that

Elaine had to disappear and they chose that particular day to act.

Clara was very worried about that third possibility.

"Miss Fitzgerald?"

Clara had been lost in her thoughts, now she glanced up and saw that an older gentleman had approached her. He had the appearance of a bank manager in his brown suit and tie. He was not very tall and a tad stout, his head seeming to have crashed down on his shoulders, leaving no room for his neck. He was almost bald except for a semi-circle of dark brown hair just above his ears. He had a permanently worried expression on his face.

"Please, sit," Clara invited him to take the chair next to her.

The man hesitated for a fraction of a second, his hands were clasped together and his fingers tapped each other, then he sighed and sat down.

"I am Laurence Mitchell, the director of this small company," he introduced himself.

"Pleased to meet you," Clara replied politely.

"I see you met Maureen. She is a very clever needlewoman, an asset to this company if ever there was one," Laurence breathed heavily through his nose, it was almost a sigh. Clara wondered if the implication was that there were a few members who were not particular assets to the company.

"Maureen was telling me a little about Elaine. Apparently, she was a rather good Lady Macbeth?"

"She was," Laurence nodded, his enthusiasm suddenly sparked. "Unlike…"

He stopped himself, but his frown towards the stage spoke volumes.

"Elaine had only been with the company a short while and had undertaken minor roles up until now. I saw she had potential and ought to be given a better part in the next play we staged. I proposed her for Lady Macbeth. Myself and the producer always choose the cast and allot roles. It saves arguments. Actors are rarely objective about their own abilities," Lawrence looked like a man who suffered greatly in his role as director. Clara could only imagine the complications his responsibilities brought to his life.

"I have already met your stage manager," Clara said sympathetically.

Laurence scowled, there was no mistaking his expression.

"I regret the day we allowed her to join the company. Our last stage manager had retired through ill-health, we were somewhat desperate for a replacement. None of the cast wanted to take on the role as it means being unable to perform on stage. Wendy had recently joined what we call our 'friends of the Brighton Theatre Company'. They are people who support us and assist with promoting our plays and fundraising for things like printing posters and repairs to the theatre. We do not make vast sums from our ticket sales and are always strapped for cash."

Laurence gave a little laugh at this assessment and Clara was now convinced that he was an actual bank manager.

"Wendy put herself forward as stage manager when she heard we needed one and, I am sorry to say, we jumped at the chance. We never really considered whether she was suitable or not," Lawrence smiled sadly. "Now we are regretting our rash decision. She is divisive and at times rather nasty. I am certain she has noted that I am talking with you and will lambast me for it later."

"Why not remove her from the company?" Clara suggested. "You are the director."

"I suppose, but that is the problem with being an amateur group. Things are rather informal. I am not sure precisely how to get rid of her. We could tell her to leave, but she does not have to and we have no real power to remove her."

Clara would not have allowed that to stop her, had she been director, but she was not and she was beginning to see how Wendy had ended up running the show, metaphorically speaking.

"In contrast, Elaine was a godsend," Laurence continued. "Elaine is clever, diplomatic and a damn good actress. There was no hesitation casting her as Lady Macbeth, though Wendy made a fuss when she learned of it. She and Elaine have exchanged sharp words more than once. Elaine will stand no nonsense from Wendy."

"Good for her," Clara said, glad there was at least one person prepared to stick their neck out. "Her disappearance must have come as a shock."

"It did," Laurence agreed. "We met here on the Saturday morning. The rehearsal went exceptionally smoothly, I was truly delighted. We finished just before midday. I announced that we should all gather again the following afternoon for a quick run through and everyone was in agreement. Elaine said her farewells and walked out the door. That was the last I saw of her."

"She made no indication she would not be available for the next rehearsal?"

"None at all," Laurence said firmly. "She was smiling as she left. She had given such a moving performance. I was feeling ecstatic about everything."

"Who left immediately after Elaine?"

Laurence gave this some thought, before he shook his head regretfully.

"I am really not sure. I was running through some logistical details with Thomas, our producer. I do recall, at one point, looking about for Wendy as I needed to discuss some stage directions and I was annoyed that she was one of the first to leave. She is supposed to wait and discuss the rehearsal with us, so we can go through any technical arrangements we might need to change or improve. But she always hurries off. Last to arrive, first to leave. That is her style."

Laurence cast an evil look at the back of Wendy's head. Clara thought it a shame the man could not manage to be more forthright to her face.

"When did you realise Elaine was missing?" Clara

asked.

"The next afternoon, when she failed to arrive for rehearsals," Laurence answered. "That was most unlike her. I was concerned immediately. She would have sent word if she was unwell. We gave her half-an-hour and then I sent John Oakes to her house to see what was the matter. It is quite a walk, but he has a bicycle. He returned and told us that he could get no answer at her door. He had looked in the windows and no one seemed to be about. He noticed that the chickens had been left out all night and the fox had got to them. That seemed very strange. Elaine was not the sort of person to be that careless."

"You were worried then?"

"Yes, instantly," Laurence's brow furrowed into deep lines of concern. "I called a halt to rehearsals and said I thought we ought to go to Elaine's house and take a look. She lives on her own, you see, as her husband is in the army and her parents moved away to help her widowed sister take care of her children. If something had happened to Elaine, no one would know."

"Everyone agreed to abandon rehearsals and go look for Elaine?"

"All except for one," Laurence rolled his eyes. "Need I say who that was?"

"Hardly," Clara smiled. "What happened during the search?"

"We discovered that Elaine had not locked her back door. The front, yes, but not the back. Who does? We went in and called out for her. I thought that perhaps she had been taken suddenly ill. But there was no one inside the property. After that we were slightly stumped. Elaine's home is remote and there are no neighbours who we could speak to. In the end, we all agreed we ought to summon the police."

"What did you think might have happened?" Clara asked him.

Laurence again considered his answer before speaking.

"I could only come to one conclusion, that Elaine had disappeared at some point on her way home from the theatre. It struck me that she never reached home. I could be wrong, but I think if she had been snatched from her house then her front door would not have been locked."

"She might have gone home and then go on somewhere else later?" Clara pointed out.

"Possibly, but I still felt as if she never made it home. It is purely a hunch," Laurence had laced his fingers together again and he held them tightly in his lap. "The chickens were still out, that is what struck me most. If Elaine had gone out again in the afternoon, she must have expected to be back before dusk. Otherwise she would have made sure the chickens were shut up and safe from the fox. Whatever happened to Elaine, it was sudden and wholly unexpected."

"What did the police say when they arrived?"

Laurence gave a small snort, clearly unimpressed by the police. Clara decided she would have to remark on this to Inspector Park-Coombs when she next saw him. It was obvious the police had not inspired confidence in this case.

"A police constable arrived after considerable delay and he wandered about the house, took some brief notes and told us to touch nothing. He would not even allow us to shut up the surviving chickens. He ushered us all away and said if no one heard from Elaine by tomorrow, they would start treating her as a missing person.

"I was appalled! I felt they should have started a search at once, but I was overruled. We were all sent to our respective homes."

Laurence fell quiet and Clara joined him in silence, thinking over what he had said. It was alarming that a woman could simply vanish into thin air and no one had any clue as to where she might have gone. It made you shudder a little.

"Had Elaine ever mentioned, or even just implied, that there was someone in her life who had a grievance against her?" Clara asked.

"Apart from Wendy?" Laurence said caustically. "No, Elaine did not mention anything. Then again, we were not exactly close friends."

"Did she have a close friend?"

"Not within the company. I don't mean to imply she was unfriendly, but she had only been here a short time. I am aware that she had other friends in the district. I recall three young women in particular. They all came for her very first performance. Elaine was extremely nervous, and they were there as moral support. I saw at least one of them at every subsequent performance."

"Do you know their names?" Clara asked.

"Unfortunately, no. I was introduced to them, but the names elude me. I was not really paying attention. I believe Elaine had gone to school with them."

Clara would have to get that information from Captain Chase or, if he could not help, perhaps Elaine's parents.

"The newspapers have implied that Elaine's disappearance was the work of her husband," Laurence said uneasily.

"I avoid paying too much attention to the newspapers," Clara told him. "Captain Chase is very keen to locate his wife."

"I see," Lawrence nodded. "Then I hope, for his sake as much as Elaine's, that she is found soon safe and well. It has unsettled everyone to imagine that a person can simply walk out a door and never be seen again. Some of the younger girls in the company have become quite agitated over it and when we have late rehearsals they are making sure they walk home together, if they can."

"What happened to Elaine is very unusual," Clara reminded him. "I doubt anyone else has reason to fear."

"But you never know," Laurence said grimly. "I recall a case last century where a string of young women vanished one after the other near Grimsby, I believe. They arrested a local man, in the end. He had abducted and killed all the women. It was awful. No doubt, when the first girl vanished, it was also said that no one else had anything to fear."

Laurence's expression suggested he was more worried that someone might abduct him, than any of the girls in his company. Clara could not think of a polite way of telling the stout man that the odds of a serial killer being interested in abducting and murdering him were so remote as to be ridiculous. She decided to say nothing on that subject.

"I intend to find Elaine as swiftly as possible, then this matter will be resolved and people will be able to walk about freely once more."

"Are you not anxious for your own safety?" Laurence asked her sharply. "You are about Elaine's age. What if her attacker turns his attention to you?"

"Then he shall make my life easier, as he will come to me rather than I having to search him out," Clara answered without hesitation.

Laurence was not impressed.

"You are taking this too glibly."

"On the contrary, I am deadly serious about my investigations. A young woman has seemingly been snatched away while walking home and I shall not rest until I know who the culprit is and can prevent them from doing the same again. There is no way I can prevent attention being drawn to my enquiries, but that may be of use to me, as often it draws out a criminal better than intensive detective work," Clara spoke plainly. "I will discover who did this and my hope is to find Elaine safe and well also. People should not have to feel worried when going about their daily business."

"Hmm," Laurence seemed unconvinced. "Well, I truly wish you luck. I would dearly love to see Elaine back in our midst safe and sound. I have my doubts about that happening, however."

"You think whoever took her does not intend to let her live?" Clara asked, somewhat surprised by the man's implication.

"I don't know, truth be told, but I think a person who abducts someone else has to be slightly insane, and insane people can do anything," Lawrence rose from his seat. "If I was Elaine's husband, I would be hoping for the best, but bracing myself for the worst."

Chapter Five

Tommy Fitzgerald walked into the kitchen. This, in itself, was something he could not have dreamt of doing just a year ago. Tommy had been shot in the war, he had lost the use of both legs, though not a single military doctor could explain to him why. It was only when he met the appropriately named Dr Cutt that he finally received answers. They were not the answers he had wanted, at least not initially. Being told he had shellshock and that the recovery of the use of his legs was a mental process rather than a physical one had been hard for Tommy to accept. But accept it he had, with some persuasion from Clara and Annie. The result was that he had found a way to bypass the mental block that prevented his legs from working. He still had a limp and on long walks he liked to take a stick with him, but he was otherwise whole.

He took a deep breath as he entered the room, absorbing the delightful aroma of a cake baking. Bramble, the small black poodle the Fitzgeralds had acquired the year before, bounced in around his feet and danced up on his hindlegs to eye up the top of the range.

"Get out of it," Annie flicked a tea towel at Bramble, though not in malice, even she was rather fond of the small dog.

"I see you have everything in hand for this afternoon," Tommy remarked, noting a second cake sitting on the kitchen table cooling. "Is that an apple sponge?"

"Yes," Annie answered casually, then she paused. "What is happening this afternoon?"

"You can't have forgotten?" Tommy laughed.

Annie's blank expression indicated she had.

"This afternoon is the opening of the O'Harris Convalescence Home for War Veterans," Tommy reminded her. "I jolly well hope Clara has not forgotten."

"She won't forget that," Annie replied with a twinkle in her eye.

Both Annie and Tommy were waiting for the moment when Clara and O'Harris finally conceded defeat and accepted they were in love. So far, they were both being far too independent and cautious. Tommy walked over to Annie and slipped his arm around her waist. He kissed the top of her head.

"Your cakes smell delicious."

"Thank you," Annie blushed, partly because of the kiss, partly because praise always made her shy.

"But why were you baking them if you had forgotten about Captain O'Harris' opening ceremony?"

"Oh, just for practice," Annie shrugged. "And I wanted to use up the last of the winter apples."

"You do not need any practice, your cooking is already perfection," Tommy told her, watching her face redden to a darker hue as he knew it would. He grinned and squeezed her. "You are the best cook in Brighton."

Annie unexpectedly winced. Tommy loosened his arm around her.

"What's wrong?"

"Oh, nothing, I just banged my side," Annie smiled. "Do you think I better whip up some scones and sandwiches while I am thinking about it? People get hungry at these things."

"I have no doubt Captain O'Harris has arranged the more mundane articles of food for the occasion," Tommy said smoothly. "Your cakes will be the finishing touch."

"Stop it," Annie flapped the tea towel at herself, trying to cool her flushed cheeks. "You really lay it on thick, Tommy Fitzgerald."

"And why not for the girl I love?" Tommy kissed the top of her head again. "We ought to talk about getting married, you know?"

"I want you to propose to me properly Thomas Fitzgerald!" Annie scolded him playfully. "Not just hint at it."

Tommy pulled a face.

"I might go down on one knee, but I think you will have to help me up again."

"You can work on it," Annie poked him with a finger. "I like things done properly and we both know that."

Tommy gave a dramatic sigh, but he knew he was not going to win. Annie had her mind and heart set on a romantic proposal and he was not going to get away with anything else. He was about to admit defeat and promise to arrange something, when Clara came in through the front door with a bang. Bramble scampered down the hallway barking in delight.

"Hello! I suddenly realised the time!" Clara appeared in the kitchen and admired the cake on the table. "Bravo Annie, always on form!"

Annie blushed again, embarrassed that it was by luck rather than judgement that she had cake ready for Captain O'Harris' event.

"I am going to get changed and then we ought to head straight over. Or did O'Harris say he was sending the car?" Clara pressed a finger to her lips. "He might have done, you know."

"O'Harris did promise to send a car," Tommy told her, amused that Clara was also forgetful of the arrangements. "Am I the only one who pays attention? By the way, where were you?"

"At the Brighton Players' theatre, on a case. A woman went missing walking home from a rehearsal there."

Annie glanced up from peering into her oven at the gently browning cake.

"That was in the papers. Mrs Chase disappeared into thin air. The papers say her husband did it."

"The papers say a lot of things," Clara countered lightly. "It is Mrs Chase's husband who has hired me to investigate. It is rather mysterious. No one seems able to explain why she would simply vanish."

"It sends a shiver down my spine," Annie visibly shuddered. "To think of someone just walking away and disappearing into thin air. I know some people are rather anxious about walking alone now."

"I suspect the culprit knew Mrs Chase," Clara comforted her. "And was after her for a specific reason. I do not think anyone else need fear the same befalling them."

Annie did not look consoled.

"You ought to get changed," Tommy told Clara and his sister agreed before disappearing upstairs in haste. Tommy turned to Annie. "Would you like some help packaging up these cakes?"

Annie had become rather solemn. She stared thoughtfully at the tiles above the hob of the range, though she was not really looking at them. A frown creased her brow.

"Annie?"

She started from her reverie.

"I was thinking, what makes a person kidnap someone else? I cannot fathom it."

"That is why you are not a kidnapper," Tommy smiled. "And, we do not as yet know what demons lurked in Mrs Chase's past."

"Is she dead, do you suppose?"

Tommy's instinct was to say 'yes', but he kept that to himself.

"Clara will figure it out, she always does. Now, boxes for cakes?"

Distracted by a practical task, Annie left behind

thoughts of Mrs Chase and her dramatic disappearance. Tommy followed her about the kitchen, getting under foot in an effort to help. Eventually he was banished and told to go get himself ready. He was in the hallway when O'Harris' private car pulled up outside.

"Time to go ladies!" He shouted out.

Clara appeared from upstairs, looking her best in a pale green dress and a white scarf. As the days still had a slight nip to them, she was wearing a cream cardigan also. Annie emerged from the kitchen with two cardboard boxes containing her cakes, she was worrying about whether she should bring her own cake knife or not. Tommy removed the cakes from her so she could don her coat. Then they were all heading out to the car.

~~~*~~~

Captain O'Harris had served in the Royal Flying Corps during the war, an organisation now formally known as the Royal Air Force. His experiences both during and after the war had demonstrated to him decisively that the provisions in existence for men who had served in the conflict and, as a result, were suffering the psychological agonies warfare produced, were wholly inadequate. He wanted to do something for those men whose injuries were on the inside, invisible to most doctors and therefore considered as fictitious. He had discussed his ideas with pioneers in the world of psychology, such as Dr Cutt, and determined to transform his old family home into a hospital for those suffering from shellshock and all its related mental ills. O'Harris had inherited a lot of money and a rambling house from his aunt and uncle. It was too big for one man to rattle around in and he found it haunted by memories of those he had cared for and lost. Transforming it, and giving it new purpose, had been a way of healing himself, as much as healing others.

O'Harris was excited. In a couple of days' time he would welcome his first handful of patients. He could accommodate ten at a time, each with his own private bedroom. O'Harris had one wing of the house converted for his personal accommodation, while the nurses on duty at night had a sitting room and there was also office space for the doctors O'Harris was employing to assist with the treatment of the men.

While patients had their own private space, they were not expected to shut themselves away from the world. Meals were to be held in a brand-new dining room, with views over the garden and a highly polished mahogany table in the centre. Each meal was to feel like a dinner party with friends – comfortable, cosy, safe. There was also a library, music room and billiards room for the men to use. During the day (and based on the recommendations O'Harris had received from his team of doctors) the patients would be encouraged to participate in activities such as woodwork and painting, or gardening in the better weather. Lessons would be offered on a wide range of subjects, from car engine repairs to the study of foreign languages. The idea was not just to bring the men out of themselves, but to provide them with new skills they could use when they left the home.

Many of the men could not return to their previous occupations, perhaps due to injury or because their old job no longer existed. Some had missed out on a proper education due to signing up to fight. By providing them with an education, both classical and practical, it was aimed to give them hope for a better future and a means of sustaining themselves.

There was no denying that the scheme was ambitious. O'Harris was well aware of the fact and he also knew that his critics were watching him closely and ready to pounce on any mistake he made. He aimed to take it all in his stride. He was doing this not for glory, but to help others like himself. Others who had seen the things he had seen, done the things he had done and been tossed aside by the British establishment the second the conflict was all over. O'Harris dearly hoped that this was the start of something that would change the way veterans of war were looked upon. If this small start could make others stop and think, then he was serving a purpose far greater than the healing of ten men.

But that was in the future. Today was about announcing the home was open and shaking hands with the most prestigious people in Brighton who had come to witness the event. The Brighton mayor was present, as were several town aldermen. O'Harris had personally invited several high-ranking members of the military; not all had come, but those who had seemed to be taking a keen interest. O'Harris was beginning to feel nervous and was relieved when he saw his driver pull up in his car and Clara step out.

"Clara!" He grinned and almost swept her up into an embrace that would have caused a few sharp glances. He resisted.

"Annie baked cakes," Clara told him, stepping aside so Annie could exit the car with her boxes. "She refused to allow anyone else to hold them on the car ride."

"You let them tip over," Annie rebuked Clara. "Here you are Captain."

O'Harris thanked Annie profusely for the cakes and escorted her and them to a table where a feast was already laid out. There were waiters on hand to serve the food, some of which was being kept piping hot. Tommy's talk of mundane food could not begin to describe the feast laid out on the tables. Clara was not even sure of the names of half the dishes. Annie's cakes were handed over and instructions were given as to how they should be placed on display. Annie's face had fallen when she saw the grand desserts already stationed on the table, including a towering jelly in the shape of a castle.

"It's all façade," O'Harris winked at her. "They will love your cake far more than all this fancy frivolous stuff."

Annie smiled gratefully at his words.

The afternoon began with O'Harris introducing himself and those who had offered to give speeches. One of which was the mayor, another was an RFC Major and lastly there was Dr Cutt, whose polite, homely tone seemed to cut through all the chaff and remind everyone how fragile mental health could be.

A ribbon had been stretched across the front door of the house and O'Harris cut it ceremoniously before escorting his guests around and showing them the newly created facilities. Clara was at O'Harris' side as he pointed out the informal classrooms where men would learn a variety of subjects in comfortable quarters.

"Just like as if they were learning in their living rooms!" He informed his guests.

Then everyone was ushered back outside to the buffet, set under marquees just in case the fine spring weather turned to rain. As the guests descended on the tables O'Harris relaxed.

"You were marvellous," Clara told him.

O'Harris laughed.

"I was so nervous," he shook his head. "I've got to make this work, you know?"

"You will," Clara reached out for his hand and squeezed it.

"Thank you," O'Harris squeezed her hand back, then his eyes strayed to the driveway. "Better late than never, here comes Inspector Park-Coombs."

Clara looked up too. O'Harris sensed her interest and chuckled.

"You have a new case, don't you? And you want to talk to him."

Clara ducked her head, mildly embarrassed.

"Is it that obvious?"

"Just a tad, look, go have a chat and I shall make up a plate for you here."

"You are too understanding," Clara replied gratefully.

"Oh, but I expect you to tell him all about my house too! Take him for a tour! I want the police to know they have nothing to worry about from my patients."

Clara gave his hand a final squeeze then departed.

O'Harris smiled to himself as he watched her walk away. Life had improved tremendously for him the day he met Clara Fitzgerald and he would never forget that. Not by a long shot.

Chapter Six

Inspector Park-Coombs twitched his moustache and smiled as Clara approached him. He seemed to be sagging in his suit jacket, which was unusual. Park-Coombs normally stood up proudly and stiffly, like an army major. Clara also noted the dark bags under his eyes.

"You look tired Inspector."

"I am," Park-Coombs gave a weary groan. "I have spent nearly every night this week in Hove, trying to nab a gang of thieves who are raiding farms for petrol and diesel, and everything else they might lay their hands on. Five have been hit so far and not a hint of who is behind it."

"That does sound exhausting," Clara said sympathetically. "You must have your hands quite full."

"Exactly. And there is all the usual stuff as well. Stolen bicycles, complaints about neighbours, mischief in the pubs. I am stretched thin Clara, I must say," Park-Coombs paused and found a reserve of energy to straighten his shoulders and stand a little taller. "Still, I am here today to enjoy myself."

"I thought you might be here on an official capacity?" Clara teased him. "Inspecting the place to see if it was secure enough, what with the mad folk going to be housed here."

"I am offended Clara," Park-Coombs looked hurt. "When have I ever given you such an impression?"

"Sorry, Inspector, it was a poor joke. Would you like a tour? Captain O'Harris has truly transformed the place and, by the time we are done, the hoards will have left the buffet and we can serve ourselves in peace."

"Why not," Park-Coombs nodded. "Last time I was in this house was after that tramp caused a fire that destroyed the dining room."

"You will see that all the damage has been repaired."

Clara showed him into the mansion and took him for a tour around all the public rooms and then the private bedrooms upstairs. The inspector nodded and made approving noises as they went around. They finally stopped back in the library, where the inspector took a closer look at the books on the shelves.

"I see the late O'Harris' works are still here," Park-Coombs tapped the spine of a book.

Captain O'Harris' uncle had been a renowned military historian who had written several books on the topic.

"It was a decision that took some consideration," Clara explained. "On the one hand, it would be odd to remove those books. Most men coming here will be aware of who O'Harris is and who his uncle was. The absence of the books might have appeared as a deliberate attempt to keep the men from reading about anything war related, which might have offended them. On the other hand, books relating to military campaigns, war techniques and the harrowing impact of conflict, albeit in an historical context, might be upsetting for those who have suffered trauma in the last war to read."

"I see, damned if you do, damned if you don't," Park-Coombs nodded. "I feel like that most days."

"In the end it was decided that the men are here as free agents and, as such, should be allowed the freedom to choose their own reading material and to make conscious decisions about what might or might not be suitable for their mental health. After all, it is foreseen that all the men will return to the everyday world sooner rather than later, and within the everyday world there are all manner of things that could upset them if they have not learned how to filter out the good from the bad.

"O'Harris is not running a monastery, where the real world is deliberately made remote. There will be no one outside these four walls to protect them. They have to learn how to protect themselves, from a psychological perspective."

"I quite understand," Park-Coombs glanced out of the library window, which faced onto the front lawn and the buffet tables. "How long does it take people to decide what to eat?"

Clara glanced past him and saw that the tables were still heaving with guests.

"I suggest we join on the end of the queue," Clara murmured.

"It mostly looked too rich for me, anyway," Park-Coombs grumbled. "I get terrible indigestion."

"Annie has made her apple sponge," Clara mentioned.

Park-Coombs brightened.

"Really? Annie's cakes seem to always agree with me. We best hurry before the gannets get to it."

They headed back outside and to the tables, joining on the end of the line of people.

"Inspector, are you in the mood for talking about a case I am on?" Clara asked delicately.

Park-Coombs shrugged.

"It's not about farm tractors being robbed of their diesel, is it?"

"No," Clara reassured him. "It is about the disappearance of Elaine Chase."

"Ah," Park-Coombs instantly knew the name. He frowned. "Vanished into thin air."

"Indeed. Her husband has asked me to look into the matter. I'm afraid he has not been very complementary about the police investigation of his wife's disappearance."

"I'm not surprised," Park-Coombs said mildly. "No one is ever pleased with us when we cannot solve the crime committed against them, or bring the culprit to justice. I am also aware that the two police constables sent to the Chase house were not our finest in uniform. They are competent, but unimaginative. Most of my best constables are on this farm raids case."

"Have you been to the house?"

"Not as yet," Park-Coombs looked abashed. "I have been up to my eyeballs, and farmers are aggressive complainants. I suppose, I found it easier to just ignore the Chase case. Truth be told, Clara, tracking missing people is one of the hardest things we find ourselves doing. Whether they disappeared of their own volition or not, it is almost impossible to track them. My stomach always goes over when I hear of a child going missing, those are the worst ones, and you know if they have been snatched the odds are you won't find them."

"But sometimes people are found," Clara pointed out.

"Oh, yes, sometimes," Park-Coombs nodded. "There was a woman in Kent who was abducted by her estranged husband. She was found six weeks later, confined in a remote cottage. There were clues to her location, however, and people had their suspicions against the husband. There appeared to be no trace of anything in Mrs Chase's disappearance."

"I have spoken with the Brighton players, well, some of them at least. None seem to have an idea as to why Mrs Chase would vanish. She seemed happy when they last saw her."

"That was the impression my constables received too," Park-Coombs twitched his moustache again, a sure sign his interest in a case had been aroused. "We ran through the usual theories; could she have gone to her parents? Had she fallen into a ditch on the way home? Had she been hit by a car and taken to hospital? All dead ends."

"The newspapers seem to have taken up the idea that Captain Chase was somehow involved," Clara pointed out.

"Not from us," Park-Coombs promised. "We quickly learned that he had been on active duty at the time of her disappearance and had not even gained his leave until the day after. I am confident this is not a case of a husband dispatching his wife. Unless he had an accomplice, of course, and accomplices are notoriously unreliable. No, I think Captain Chase is innocent in this matter."

"I do too," Clara said. "But that leaves me with no idea who is responsible for this crime. I am convinced Mrs Chase was snatched. She had no reason to abandon her husband, and her mood as she left the rehearsal indicates that she was happy and excited about participating in the performance. She disappeared with only her handbag, taking no extra clothes or provisions. Equally, she left her pet chickens to fend for themselves. Something I am told would have been out-of-character. No, Mrs Chase did not expect to disappear, I am sure of it."

"And yet she is gone," Park-Coombs reminded her. "Her friends seem to think she had no real enemies to speak of, and I cannot for the life of me discern a motive. She is not rich to be ransomed."

"Perhaps it is not her the abductor had a grudge against," Clara remarked. "We have focused on Mrs Chase, but what if she is just a pawn in someone's scheme of revenge against another? Her husband, for instance, or even her parents?"

"A good point," Park-Coombs mused, and his moustache twitched again. "Captain Chase has been serving in Ireland. He is Anglo-Irish and that attracts dislike, even hatred, from certain quarters. If Mrs Chase had vanished in Ireland, I would certainly have been considering that this was a revenge attack against her husband. But Brighton is a long way from Ireland."

"Irish bombs were placed in London," Clara pointed out. "How far is too far? All it takes is for someone to know someone and to decide to attack Captain Chase."

"If that was the case I would expect there to be talk," Park-Coombs was unconvinced. "No point in making an attack against Captain Chase if he does not know why. I would expect there to have been threats and letters about his wife's disappearance."

Clara agreed that that was logical. Political statements only worked when people knew what they were about.

"However, it remains likely that it was an enemy of the family, rather than specifically an enemy of Mrs Chase, who committed this crime," Park-Coombs hesitated. "Unless we are dealing with a madman who is abducting women at random."

"That is unlikely, isn't it?"

"Unlikely, yes. Impossible, no."

Clara did not like that idea. A random abduction, based on no more than opportunity would leave little in the way of clues. Equally, it could mean that more abductions were to follow.

"Do you think she is dead?" Clara dropped her voice and asked the inspector.

He took a long while to answer.

"My police instincts tell me that is the most probable outcome. But I would like to hope there is a chance she is not. Then again, I am doing nothing about the case, so if she is alive and I am doing nothing to trace her, that adds a burden of guilt onto me. I suppose, it is easier to imagine she is deceased."

"There must be something, Inspector? Surely a person cannot leave no mark of themselves behind?"

"We came to the conclusion, after we had ruled out that she had not gone to her parents or had been involved in an accident, that she had disappeared on her walk home from the theatre," Park-Coombs paused. They had reached the edge of the buffet table and he was looking at the remains of food in the dishes. It appeared that almost every platter had been picked clean. "Are those plain sausages? I suppose I could eat one."

He took three and placed them on a plate.

"You were saying that you thought Mrs Chase had vanished while walking home?" Clara nudged him.

Park-Coombs was examining some small open pastries.

"What are these?" He asked a waiter.

"Chicken and mushroom pastry puffs. The chicken being cooked in a white wine sauce," the waiter replied obediently. "They are hot and go well with the saffron rice we are serving."

Park-Coombs looked uncertain for a moment, then held out his plate.

"Give me a couple, and a good dollop of that rice. Are those potatoes?"

"It is a potato and leek gratin, sir."

"A dollop of that too."

"Inspector?" Clara politely coughed behind him.

"Are those miniature Cornish pasties?"

"They are, sir."

"Two of them, actually, three. I haven't had a pasty in years. My wife can't master the pastry. With you in a minute, Clara."

Park-Coombs worked down the line, picking up something from nearly every platter or dish. Clara gave a small sigh, then gave in herself and started filling a plate. With a fork in hand, Park-Coombs trundled over to a raised stone flower bed and perched on the edge. Clara sat beside him and turned her face upwards with her eyes closed and allowed the mild sun to warm her.

"You didn't get much," Park-Coombs compared his overloaded plate to her token effort.

"O'Harris said he was keeping a plate back for me," Clara replied. "Now, tell me what you found on the road between the theatre and Mrs Chase's home?"

"Ah!" Park-Coombs munched into a Cornish pasty. "We traced her route. At one point it was quicker for Mrs Chase to go cross-country than to follow the road. She was known to take this shortcut. There is a stile leading into a field and across a stream. The stile is situated in a wall right beside the road. On the verge next to this stile, which Mrs Chase almost certainly would have used, there were tyre tracks in the grass. They were narrow and suggested a car, rather than a tractor or lorry. We have not been able to trace this vehicle.

"I postulated that someone drove up onto that verge when they saw Mrs Chase crossing the stile and offered her a lift. It was a damp day and there was rain in the air. Mrs Chase might have considered a car ride better to getting wet or her shoes muddy. There seemed no other reason that a car would have mounted that verge. The roadway is wide at that point, wide enough two cars can pass by each other easily. Not that that happens often. From the nature of the tracks, and the way they were pressed into the verge, it seemed the car had been coming from behind Mrs Chase."

"Possibly following her?" Clara asked.

"Perhaps, or it was just coincidence," Park-Coombs tried his chicken and mushroom pastry. At first his mouth drooped in seeming disapproval, then he smiled. "Rather good."

"Does anyone in the Players own a car?" Clara asked.

"No," Park-Coombs shrugged.

"If she was taken by car, she could be a long way from here," Clara sighed. "That is not good."

"You see why we were stumped?" Park-Coombs said. "I had men scouring the hedgerows and fields for anything, but not a hint of what might have occurred."

"Mrs Chase went somewhere," Clara said firmly. "And there has to be a clue."

"Missing person cases are the hardest," Park-Coombs reiterated his earlier statement. "I appreciate that is not what you want to hear."

"I value your honesty, Inspector, you know that," Clara toyed with the rice on her plate. "But I can't give up. I have to hope that somewhere out there someone knows something. Mrs Chase did not disappear without a trace, that is impossible. I will solve this and, if she is still alive, I will find Elaine Chase and bring her home."

Chapter Seven

When the opening ceremony was over and the guests had gone home, Clara approached Captain O'Harris to ask a favour. He listened, intrigued.

"Naturally we can take a drive along that road," he said. "But surely any trace of Elaine Chase will be gone by now?"

"Maybe," Clara Admitted. "I would just like to get a feel for the route."

Captain O'Harris had no objections, so they set off in the car with Jones driving; that way they could both keep their eyes pinned on the road for clues. The evening was slowly pulling in, casting long shadows. Clara was staring so hard at the hedges and the verge that clumps of grass or odd stones started to turn into Elaine Chase's shoe or a piece of her clothing. She had to blink and shake her head.

"This is the stile," Clara called out to Jones.

Jones pulled the car up along the side of the road. The marks of the tyre that the police suspected was connected to Elaine's disappearance were still visible. Clara stepped out and walked towards them, bending down to get a better look.

"Can you recognise a car from its tyre tracks?" She

asked O'Harris.

"Sometimes," he nodded. "You can certainly tell what type of vehicle bore these tyres. When I was a spotter in the war, one of the things I was always on the lookout for were the marks left behind by vehicles. You could learn a lot, especially if you were trying to trace recent movements of big guns."

O'Harris crouched by the marks in the mud. They were well defined, the ground having been just right to take a detailed impression.

"It's not a Dunlop, I have those on my car," O'Harris pointed to the car, then he peered closer at the ground. "I think this is a Squires."

"Squires?" Clara asked.

"They are a rubber tyre company here in Brighton. They make their own brand of tyres. Not of the finest quality, if I am honest, but they are cheaper than the big names. Of course, you end up buying more of them than of the better tyres as they last barely a moment. Here, look, this tyre is not very old, the tread is very well defined, but there is a round nick out of one of the rubber treads."

O'Harris was pointing to a section of the mud. The tyre had a series of angled squares and grooves across its surface to provide traction. One of the angled squares had a noticeable semi-circle missing from its edge. When it had gone into the soft mud the damaged square had left its own unique pattern, like someone had taken a bite out of it.

"I'm sure this is a Squires, but let's ask Jones. Jones!"

Jones the driver hopped out of the car and came around the front. He stood beside O'Harris.

"Sir?"

"What make would you say the tyre was that left these marks?"

Jones crouched down beside his employer. He frowned as he studied the impressions.

"Looks like a Squires," he said. "They always have a

ridge down the middle. I wouldn't buy one."

"Then I am looking for a car with Squires Tyres," Clara reiterated. "And when I find that, I need to see if one of the tyres has a notch out of it."

"It will be the front left," Jones added helpfully. "They would have pulled onto this verge from the direction we have travelled. The front left went onto the verge as a result, but when they pulled off the back tyre did not travel so far up the verge. Its marks are here, barely discernible."

Jones pointed to where the road met the verge and a faint impression of tyre tracks was visible. Clara had not spotted it herself. She was glad she had brought the two men, both with a good knowledge of vehicles and sharp eyes.

"I might just be able to trace this car then," Clara said, slipping a notebook from her handbag. "I am going to make a drawing of the tread so I know what I am looking for."

"Let's hope the damn thing hasn't developed a puncture since and had to be replaced," O'Harris laughed. "For a whole lump of rubber to come off like that is shocking. Remarkable the tyre has not already failed."

"Squires make their tread deep," Jones replied. "Namely because the rubber is poor and prone to breaking off in chunks as you see. It perishes so fast too. Surprisingly, really, that people don't realise, but, of course, the tyres are cheap."

"Do you people never stop talking?" A slurry voice yelled at them from behind the stone wall that bordered a field. "Can't you see when a fellow is trying to catch some shut-eye?"

Clara rose and peered over the wall. On the other side, sitting on the ground, was a gentleman who could only be described as a tramp. He had been lying on the ground, his old, tatty coat folded into a pillow for his head. He moodily looked up at Clara with ancient watery eyes. A thick stubble clung to his haggard face.

"How can a man get peace when folk are rabbiting on about tyres?" He complained to Clara.

"Good evening," Clara smiled to him. "I apologise, I was unaware anyone was behind this wall."

"This is my resting spot," the tramp informed her. "I sleep here every evening in the fine weather. After a long day of hard work, I need my sleep."

Clara restrained herself from asking precisely what sort of hard work the man did.

"You sleep here all the time?" She asked him.

"Didn't I say so? Always in the evenings, sometimes midday too. That is what they call a siesta in hotter climes. Very good for you too."

Clara had an idea.

"You must see plenty of people going over this stile? Seeing as it is right next to your sleeping space."

The old tramp shrugged.

"It's inconvenient, I'll grant you that. Whoever put a stile there, hmm?" He patted the ground beneath him. "This is the perfect place to sleep, apart from that stile. Sheltered from the wind, warmed by the sun and the farmer doesn't mind me being here. I keep an eye on his sheep for him when they are in this field. I used to be a shepherd, you know?"

Clara was not terribly interested in his life history, she was, however, interested in who precisely he had seen coming over the stile.

"I imagine the farmer appreciates you taking note of who uses this stile?" Clara said. "Just in case someone might cause harm to his animals? Some people aren't very nice."

"That is true," the tramp nodded. "I have had to warn off a few people. There was a fellow with a dog thought he could just traipse through the field and let his hound molest the sheep. I told him."

"And some people must use this route quite regularly?" Clara persisted.

The tramp sniffed somewhat haughtily.

"There are indeed those I am familiar with. I watch their comings and goings. Some are nice enough to speak to me, recognising a poor fellow who has fallen on hard luck. Others won't give me the time of day."

"That is a shame," Clara sympathised. "Do you know a lady who uses this stile as a shortcut to her home, her name is Elaine Chase?"

The tramp scratched at his mop of grey hair. It sounded like someone rifling through straw.

"Elaine Chase? Yes, I do see a lady cut across here often enough. Young, pretty. Usually says hello. Haven't seen her in a while."

"That is because she has been abducted," Clara dropped her voice, though there was no one around to overhear her. But she guessed, correctly as it happened, that to attract the old tramp's full attention it was best to act as if some great conspiracy was afoot.

"Abducted!" The tramp hissed through his teeth. "Now, that explains why the police were all around here the other week."

"You didn't speak to them?"

The tramp gave Clara a stern look, implying that she had just said something incredibly stupid.

"I do not lower myself to speaking with those bluebottles," he informed her coldly. "I saw them making such a fuss along the roadway and I decided to take myself off for a while. No good comes of speaking to the police."

Clara imagined that to be very much the case for the old tramp. Had he been found at the spot he would have been questioned, possibly even suspected for the disappearance. Trouble would only have ensued. Clara, however, did not think the tramp had abducted Elaine, for a start where would he take her? If he kidnapped her for nefarious reasons, he would have had to have killed her afterwards and then dumped the body. More than likely they would have found Elaine by now had that been the case. No, she did not think this was the work of a tramp.

"I don't suppose you recall the last time Elaine used this stile?"

"I have a very good memory," the tramp said, his haughty tone returned. "I used to be in a glass factory that made milk bottles. I was the bottle counter. Great responsibility that, keeping all the records in order. I used to have to count over a hundred bottles a day."

Clara resisted smiling, she was sceptical of his story but did not want it to show.

"But what about the last day you saw Elaine?" She asked instead.

The tramp sniffed, and then rubbed his nose with a finger.

"Let's see, it was over a week ago. I keep firm track of the days, that is terribly important. First sign of losing your mind if you can't tell what day it is. I used to work for a calendar printing company, you know. We made all sorts of calendars and diaries too. I was in charge of writing up the section on important dates at the front of the book, like when Easter was or the king's birthday."

The tramp sat up a little straighter, pride creeping over him as he reflected on his former days of proper employment.

"Which day of the week was it Elaine last crossed this stile?" Clara tested him.

He scowled at her.

"It was a Saturday," he said. "I don't have a watch, but I can tell you it was about noon, the sun being right up in the sky. She stepped over that stile and smiled to me, as she always did. 'Nice weather,' she said."

"And then she carried on walking home?" Clara asked, starting to wonder if the car tracks were a complete red herring.

"No, she was going to, but then this car pulled up. Damn noisy things cars!" The tramp spat on the ground. "Worst thing ever invented! Do you know how many times I have nearly been knocked down by a car? Twelve times! Miracle I am alive at all! People tear about the roads, no respect for those on foot. I used to be a bicycle tester, you know, but I had to give it up because of people driving cars too fast down roads. My nerves were shot by the strain."

Clara gently smiled.

"I apologise if our car disturbed you."

The tramp huffed to himself.

"What happened when the car pulled up as Elaine was crossing the stile?" Clara asked next.

"Someone called out to her," the tramp said. "Didn't catch the name they called, guess it might have been Elaine. Well, she turned and looked back anyway. And then the person in the car asked if she would like a lift as it was going to rain. I could have told them it weren't going to rain, yes there were grey clouds in the sky, but they weren't the right sort of clouds for rain. I used to referee for football matches and I got very good at telling the weather. I always knew when the lads were in for rain and when they would stay dry. They thought I was some sort of magician with my ability to predict the weather."

"What did Elaine say when she was called?" Clara asked.

"She hesitated, I saw that right enough. You ask me, she wasn't sure about getting in the car with the person who called her name. She almost carried on walking, but the person was persistent, told her it was silly to risk getting wet," the old tramp paused and for the first time his face became bleak and lost its sternness. He seemed to be realising what had occurred. "I could have spoken up, couldn't I? I could have said it weren't going to rain and she ought to carry on walking rather than get in that car. But I didn't and now she is missing."

"You could not have known," Clara reassured him.

"Nice woman too. Never a mean word. I had a cold once, I was sat here watching the sheep, miserable as sin because I felt ill and she crossed the stile and noticed me. She handed me her handkerchief, told me to keep it. I still have it."

The tramp rummaged in his pocket and produced a soiled piece of cloth. Once it had been a pure white handkerchief with the edges embroidered with lemon cotton thread. There was a set of initials on the handkerchief. The tramp showed them to Clara.

"There you are, it was her. E. C."

They were certainly the initials of Elaine Chase.

"Has something terrible happened to her?" The tramp asked, his face grim and all his bravado evaporated.

"I don't know," Clara confessed. "I am trying to find that out."

"That's why the police were here," the tramp muttered to himself. "Because of that car."

"Did you get a look at the person in the car?" Clara asked.

The tramp shook his head once more.

"I never rose from my spot here. I didn't see the point."

"That's a shame," Clara sighed. "Either the person in the car was the last person to see Elaine Chase before she was taken, or…"

"They took her," the tramp interrupted. He was glowering now, his fist clenching around the handkerchief. "I would wring their bloody necks if I could! What is the world coming to?"

Clara had no answer for that.

"Are you going to trace this person with the car?" The tramp asked.

"I hope to try," Clara replied.

He narrowed his eyes to little slits.

"I might not have seen that car, but I would recognise its engine anywhere. I have exceptional hearing, I used to be in charge of quality control in a gramophone factory."

"Well, if I track the car I shall have to fetch you to listen to its engine," Clara smiled, turning away to rejoin O'Harris.

"There is one other thing," the tramp called out. "Probably important too."

Clara glanced back.

"I may not have seen who was in the car," he said. "But I heard them. That was a woman's voice I heard."

The tramp met Clara's eyes.

"It was a woman who offered Elaine a lift, and that means it was a woman who abducted her!"

Chapter Eight

Annie was satisfied that her cakes had been enjoyed by the guests at Captain O'Harris' opening ceremony. She felt triumphant, as though she had redeemed herself as a cook. Redeemed from what? She could not say, but that was what it felt like. As if she had gone from being an everyday home cook to something a little bit more special. Brighton's mayor had eaten her cake and remarked on how light the sponge was. She had overheard him. Could there be any better indication that she had excelled herself?

That evening, as she rounded up the chickens to their coop for the night, she felt strangely alive. A warm glow came over her. She had always known her cakes were very good, now it had been proved. All that was left was to win the baking competition, which was surely now a certainty?

Annie heard footsteps from behind the fence that separated the Fitzgerald yard from the garden next door. She guessed that Olive, the maid for the Bramwells, was coming out to retrieve the washing from the line. Annie knew it was boastful, but she desperately wanted to tell someone about her victory that day, someone who would truly appreciate what she had achieved. She could tell

Clara and Tommy, and they would congratulate her and speak well of her baking skills, but they wouldn't truly understand. For them a cake was something to eat, not revel over. They did not know what it was to be defined, albeit by oneself, by the ability to bake well.

"Olive!" Annie hopped to the fence and glanced over.

Olive was indeed heading out into the garden to retrieve her washing, but she was not alone. Jane Jenkins was with her. Jane was a few years older than Annie and worked as housekeeper to the family at No.34. She was a sharp-faced woman, the sort you did not expect warm words from. Annie could safely say she had never received any from her.

"Evening Annie," Olive was the youngest out of the trio. Just turned eighteen, she was still learning the ropes of being a domestic servant. Annie had been very kind in helping to teach her the best way to go about her daily tasks and they were friends, though not particularly close. Unfortunately, Jane Jenkins had also latched onto Olive, much to the latter's chagrin.

She cast an apologetic look in Annie's direction. No one in the road could fail to know that Annie and Jane were at permanent loggerheads. It was not plain where the discord had begun, some thought it was when Jane had carelessly suggested that Annie had received more than her typical ration of sugar one week, the implication being that Annie had an arrangement with the greengrocer. This idle gossip, which was a complete lie (Annie's ration had in fact been short the week before due to supply problems and the grocer added the shortfall to her next week's ration) had filtered back to Annie and caused her a good deal of affront. By then it was the story on everyone's lips – well, everyone who worked as a maid, cook or housekeeper down the road, anyway. Infuriated, Annie protested to whoever she could and eventually confronted Jane. From then on, they had been the bitterest of enemies.

"Annie," Jane wandered over to the fence and pulled

her unpleasant little smile. It always made her look stuck-up and self-satisfied. As if she were the Queen of Sheba. Annie felt it grate on her nerves a little. "I imagine you have seen the advertisement in the Brighton Gazette for a baking contest?"

"I have," Annie confirmed.

"Are you entering?" Jane asked coolly.

"Would seem a shame not to," Annie replied nonchalantly.

Olive glanced between the two of them, anxiously waiting for something to happen.

"Let me guess, you will be going for best Victoria sponge?" Jane said smugly.

Annie felt herself bristling inside, though she could not quite see the catch in the comment.

"I will be," she answered. "Toughest category. Only the best of the best will win."

"That's what I was thinking too," Jane appeared to be smirking. "I thought I would enter that class. As they have decided not to have a scone competition. I suppose they perhaps felt they needed a change, considering I had won that category hands down for three years running. Blind tasting too, no one knew who made each scone. Makes it more impressive when you win."

Annie bit down on her tongue, but she wanted to tell Jane that when it came to sponges she would not be so victorious. Scones were one thing; most people couldn't make a decent scone. They either made them too dry or too hard or too cloying in the mouth. All you had to be able to do was make a semi-decent scone to win such a class. Now Annie wished there was a scone contest, so she could enter it herself and demonstrate what a real scone should taste like.

Sponges were different. Lots of people could make a reasonable sponge. To win such a class you had to be able to produce something divine, something exceptional. Annie knew she was capable of just that.

"I shall enjoy winning that category then," Annie said

boldly, knowing her words would be incendiary and not caring.

Olive was attempting to slip away and get in the washing, desperate to be out of the firing line.

"You did hear me say that I would be entering that class?" Jane asked snidely.

"I did," Annie retorted coldly.

"Have you tasted my raspberry jam? I have been told it is the perfect combination of sharp and sweet. It offsets my golden sponge perfectly. I just thought I ought to tell you, so you will not be too disappointed."

"I'll have you know my sponge has had the approval of the Mayor of Brighton himself," Annie countered. "I intend to use strawberry jam, as it is more traditional. Though, it is also a good deal harder to make. Strawberries can become overly sweet in the process and need a delicate touch to bring them back to perfection."

"Raspberry or strawberry, both are acceptable in a Victoria," Jane snorted.

"And will you be making butter icing for the filling or using fresh cream? I personally find butter icing more in keeping, but some cannot resist going along the cream route."

"I prefer fresh cream," Jane snapped back. "It is an art to get the cream whipped to just the right consistency. Not too stiff and not too runny. I can see why you might opt for butter icing instead. It is harder to go wrong."

"Cream can be so bland in a sponge," Annie replied, any attempt to be polite now lost. "I always consider it a somewhat lazy filling, unless you do something interesting with it like piping it into an éclair."

"Whipped with sugar it is heavenly," Jane said defiantly. "Only a cook with little respect for the finer things in life would say otherwise. Simple does not mean lazy or bland, just as time-consuming work does not make a dish more special. You ought to remember that Annie. When it comes to tasting a cake, no one takes into account the amount of hours you put into it. All they care about is whether it is sweet and light and altogether so delicious you could eat slice after slice without stopping."

Jane crossed her arms firmly across her chest.

"If you do not understand that, I suggest you try your luck at the best fruit cake class."

"I understand perfectly," Annie snapped. "Don't think I do not. When my sponge wins you will be weeping into your whipped cream!"

Olive drew a sharp breath backwards through her teeth and looked like she was contemplating diving for cover. Annie was not done, however.

"You think you are the best cook in Brighton, Jane Jenkins, well let me tell you, you are not. It takes more than a few scone contests to prove that. Your arrogance and your lies are bad enough, but don't think for a moment you can criticise my cooking and get away with it. This competition will prove which of us is the best and that will be that," Annie pointed a finger at her rival. "I am not afraid of you Jane Jenkins, nor your sponge."

"Then you are a fool!" Jane snapped back. "I didn't win those scone contests by fluke! I am an exceptional cook, an artist at sweet things and I shall show you Annie! I shall make you regret calling my cream lazy!"

"You can do that, go ahead!" Annie shouted, losing her temper at last.

Jane was laughing at her.

"You have no idea! None at all! I was going to wish you luck, but what would be the point? You aren't going to succeed, not while I am in the running!"

"Please!" Olive interjected, finally unable to bear the argument anymore. "You don't need to be like this. It is only cake."

"Only cake!" Both woman snapped in unison at Olive.

She ducked her head and tried to vanish into the hard ground of the yard.

"You watch out Annie," Jane snarled one last time at her rival. "I shall show you up and you won't be able to hold your head high in Brighton again!"

"Preposterous! I would like to see you try!" Annie threw back at her.

"You can't be talked to rationally!" Jane scoffed. "Well, we shall have our answer when the cake contest comes around! Until then I have nothing more to say to you!"

Jane stalked off to the back door of the house and disappeared. Annie was fuming, her fists were clenched at her side. She felt like she could not take a deep breath. Olive shuffled her feet on the ground, then mumbled about getting in her washing.

"I apologise Olive for snapping at you," Annie said hastily as the girl moved off.

Olive turned back. She gave a long sigh.

"I know I am not like you or Jane. I ain't clever enough to make splendid cakes. I just get by. But I do think that fighting like this over a baking contest ain't good for you. You are both brilliant bakers, why do you have to be better than each other?"

Annie's anger melted away a little at Olive's soft words. It was true, of course, why were they fighting over sponges? Of all things to start a private war over, the Victoria sponge had to be the most peculiar. But Annie couldn't help it. Just thinking about Jane Jenkins made her blood boil. She had to beat her in this cake contest, it was the only way to stop all this nonsense – wasn't it?

"I can't explain it Olive," Annie said after a moment. "Maybe one day you will come across a person who just rubs you up the wrong way. I have to be successful at this, its more important to me than I can explain."

Olive looked a little saddened by this answer, but she did not contradict it.

"I wish you luck Annie, but I also wish Jane luck. I won't take sides."

"I understand," Annie said, though she didn't, not really. She was hurt that Olive was not sticking up for her and taking Annie's part in the struggle against Jane.

"If Jane wins, I know you are going to be upset," Olive said steadily. "I rather hope neither of you win, then you will be united in defeat. Better than one of you lording it over the other."

"I wouldn't lord over Jane," Annie snorted.

Olive gave her a look that implied she thought differently. Annie had to look away as Olive was hitting a little too close to the mark.

"Worse thing out would be if Jane won this contest. She already has too high an opinion of herself," Annie grumbled.

"Oh, how I wish there was no baking contest!" Olive flung up her arms. "Well, I have to get dinner ready and served. Fortunately, no one asks more of me than that I make a wholesome and tasty supper. Nothing fancy, just good, English food. I can live with being a very average and humble baker of cakes. And my scones are largely edible, but unremarkable. For that I am grateful. Good evening Annie."

Olive gathered up the washing and headed back indoors. Annie stood by the fence for a while, contemplating what Olive had said. Was she being irrational about a cake contest? No, surely not. This was important. Olive was too young to understand. You had to make your mark in this life, you had to take pride in what you did. Besides, Jane had never slandered Olive like she had Annie.

Annie walked back to the chickens and finished shuffling them into the coop for the night. Her excitement for the cooking contest had abruptly diminished. She felt uncertain and uneasy. Her mother had always warned her about being proud and boastful, it was not just a sin, but it had a way of coming back at you. Annie started to see what she had meant. She closed up the coop and headed to the kitchen door.

Her side twinged again. It had been good all day and she had concluded that she had pulled something earlier. Now it nagged a little, but not anything that would distract her from what she was doing.

Just inside the kitchen door, sitting on the wooden

draining board next to the deep sink, was a basket of eggs. She had collected them with satisfaction, thinking how fine a cake they would make. She had used them in the sponge the mayor had praised.

Why was it wrong to take pride in one's work and endeavour to do one's best? Surely that was what a person should do? It was all very well being little Olive, satisfied with making average meals, but they were put on this earth to be the best at whatever talent they had been God given. Annie remembered that from a sermon she had once heard. This was not about being boastful or showing up Jane Jenkins. It was about demonstrating the pride she took in her work, the consideration and the skill. She would make her finest sponge and let others decide on its worth.

Annie felt a little better. Jane Jenkins just brought out the worst in her, that was all. She should avoid her in the future.

Smiling to herself, Annie set about making a nice pot of tea.

Chapter Nine

A woman had been in the car.

Clara sat contemplating what she had so far learned in the Elaine Chase case as the early evening sunlight lanced through the window and fell pleasantly on her stockinged feet.

There had been a woman driving the car. The tramp was sure of it. He had heard a woman's voice call out to Elaine and offer her a lift. That raised a variety of interesting possibilities. First, it could be that the woman was a mere bystander to events. She could have quite innocently offered the lift and after Elaine had been deposited safely at home she had vanished. In which case, it would seem very odd that the woman had not come forward to present this evidence to the police. She could be the last person to have seen Elaine before she vanished.

Then again, she might be the very person who caused Elaine to vanish. That, to Clara, seemed the greater probability. What precisely was the woman's intent? If a man had snatched Elaine then indecency would spring to mind as a motive. He wanted something from Elaine that she would not willingly give. But that was less likely with a woman abducting Elaine – though Clara ruled nothing out, these days the world was a lot more complicated.

Clara turned away from motive and back to fact. There had been a car and it had left a tyre imprint on the verge. She knew Elaine had climbed into that car, and that the tyres were from the Squires Garage, here in Brighton. The company would hopefully have records of their customers and what they had purchased. There were not that many car owners in Brighton, it was an expensive business owning a car. If she could track down the car, then surely she could track down the last person to have seen Elaine before she vanished? Perhaps even the person who made her vanish? Clara liked that possibility.

Clara absent-mindedly glanced up as the doorbell rang. She heard Annie heading to answer it and Bramble give an excited yap, before she went back to her work.

Facts. Elaine Chase had no known enemies, as far as her friends in the Players could say, though Clara had far from interviewed them all. Most had avoided her during the rehearsal. She would need to track them down individually. Fortunately, the director had given her a list of everyone in the company and their addresses. She had a feeling he was desperate for his lead actress to be found before opening night and, having seen her under-study in action, Clara understood why.

Elaine had to have an enemy. No one liked to admit to such a thing, but even the nicest, most innocuous of people offended someone at some point in their lives. Jealousy could make a person your enemy just as easily as a real offence. Sometimes it was worse, because it was impossible to apologise to someone who was jealous of you, but you could apologise to someone you had offended. There was always someone out there who disliked you. Clara did not believe there to be a soul in the world who was not hated by someone else. Even Jesus had enemies.

"Clara, a visitor for you," Annie appeared in the door of the front parlour.

Clara looked up and saw that the visitor was Agnes, the Scottish lass who had recently taken on the daunting task of becoming Brighton's first policewoman. She was in uniform, a dark tunic over a long dark skirt, with brass buttons smartly polished and a cap to finish the ensemble.

"Evening, Clara," Agnes looked very practical in her heavy-duty shoes. Her wild red hair had been tamed by some form of magic into a very neat bun. Clara grinned at her.

"Nice to see you getting along all right," she said.

"It's been an interestin' few months. A few of the boys have not taken too kindly to a lassie among them, but I am winnin' them over slowly. Inspector Park-Coombs asked me to bring a copy of one of our files over to you. He also said I could offer my assistance, in a professional capacity."

Agnes handed over a brown cardboard folder.

"This is all the material the police have gathered so far on the Elaine Chase disappearance?" Clara asked.

"Exactly," Agnes replied. "Crying shame, that one. Poor maid goes vanishing into thin air and not a soul can say why or how."

"Take a seat, Agnes," Clara remembered her manners. "Would you like some tea?"

"I am on that," Annie announced from the hallway. "I don't suppose Agnes has had any supper yet, either. I know the long hours the police work."

"Aye, it has been a day and a half," Agnes laughed. "I've got some cold meat at home, though."

"You shall have a plate here and that is that," Annie declared firmly, and then she hurried off to her work.

"Grand lass you have there," Agnes said to Clara.

"She is the only reason I do not starve to death," Clara responded with mock solemnity. "Annie makes everything I do possible. Now, what has Park-Coombs sent me?"

Clara opened the brown folder and found it contained the statements of everyone he had contacted and interviewed in the search for Elaine, including all the members of the Players and her parents and sister. There was also an interview with Captain Chase, along with a copy of a complaint he had made to the police that they were not doing enough to find his wife.

"It scares me a little to think someone could just disappeared into thin air," Agnes said, slumping further down into the chair, exhaustion overcoming her. "Do you have no leads, yourself?"

"Maybe one," Clara replied. "I now know that Elaine was offered a lift in a car by a woman after she left the theatre. She accepted the lift and it would seem whoever the person in the car was, they were the last person to see Elaine before she vanished."

"Or they made her vanish."

"Well, yes," Clara nodded. "To be honest, I suspect that more than this being a coincidence."

"I went up to interview the parents. The inspector thought it would suit a woman's touch."

"What were they like?" Clara asked.

Agnes folded her hands in her lap, her eyes were drooping slightly as if she was in danger of dozing off.

"Honest working folk. Rather on edge though, nerves worn thin by life. The sister had lost her husband in the war and was struggling to cope with her young bairns. She had been ill herself. I didna ask, but I got the impression she is a sufferer of the old tuberculosis."

"Oh dear," Clara said with heartfelt sympathy for the poor woman. TB had the potential to be a killer; a prospect a widow with young children must find terrifying. "I'm surprised she did not move down to Brighton, the sea air is supposed to be good for TB, and then she would be near her sister too."

"There is an ailing mother-in-law complicating matters," Agnes explained. "The woman seems to have lost her mind, reverted to a state of childlike simplicity. They told me it was the grief of losing a husband and a son in the war. Her daughter-in-law had been looking after her and had even brought her into her home. I think it was felt it would be too much to try to move her too. It was easier for the parents to go up there."

"A very difficult situation," Clara nodded, thinking that for some people life seemed to throw up endless hurdles. "The disappearance of Elaine must have hit them all hard?"

"The parents were devastated," Agnes agreed. "They seemed to almost at once jump to the worst possible conclusion. I think life has been so hard on them that they always see the most dire consequences of any situation first. I tried to convince them that Elaine could still be alive, but I sensed they had already concluded she was lost to them too. They asked a few questions, mainly about what had happened and where Captain Chase was. Of course, he was only just heading back from Ireland."

"The Irish connection," Clara mused. "I have wondered about this being a revenge attack on Captain Chase by Irish rebels."

"No evidence of that," Agnes said. "Not yet at least. I asked when the parents had last heard from Elaine, and they said she had written to them only the day before she vanished. They had her letter to hand as they had only just been reading it. They let me look at it, but it was all very normal stuff. Talking about the price of bread, the good laying of the chickens and asking about everyone's health. She mentioned the play she was in a lot too."

"Elaine was proud of her role in Macbeth," Clara sighed. "Another reason to suggest she would not leave the county voluntarily. Did the parents have any concerns about their daughter?"

"Not particularly," Agnes shrugged. "They liked Captain Chase and felt he was a good man. Elaine was in fine health. Perhaps the only upset was that the marriage had yet to be graced by children. Elaine apparently loves bairns and wants some of her own. Reading between the lines, I think arrangements had been made that if anything happened to her sister, Elaine would officially adopt the little ones."

"And now they fear that prospect is gone too, and

another means of securing the children's future lost," Clara understood. "I suppose they could offer no indication of anyone who would wish Elaine harm?"

"On the contrary, they did suggest one person. We went and interviewed her."

"Her?" Clara asked sharply, she quickly looked through the folder. "Is this it?"

One of the interviews had a hand-written note at the top which stated, in Inspector Park-Coombs' familiar scrawl, that the person questioned below remained a significant suspect. The name of the interviewee was Mary Worthing. Clara had not come across that name in her own investigations.

"Who is Mary Worthing?"

"The landlady of the White Rose," Agnes answered her. "She also happens to be the person who sold the Chases the cottage they now live in. I understand it used to belong to her mother and she sold it to them with the proviso that they made no more than the most necessary alterations. Of course, one person's view of what is necessary can be very different from another.

"Elaine Chase showed her parents the cottage not long after she bought it. Structurally it was fine, but the décor was tired and someone had sub-divided a couple of the rooms with cheap plasterboard. They set about stripping the place and making it a home. The plasterboard was taken down, the furniture which had been included in the sale was either dumped or sold. Just a handful of nice pieces kept. The wallpaper was removed, the curtains replaced and all the windows and doors given a lick of paint.

"It looked smart as polished silver when it was done, but when Mary Worthing called around to see how they were getting along she blew her lid. Her idea of necessary was apparently airing the rooms and maybe changing the bed linen. She was upset that every trace of her old mother had seemingly gone from the cottage. She let loose on Elaine, screaming and shouting, calling her names no one should be called and making all sorts of nasty threats. Captain Chase was thankfully home and kicked her out of the house and told her to never come back.

"From what I heard, her parting words were that if she ever got the chance she would make Elaine vanish from that cottage just like she had made her mother vanish. Nasty woman. She was interviewed but denied everything, of course. Reckoned she had not seen Elaine in months and kept away from the cottage these days."

Clara was intrigued. Mary Worthing sounded volatile and vengeful enough to do something as crazy as kidnap a person. Had she waited for just the right opportunity and snatched Elaine from the road as she had threatened to do?

"If you go to interview her, Clara, watch yourself. She has more than one screw loose. Some of the lads were saying she had threatened them with a knife when they raided the pub for opening too late. She had scared the life out of them."

Clara had no doubt about that. Someone incensed and wielding a knife was most certainly cause for alarm. She wondered how the inspector had persuaded the woman to speak to him. She noticed that the interview, which had been noted down verbatim, included a lot of asides where the inspector had remarked on Mary's aggressive temper and liberal use of foul language.

"If you need to go see her, I would be happy to accompany you," Agnes offered. "You ought not to confront her alone."

Clara was not perturbed by Mary's hostility, but she appreciated Agnes' offer.

"She sounds a promising lead."

"The police thought so, but couldn't find much. Besides, we've been side-tracked by this farm thieving business."

"Inspector Park-Coombs mentioned that," Clara remarked.

"Real nightmare," Agnes shook her head. "They'll have men stationed across Hove again tonight to try to catch the beggars. More than one farmer has threatened to shoot the thieves if he sees them."

"Which would not be good for anyone," Clara frowned.

"People are too slapdash with their security," Agnes said nonchalantly. "They think a closed door will be enough to stop someone. Amount of farmers that have been told to padlock things and still leave their tractors out in the open inviting trouble. I walk into these farmyards and feel a wave of disbelief come over me as I look at everything just lying about. Thieves' paradise."

Annie returned at that moment with a tray of food for Agnes. It included a plate of beef cutlets in gravy with bubble and squeak, and on a smaller plate a slice of Annie's apple sponge. Agnes' eyes lit up.

"A rare feast!" She declared, taking the tray gladly.

Annie blossomed with pride and then hastened away to fetch the teapot. Agnes set to work on her food like a famine victim.

"I appreciate the inspector sending me all this over," Clara spoke, tapping the papers before her. "I never like to think I am stepping on his toes."

"On the contrary, the inspector is mighty sick of this case. Not a single real lead to find Elaine, but a lot of dead-ends," Agnes glanced up from her food. "He would appreciate it if you could solve this case."

Clara frowned as she looked at the papers and thought of all the work that had already gone into this affair and achieved nothing.

"Well, I shall certainly try," she said, hoping that dedication and determination alone would be the key to solving this matter.

Chapter Ten

The following morning, Clara and Tommy caught the bus and headed to the Squires Garage. When Tommy had learned that Clara was going to look at cars, or rather to talk to people who worked with cars, he could not miss the opportunity. Tommy's greatest desire was to own a car, something brand new and sporty. Unfortunately, he did not as yet have the money to do so.

The Squires Garage was situated right in the middle of a row of Victorian terraces. It seemed an odd place to put such a busy workshop, but there it was, and the neighbours did not seem to be complaining about the noise or the smell of oil and petrol. Once the garage had been a blacksmith; the houses had grown up around it and when cars began to seriously replace horses the former blacksmith had sold his premises to a man who wanted to start a garage. Mr Humphry Squires came from a boatbuilding background, his grandfather had started a wet and dry dock where fishing vessels could be built or repaired. The fishing industry in Brighton was not what it had once been after the war and Humphry felt it was time to move on. Cars seemed to be the future and he knew plenty of men who could service and repair ship's engines. It just took a little bit of adapting to move into cars.

Humphry had briefly toyed with making his own car – The Squires' Dragon. But his company was too small and it would be impractical to compete with the big name manufacturers. However, he did spy a gap in the market for cheap tyres; motorists seeming to go through the things at an alarming rate. Squires' Rubber Company was thus founded, making tyres for cars, lorries and bicycles. People liked the fact they could buy locally, rather than ordering in a tyre from another producer. They also liked the price. There were, of course, those who queried the quality of a Squires' tyre and still insisted on ordering in a Dunlop or something similar, but Humphry found that, by and large, people liked his cheap and cheerful wheels.

Walking into the courtyard of the garage, Clara was struck by an overpowering smell of petrol. A puddle of water just in front of her shimmered with green, blue and pink swirls, indicating that something had leaked recently. To her right there was a smart town car, low-slung, convertible roof and painted in an electrifying blue. It had white fenders that reared up over the black wheels like a wild horse. One of these fenders was badly dented and scuffed. It appeared to have struck a big, solid object and been buckled in on itself. It nearly curved backwards into the tyre. Clara ran her fingers over the damage, her mind as always puzzling out what had occurred and debating whether a person being run down could cause such a dent.

"Sheep on the road."

Clara looked up as a gentleman in brown overalls walked towards them. He was wiping his oily hands on an equally oily cloth.

"Sir Hugo was driving at the time. Only ever takes it out on Sundays. Spitting feathers he was when he brought her in," the mechanic patted the car affectionately, like it was a pet dog. "Farmers ought to take better care of their livestock fences. Sir Hugo nearly had a heart attack at the shock. It folded the metal back on itself, will need a whole new fender, at least. We haven't even got to checking the suspension and steering for damage yet."

"And the sheep?" Clara asked.

The man looked at her in bafflement, the sheep had never crossed his mind.

"Are you looking to buy a car?" He asked instead.

"Possibly," Tommy said before Clara could interject. "All depends on price."

"Naturally, naturally," the mechanic nodded. "What sort of budget do you have?"

Tommy cleared his throat and looked a little bit sheepish.

"I believe I have around fifty pounds in my bank account," he said, trying not to sound embarrassed.

The mechanic's face, formerly enthusiastic, now fixed into a look of disappointment.

"Sir Hugo drives a Crossley, that sells for around £850. A basic Sunbeam is about £650. We occasionally have cars for resale between the £400 and £600 mark."

Tommy shoved his hands into his pockets.

"Well, I never thought motoring was cheap."

"Actually, we are not here to buy a car," Clara interrupted finally. "I would like to speak to whoever deals with the sale of car tyres."

The mechanic frowned, clearly confused as to why a person who did not own a car would be interested in tyres.

"We do have a nice range of bicycle tyres," he said, thinking that had to be the answer.

"Who would I need to speak to?" Clara persisted without offering further explanation.

"Mr Benson," the mechanic replied. "He is in charge of our car parts sales. Lots of people like to tinker with the cars themselves and just come along to buy a part. He is just through that door there."

The mechanic pointed to a brown door in the side of the building. A sign nailed to the door declared this was the Spares and Other Sales Office. Clara and Tommy headed over, Tommy looking glum.

"I feel a fool now," he muttered.

"Silly price for a lump of metal," Clara consoled him. "If they want the car to really take off, manufacturers will have to start making them more affordable."

She entered the office and saw an older gentleman perched behind a high counter. He was wearing a long brown jacket, rather like the sort shopkeepers wore and he had a thick pair of spectacles pinching the bridge of his wide nose.

"Can I help?" He asked, looking up from a catalogue he was browsing.

"I hope you can. I am trying to unravel a mystery," Clara smiled at him. "Someone drove onto my garden the other day and destroyed my flowerbeds."

"Oh dear," the salesman said sympathetically.

"Indeed, and they did not have the decency to even leave a note stating who they were and offering to pay for the damages. Fortunately, I know someone with a bit of car knowledge and he is convinced that the tyre was a Squires. Now, if I could track down the person who bought those tyres I could find my culprit and have them reimburse me for my flowers."

"I see," the salesman said, though his frown suggested he didn't. "We sell a lot of tyres. At least one full set a fortnight."

"I only need to know who has bought one very recently. The tyre itself had a distinctive notch missing, so I shall be able to identify it when I see it. I just need to know where to look."

The salesman seemed a little uneasy about all this.

"I'm not sure I can just give you the names of all our customers."

"I only need to know who has bought new tyres in the last three or so months," Clara continued, hoping to wear him down. "You keep those records, I imagine?"

"I do," the salesman was not budging. "Look, I think I

ought to run this by Mr Squires."

"I don't intend to cause trouble for anyone who is not involved," Clara promised, but to no avail.

The salesman politely asked her to wait while he went through to a back room.

"This is not going well," Clara admitted to Tommy.

"Maybe you should have told him the truth?" Tommy suggested, but he didn't look convinced by his own answer.

"I couldn't risk it. I don't want everyone knowing what I am up to."

"I don't think he will let you see that list of names without a better reason than a damaged garden."

Clara pulled a face. She had hoped a touch of gentle persuasion would do the trick. The salesman was returning and his expression looked rather grim.

"Mr Squires thinks he ought to speak with you. Would you mind going through to his office?" The salesman lifted a hatch in the counter to enable them to pass through.

Clara tried not to sigh aloud as she was escorted into the office of Humphry Squires. The garage owner was sitting behind his desk apparently going through his books. He rose up and smiled at his two visitors, which was somewhat reassuring. He was wearing a yellow checked suit and red tie, it made him look rather overdressed for a day of work. He was in his late thirties with slicked back black hair and a moustache so thin it might have been pencilled onto his upper lip.

"Thanks George," he said to the salesman who disappeared from the room, closing the door as he went. Humphry turned to Clara. "Something about a ruined garden, is it?"

"Actually, it is more complicated than that," Clara decided she would have to be honest with the man if she was going to get anywhere. "I am investigating the disappearance of Elaine Chase."

"Oh, I read about that in the papers," Humphry

nodded. "I thought the husband was suspected?"

"Only in the imaginations of gossiping journalists," Clara said with a suitable amount of disdain. "Captain Chase could not have been involved. However, I have learned that on the day she disappeared Elaine was offered a lift in a car. A car with new Squires tyres. I am trying to track this car and the person who gave Elaine that lift as they might be a vital witness."

"You are not the police, though?" Humphry raised an eyebrow curiously.

"I am a private detective, but I can assure you my activities are known to the police and have their approval. If you wish to call Inspector Park-Coombs…"

"That won't be necessary," Humphry waved a hand. "You really think tracing this car might help?"

"When a woman has apparently been snatched away from her home, you cannot afford to miss any lead."

"All right," Humphry said, having given the matter due thought. "Bear with me a moment and I shall fetch the tyre sales register."

He disappeared from the office and Clara allowed herself a sigh of relief.

"Honesty is the best policy," Tommy mumbled, wandering to the wall and looking at a calendar with illustrations of cars. "How basic do you suppose a basic Sunbeam really is?"

Clara had no opportunity to answer as Humphry returned with a large ledger. He placed it on his desk with a thud.

"We sell quite a few tyres. More one-offs than sets. We recommend changing them in pairs, naturally, but not everyone wants to," he opened the book and took a look at the list. "We do different types to suit different makes. Did you happen to get a good look at the tread?"

Clara automatically produced her notebook with the sketch she had made of the tyre's pattern. Humphry looked at it and smiled.

"That is our Indian 230. Tends to be more suited to

road cars rather than sports cars. One of our more robust models and recommended if the vehicle regularly travels off tarmacadam roads," he was thumbing through the sales ledger as he talked. "Here we go, we sold twelve of those tyres in the last couple of months. Four were a full set change for Mr Brown's 1910 tourer. He was off on holiday to the Isle of Wight, always takes the car and travels around. He won't be back until the end of April."

"When did he leave?" Clara asked.

"I believe he said he was leaving on the Saturday, the tyres being fitted on the Thursday before. He has certainly been gone over a month."

Clara could exclude him then.

"The other 230s were sold either in pairs or as singles. That boils down to five different customers."

"Are all of them residents of Brighton?"

"Mr Finch resides on the far side of Hove. He is a farmer and dreadful for considering his car a tractor. You should see the damage he does to the suspension. My mechanics groan every time that car rolls in. He must run it at full speed across fields. No consideration for the undercarriage at all."

"How many of the customers are women?" Clara asked.

"Two," Humphry ran his finger down the ledger. "Mrs Anderson bought a pair and Miss Erskine just bought a single. Shall I write these all down?"

"Please do," Clara was feeling more hopeful now she had names to work on, especially as two were women. Of course, she could not rule out that a man owned the car and that it had been driven on the fateful occasion by a female relative or friend. But she had more leads than she had done a few minutes ago.

Humphry finished the list and handed it to Clara.

"I do hope you can find this poor lost woman. It brings a shiver to the spine to imagine someone being snatched like that," Humphry did not look particularly spooked as he sat back in his chair. "My wife has been rather uneasy about walking home alone from her mother's ever since. I go collect her in the car. That, of course, is a very good selling point. They are a secure means of transporting yourself safely home. Had Elaine Chase been in a car of her own, she could not have been snatched."

"You could use that as an advertisement," Tommy said, aiming not to smirk. "Cars keep you safe."

"Yes, I could!" Humphry said with sudden elation, completely missing Tommy's sarcasm. "You know, I think the world will be a far safer place once everyone has a car. Think how few accidents there will be if everyone is in one? No pedestrians to knock down, no cyclists to collide with. The car will reinvent road safety, why, what a great line!"

Clara was smiling as she thanked Mr Squires for his time. He was only half-listening, fully absorbed in his own vision of the future and the promotion of his business. Tommy and Clara let themselves out of his office and nodded to George as they went back to the courtyard. Clara folded the list of names Humphry had given her and placed it in her handbag.

"I take it Mrs Anderson and Miss Erskine are top of your list of suspects," Tommy asked with a smirk.

"As women with cars they naturally have to be, but I rule nothing out and their names are unfamiliar to me. For the moment I do not know what connection they might have had with Elaine."

"So, what next?" Tommy asked.

Clara smiled.

"I feel it is time for some refreshment and I happen to know just the place."

Chapter Eleven

Clara stood before the door of the White Rose and considered the prospect. A lick of paint would not have gone amiss. They were close to the harbour and the smell of salt and seawater struck you at once. It had also struck the paintwork and caused it to peel considerably. A forlorn sign hung over the door, so battered by age and the elements that it now informed the world that this was the hit ose. Presumably Mary Worthing largely existed on regular trade and was not concerned that her damaged sign made it appear as if her pub was on the shortlist for repossession. Or, possibly, demolition; for one of the front windows was boarded up and several of the small glass panes in the front door had been smashed and covered over with paper and tape.

Tommy studied the façade with a grimace.

"Bit of a dive."

"It doesn't really inspire hope," Clara admitted. "Had I just walked past I would have thought it was closed."

"You sure it is not?" Tommy reached out for the door handle as he spoke and turned it. The door opened with a groan – it was too dramatic to be termed merely a creak – and the soft sounds of people inside could be heard. There was a second door after the first, creating a little porch and explaining why the glass in the outer door had been so rudimentarily repaired.

Tommy opened the second door and the noise increased. People were talking and glasses clinked. However, it was not the lively chatter often heard in pubs, rather it was almost as if everyone was keeping their voices down. A faint smell of stale food, namely cabbage, drifted in their direction and there was more than a hint of beer in the air.

Entering the pub, which was dark after the bright day outside, (the windows that weren't boarded up were so filthy they did not allow any light in) they found themselves facing a long bar. To the left and right were tables and chairs. Drinkers sat in groups, many of them wearing the garb of fishermen or dock workers. There was an underlying hint of fish in the pub's personal aroma. No one was sitting at the bar, aside from one old man who was perched on a stool at the very end and seemed to be half-asleep from the way his head tipped over his pint.

The person behind the bar was a stout woman in her fifties. She had raven-black, coarse hair, interspersed by tendrils of white. It was hard to imagine a time when she might ever have been called pretty; her nose was bulbous and sunk between her fat cheeks, a wart swelled to one side. Her eyes were also deep set and shrouded by deep wrinkles. Her lips pulled into a scowl, even as she polished a glass with an old cloth. Everything about her seemed solid and imposing. The thick arms were muscular, the hands as big as a man's and swollen up. Her form was that of an apple-shaped lump, hidden as much as possible by a loose blouse and a large skirt. She suddenly slapped one hand down hard on the bar, making everyone jump.

"Alfie! You fall asleep and knock another of me beer mugs off the bar and you'll be for the high jump!" She screamed down the bar at the old man whose head now hung perilously over his glass.

Alfie jumped with everyone else and looked at her in stunned amazement.

"I must have just nodded off…"

"Not over my beer mug! I don't need another smashed! Put it to one side if you are going to fall asleep on my bar or go home to your bed!"

Alfie mumbled his apologies and moved the mug to one side. It was not many moments before he appeared to be drifting off again. However, now Mary Worthing's attention was on her new arrivals.

"What can I get you?" She asked gruffly, looking as if this was a tiresome task she did not want to be bothered with.

"What are you serving?" Tommy asked with a smile.

"Beer," Mary sneered.

Tommy corrected himself carefully, his smile not fading.

"I shall have a beer then. Clara?"

"Tonic water?" Clara asked, feeling that was a forlorn hope.

"You can have tap water and I'll blow some bubbles in it," Mary Worthing snapped at her. "This is a pub. I serve beer, it's all I serve."

Customer service was not something Mary had clearly ever heard of.

"I'll have a beer," Clara said pleasantly, intending to palm it off on Tommy the second she could.

Mary Worthing began pulling two pints. Clara and Tommy perched on bar stools, the velvet covering rather sticky as they sat on it. Mary set the two beer mugs before her new guests and demanded payment. The beer looked to be swirling with small flecks of something, its quality presumably only compensated for by the low price.

Clara was intent on asking Mary a question or two, but she was putting off the moment as the woman seemed so volatile and disagreeable. She thought a direct approach might be unproductive. After timidly sipping the beer, and endeavouring to not pull a face, she came up with a solution.

"Is it possible to reach the western cliffs through the harbour?" She asked Mary Worthing casually.

The woman huffed.

"Course it is. Just follow the harbour wall and head up the steps. But ain't much worth looking at over there. Unless you are one of those folks who like to look at 'views'."

Mary said this as if it was something lewd.

"Actually, I have a friend who lives in a cottage along the cliffs. We are down on holiday and thought we would surprise Elaine," Clara pretended to sip more of her beer, leaving the statement to do its work. It didn't take long.

"Elaine Chase, that would be?" Mary asked, pausing in the act of putting more glasses away.

"Yes," Clara smiled. "Do you know her?"

Mary's face warped into a look of pure hatred and Clara was sure she heard a few people get up and move further back from the bar. Clara had heard the expression 'red rag to a bull', but, until that moment, she had never seen it so plainly enacted.

"Yes, I know that little cow! She bought my dear late mother's cottage off me and went about destroying all memory of my old mum!"

"Oh," Clara said quietly.

"She told me she would only make necessary changes, that was our arrangement. Next thing I know she has stripped the house of everything! Everything! Did she ask me if she could get rid of my mother's furniture before she sold it? No! My mother spent years getting that cottage just as she wanted it and it wasn't for Elaine Chase to alter that! Just 'cause she thinks she has a right to! Looked me straight in the eye and said 'I do own this house, my dear.' I almost spat in her face! My mother must have been turning in her grave watching her floral wallpaper come down in shreds."

Clara remained mute during this tirade. Mary

thumped her fist on the bar.

"There was nothing wrong with that furniture or the wallpaper! It was completely serviceable and she should not have changed it. I walked into the place and I found my mother's presence completely gone! What sort of evil creature would do such a thing? She took my mother from me more certainly than death itself."

Mary bit at her lower lip and there was a hint of tears in the fierce eyes. The tyrant had emotions, just like anyone else.

"People are cruel and inconsiderate, that is what it is!" She snapped at Clara. "I went back to my poor dead mother's cottage on the second anniversary of her death, intending to remember her. I wanted to sit in her favourite armchair. Instead, I strolled in to a completely different house. My ma had been stolen from me, completely and utterly!"

Mary's mouth had almost turned in on itself as she battled her grief, she rather looked as though she was sucking a very bitter pill.

"I wouldn't have sold the place if I didn't have to. People don't understand. I couldn't live there and run this place and I couldn't afford to have it sit there empty. I had to sell. I ain't rich," Mary shouted this at Clara as if she had been accused of being wealthy in the past.

Clara kept her face sympathetic, hoping to elicit as much as possible from the woman. She had a hunch this was a complaint that Mary regularly ranted upon to her customers and they knew the ire it would provoke within her.

"She put chickens in the garden," Mary's tone had gone from ferocity to misery. "My mother hated birds and to think of chickens clucking about her flowerbeds boils the blood."

"I didn't know all that," Clara said to fill the silence that followed and to provoke something more. "Elaine is not normally so inconsiderate."

"She had no heart," Mary snorted. "Anyway, you don't

want to be going all the way along the cliff to her cottage, not after what happened."

Clara feigned confusion.

"Elaine only went and vanished!" Mary responded, a look of satisfaction coming onto her face. "Police have been nosing around, even came in here to ask questions. Disappeared into thin air."

"That is awful!" Clara gasped. "Why, I had a letter from her not so long ago."

"It happened recently," Mary nodded. "The story goes she was walking home and just vanished. I personally think she has done a runner from that husband of hers. I didn't like him either. Rude and arrogant, he was. Not surprised she opted to leave him."

"How remarkable!" Clara continued. "Did she not leave any indication of where she had gone?"

"No," Mary slapped a meaty hand on the bar again, it seemed to be a favourite gesture. "And that's another thing, I wanted back some of the flower pots in the garden. Wanted to save my mother's flowers before that woman sold them. Elaine refused to let me near the cottage when her husband was not around. He is controlling, I see that."

Mary narrowed her eyes and clucked her tongue.

"He was due home on leave and I was to go over on the Saturday and collect my flower pots. Well, the week before she disappears! And now I can't get my flower pots because Captain Chase is in the doldrums and keeps insinuating I might have had something to do with Elaine vanishing!"

"Oh dear," Clara said. "Why would he think such a thing?"

"Malice!" Mary huffed. "And the police have filled his head with ideas. Then there are the papers going on about him making Elaine disappear. He is angry and looking for someone to blame. He seems to think his wife too perfect to have enemies other than me!"

"What do the police make of it all?"

"Useless, as always," Mary laughed. "I wouldn't trust them to find a lost penny, let alone a person! I always say you have to sort out your own problems. I have no time for the police. They actually came here to question me! I had half a mind to run them out of the door! Who did they think they were?"

"Well, this has certainly changed my plans," Clara commented. "I feel absolutely awful. Thank goodness I came in here and spoke to you, else I would have made such a fool of myself."

Mary puffed herself up, pleased to think she had been of considerable use to someone. She was the sort of person who needed their ego massaged regularly.

"Was bound to happen, considering what Elaine was like," Mary said solemnly. "But, what a nuisance for me! I keep fearing Captain Chase will sell on the cottage and then I will have no link to my mother whatsoever."

"Might he sell?" Clara asked casually.

"Can't see him staying, what with all those silly rumours flying about. He is in the army, anyway, and won't need the cottage without his wife."

"Elaine might be found," Tommy interjected. The talk of Elaine as if she was dead and gone had been troubling him for a while.

Mary looked at him as if he was rather dull and had not grasped the situation.

"People vanish for a reason and they don't come back. My old father disappeared one night when I was just a girl. Walked out the door and never came home. After a few days my mother said good riddance and that was that," Mary smiled to herself. "Wherever Elaine went, whether she went alone or with someone else, she ain't coming back. I expect she was tired of the husband always being away in the army. It's a lonely life being a soldier's wife, and her parents had moved away to help out her sister. I hear tell she is something of a liability too. Anyway, I know for a fact Elaine was spending considerable time with Walter Stone. He is another of the actors with the Brighton Players. Elaine was a member too."

"Yes," Clara agreed. "She wrote to tell me she was playing Lady Macbeth in the newest production."

"And Walter is Macbeth," Mary added. "I was asked to put up a poster for the production, it's in my lobby. He is listed on it. Still has Elaine's name on it too, mind. She disappeared after the posters were printed and they couldn't afford new ones. I smirk at it every time I go past to lock and unlock the front door."

Mary Worthing had an unpleasant grin on her face.

"I don't tend to listen to such gossip about friends," Clara said quietly.

"It's fact, not gossip. Walter Stone lives in West Street and people have seen Elaine going there of an evening. He is a bachelor, a handsome one at that. Doesn't take a genius to conclude the obvious."

"But Walter Stone has not disappeared," Clara pointed out.

"Not yet," Mary wagged a finger at her. "That would be too suspicious. No, she has gone ahead and he will join her after this performance of Macbeth, mark my words. The husband probably knows too, but isn't saying because he feels a damn fool."

"Oh dear," Clara repeated herself, feeling that the waters had suddenly become murkier. Until now there had been no hint of impropriety on Elaine's part, everyone had spoken of her as being above suspicion of such a thing. Could it be they were all wrong?

"Always the quiet ones," Mary said, still smirking.

Chapter Twelve

"A complicated character," Tommy reflected as they left the White Rose. "Not a woman I would want to meet on a dark night, unless armed with a machine gun."

Clara chuckled.

"I would prefer not to meet her anywhere, but apparently she is capable of running a business," Clara glanced behind her. "Well, to a degree."

They paused on the street, watching a group of passing dock workers traipsing along the other side.

"No one else had mentioned Walter Stone," Clara said.

"Nothing like a sworn enemy to reveal the real truth about someone," Tommy replied with a hint of irony to his voice. "Is it possible Elaine was having an affair?"

"I really do not know the woman enough to say," Clara sighed. "Her friends and parents wish me to believe she was perfect, but no one is perfect. Everyone has their chink, the part of their façade that does not glisten as brightly. Maybe Walter Stone was Elaine's chink?"

"He didn't speak to you at the rehearsal?"

"No. Now I look back, he almost seemed to be avoiding me. But that might be a case of me reading too much into things," Clara paused. "Let's go see if he will speak to me now. He is probably at work, if he works, but his landlady will know where that is."

They turned right and walked in the direction of West Street. The road was long and partly lined with houses and partly with shops. Elaine had not specified an address for Walter, so Clara walked into a greengrocer's and asked if they knew which house Mr Stone resided in. Luckily, they did; Walter bought an apple from the grocer every morning and his landlady was a regular customer. The grocer was one of life's great talkers and he started to regale Clara with a lengthy description on the woman's shopping habits and character before she could extract herself.

"Well?" Tommy asked.

"Just a few doors down."

They walked up the road and paused before a humble, but well-tended white terrace. A tile on the garden wall announced that this was Hyacinth House. Clara knocked on the door and, after an interval of about a minute, a tiny woman opened it. Clara did not often have to look down to meet a person's eyes, she was not considered tall in any stretch of the imagination and largely she spent her time looking up. The woman on the doorstep, however, was even smaller, possibly over a foot shorter than Clara.

She wore a housecoat to cover her dress while she went about her chores, it nearly dusted the floor for her. Aged somewhere in her seventies, the woman's hair was pure white and cut into a short bob that did not entirely suit her. She looked up at Clara with bright, sparkling eyes.

"Hello," she said.

"Apologies for the interruption, but I am trying to locate Walter Stone," Clara explained quickly.

The woman smiled.

"Interruptions are fine, my dear, when I am dusting. It is my least favourite task," she said pleasantly. "Walter is at work at the moment."

"Where does he work?" Clara asked.

"The printing firm two streets over. He is a

typesetter," the woman explained. "What is it you wanted to speak to him about?"

"It's a delicate matter," Clara lowered her voice. "I am looking into the disappearance of Elaine Chase, and I hoped Walter might be able to assist."

"Oh, yes, that poor woman," the landlady pressed a hand to her mouth as if she felt suddenly unwell. "Elaine was a dear person. I felt awful when I heard what had happened."

"She came here?" Clara asked innocently.

"Quite often these last weeks," the landlady nodded. "Walter and Elaine were putting in extra rehearsal time. They are both in Macbeth. It was Elaine's first big performance and she was a little nervous. Walter was helping her prepare."

Clara wondered how honest an assessment of the situation that was. She decided Walter's landlady might just have some knowledge that could be useful.

"Might we come in for a chat about Elaine? You might be able to help us."

"Why of course!" The landlady stepped back from the door so they could enter. "I would do anything to help find Elaine. Please, go sit down and I will make some tea."

Clara and Tommy settled into the front parlour, which reminded them of their grandmother's house. Every item of furniture had a cover; even the tea table had a velvet cloth with tassels over it. The mantelpiece displayed various low-quality porcelain figurines, mainly shepherds and shepherdesses, or similar labouring class characters. Everything was immaculate. The dust the landlady had referred to was impossible to see. Clara took note of several photographs in frames featuring two women, one clearly their host, the other very similar in appearance. Clara guessed it was a sister.

When the landlady reappeared with a tea tray, Clara spent a few moments making formal introductions of herself and Tommy. She explained in as vague a fashion as possible that she had been hired to look into Elaine

Chase's disappearance, and what she currently knew about that event. She did not reveal that Captain Chase was the one to hire her. She felt it was prudent to avoid saying his name as it might make the landlady more reluctant to talk of any potential indiscretion on Elaine's part. For that matter, she was not certain if the landlady was aware that Elaine was married. It might have been tactfully overlooked.

"I think it is wonderful someone is finally looking into this dreadful crime," the landlady said when Clara was finished. "My name is Patricia Rownley. I have been Walter's landlady for about three years. He rents the rooms on the two floors upstairs. I cook and clean for him. He is a very nice young man. Sometimes, when he has nothing else on, he will come and take afternoon tea with me on a Sunday. I appreciate the company. I have been very lonely since my sister passed away."

"I noticed the photographs of you and another woman. I thought it might be your sister," Clara said.

"Her name was Mavis. We lived here together after our parents died. Mavis was a few years older than me. She died in 1917. Cancer," Patricia paused thoughtfully. "Renting out the upper rooms was partly a means of practicality and partly a way of providing myself with company. The thought of a home silent of another's voice filled me with dread. Walter has been the perfect tenant in that regard."

"And how long have you known Elaine Chase?" Clara asked.

Patricia did a quick mental calculation.

"You know, it will be a year in a couple of weeks' time. Elaine came over one Sunday afternoon and Walter introduced us. She had recently joined the Brighton Players and was getting used to it all. She was rather nervous about going on the stage for the first time," Patricia smiled to herself. "I made tea and we sat and talked for perhaps a couple of hours. I thought she was a lovely young woman. Intelligent, kind and with a sense of humour. I liked her a lot."

"And since then she has come over quite often?" Clara suggested.

"I would say most weeks she pops in for a visit. Usually on a Sunday after they have been rehearsing. Walter and Elaine always take tea with me first before going upstairs to practice. Walter told me, in private, that Elaine had the makings of a first-class actress. He almost felt she was wasted in amateur performances."

"Sounds like a charming woman," Tommy said. "The sort any man would like to meet and take home for tea."

"She is all those things and more," Patricia agreed. "I cannot fathom how anyone could take against her. There was not a cruel bone in her body. I remember, one day last winter, I was rather under-the-weather and struggling with my usual housework. Walter had been keeping an eye on me, but had to go to work. I felt so awful that day. I cannot describe it. I wondered if I was dying a little, I seemed to have no strength. And then Elaine turned up on the doorstep with a kettle of chicken broth. Walter had sent a message to her, saying how he was worried about me and asking if she could pop in and check I was all right.

"She did more than that. She kept me company all that day and the next. I can't remember the last time someone took care of me like that, not since my sister was living at least."

Tears welled in Patricia's eyes.

"That woman pulled me back from the brink, I am sure of it. And I will personally thrash anyone who has laid a single hand on her. No matter if they are a man or woman," Patricia sat up a little higher and her determination was palpable.

"Tell me about Walter," Clara asked. "I have seen him act, but not had the chance to speak to him."

"Walter loves the theatre," Patricia quickly warmed to her topic. "He goes to London to watch the latest productions whenever he can. He has suggested taking me, but that is such a long way away and I don't go far these days. I do always go to the opening night of the Brighton Players' performances. Walter is very often leading man, he is a competent actor, maybe sometimes a little over-dramatic. I've told him as much."

Patricia blushed.

"He laughs sometimes when I say these things. He says I am his best critic, because I do not pull my punches. No one will tell him what he is doing wrong at the Players because they are scared he might suddenly leave and they would be without a leading man," Patricia leaned forward conspiratorially. "You may have noticed that most of the members of the Players are women or old men. Walter invariably gets the lead male roles by default. The women tend to fight over who gets to act alongside him. He is handsome, you see."

"Did Elaine fight over him?"

"Elaine is married," Patricia grinned, revealing that she knew more than Clara had first thought. "But, it wouldn't surprise me if she did have a little thing for Walter. Her husband is in the army and it is lonely for her. She said as much to me. Her cottage is rather remote, and a lot of her friends are too busy during the day with their families to be able to offer her much time. She doesn't like to impose. I told her she could come here whenever she wished."

Patricia paused again, that thoughtful look returning.

"I sensed that Elaine often avoided her friends too, the ones at least who had a family. Elaine wanted a baby, though she never made a fuss about it. I just saw it in her eyes when she talked about a friend's new child. There was this little flicker of sadness," Patricia tilted her head to the side. "I suppose, it takes a person who has suffered the same sadness to notice it. Neither I, nor my sister married. It was not a conscious choice, just how fate dealt our cards. I had always thought of having children.

"I hoped that my disappointment would not also be Elaine's. She did at least have a husband, which is half the battle."

"Did she ever speak of Captain Chase?"

"Oh, all the time," Patricia said. "There was all that nonsense in the papers about him being responsible for her disappearance. Elaine would be heartbroken to read such rot. She loved him as dearly as any woman can love a man. I have no doubt in my mind about that. She was always worried about him in Ireland, scared for his safety. And then it was Elaine, herself, who was snatched."

Patricia shook her head, a part of her still unable to comprehend that fact.

"When you last saw Elaine, was she upset or concerned at all?" Clara asked. "Maybe she had been followed recently? Or had been worried about being alone at home?"

"No," Patricia shook her head harder. "Nothing like that. I am certain Elaine would have told me if that was the case and I would have insisted she stay with me until things were resolved. She was a friend to me as much as Walter, Miss Fitzgerald, I would have done anything for her."

"When did you learn she was missing?" Clara asked gently.

"The Sunday after it happened," Patricia's face fell, her mind returning to that day when she heard the awful news. "Walter came home and looked as white as a sheet. He said Elaine had not come to rehearsals, which was extremely unusual. All the Players had gone to look for her at her cottage. There was something not right about the place. The chickens had been had by the fox and there were signs that Elaine had suddenly sprung up and left. They informed the police, they were that upset."

"I have spoken with the police. It is safe to say they are stumped," Clara explained sadly.

"I told Walter a search party ought to be arranged and he agreed. I went with him and a number of the Players to search all the roads around the cottage," Patricia hesitated. "I've had this awful feeling ever since it happened, something in the pit of my stomach."

She pressed a balled fist into her belly, as if the feeling now bothered her.

"Elaine's house is so very near the cliffs. You can hear the waves crashing below all the time. I stood in her garden that Sunday evening and I found myself looking out over the ocean and a feeling of desolation swept over me. I don't know…" Patricia bit her lip. "Maybe it was my own feelings at play. I was upset, frightened, worried. I couldn't think that anyone in Brighton would wish Elaine harm. I walked across the road and towards the cliff edge. The sea seemed dark below and swept right up to the rocks of the cliff, and the gulls were crying overhead so shrilly."

Patricia knotted her fingers together, the action seeming to give her strength to continue speaking.

"The more I looked, the more I thought of that secret sadness in Elaine, the one she hid so carefully," Patricia's knuckles had gone white. "What if, I asked myself, Elaine could not handle the sadness anymore? What if, in a sudden moment of madness, she had stood on that same clifftop and looked out across the ocean, and…"

"You think Elaine committed suicide?" Clara asked quietly, the question did not seem one that should be spoken loudly.

"They would never find the body. It would be swept straight out to sea," Patricia hung her head and the tears finally fell. "Surely that makes more sense? I've told no one my fears until now. I have this gnawing anxiety inside me. Could it be that Elaine jumped?" Patricia met Clara's eyes. "I very much fear that is the case."

Chapter Thirteen

Suicide.

That had been the furthest thought from Clara's mind. Patricia's revelation had knocked her for six. After leaving the house in West Street, she and Tommy had walked to a nearby park and sat down for a moment. Clara needed to think and to reassess the situation.

Tommy sat in silence beside her, waiting for Clara to gather her thoughts, giving her the time she needed to regain focus on her case. Clara appreciated the silence, but she was struggling to get her head around the possibility that Elaine Chase might have jumped from the clifftop and be gone for good. There might be no kidnapper, no one to blame, except circumstances and some unknown reason for Elaine to suddenly find life overwhelming.

It was Patricia's certainty that had made Clara so uneasy. The woman had been a good friend to Elaine and knew her a lot better than Clara did. Had she sensed something bubbling beneath the surface which she could not quite define? An instinct, a hunch, that Elaine was not as happy as she appeared. Maybe she sensed that Elaine was worried about something, or could Patricia have been lying when she indicated that Elaine and Walter's relationship was purely professional? If Elaine had been having an affair, could the imminent return of Captain Chase have caused her so much guilt over her conduct that she jumped rather than face her husband?

"She might have jumped," Clara said out loud at last.

Tommy glanced at her. He was altogether too familiar with the darker parts of the human mind.

"The evidence is not conclusive," he said carefully. "She lived near a cliff. She vanished suddenly, and Patricia had a funny feeling near the clifftop. I'm not sure it would convince an inquest."

There had, as yet, been no inquest in the Elaine Chase mystery. There was no body for an inquest to be held over, for a start, and people still hoped she was alive. Clara imagined an inquest being held and the evidence being proposed for suicide.

"She did not leave a note," Clara continued. "Not that suicides always do leave notes, if they are suddenly swept up with the madness of the moment. And her handbag was missing, meaning she probably had it with her. If she walked straight out of her house and to the cliffside to jump, why take her handbag?"

"The flipside to that argument is that suicide is not a rational act, therefore why should the person's actions when committing it be rational?" Tommy said. "We had more than enough suicides in the trenches to make you rethink what you thought you knew about such things. Not to mention the odd ones which you could not quite say whether they were the result of a stray German bullet or a man taking his own life.

"We found a fellow once with a bullet to the back of his head. He was either shot by someone on his own side or he somehow shot himself. We never did work out the matter satisfactorily."

"Would Elaine have left the chickens to their fate had she decided to kill herself?" Clara mused.

"Better to let them take their chances with the fox, then to lock them in their house and leave them to starve," Tommy replied.

"The front door was unlocked," Clara remembered. "Though, many people do not lock their doors, especially when they live outside of town. And then there was the woman in the car who offered her a lift. Did she actually drop her at home and then Elaine later decided to end it all?"

"I know it is not what we want to think," Tommy said gently. "We are hopeful Elaine is alive and can be saved. But the possibility remains. I suppose, though not conclusive, the evidence does fit a suicide."

"And yet I must not be tempted to think that. It will sully my investigation and point me in the wrong direction. I must continue in the belief that Elaine Chase is alive and being held prisoner somewhere. It would be hideous if I accepted the idea that she had committed suicide when she could really have been saved," Clara closed her eyes for a brief moment and tried to focus her thoughts. "Let's pay Walter Stone a visit and talk to him. Perhaps he will offer some insight."

Walter Stone worked for a printing company a short walk from West Street. Clara would not normally disturb someone when they were at work, but she felt that as each hour ticked by, Elaine Chase's fate became less promising. Time was of the essence.

The printing company was set back in a concrete yard. A delivery van had just pulled in with rolls of paper and there were men unloading them. Clara stopped to ask someone where she could find the main office and was given directions through the main doors and up a metal staircase. A brown door at the top had 'office' painted on it in white paint. Clara knocked and a voice within asked her to enter.

Behind the door a suite of three rooms served as the administrative hub of the company. The first office was used by the head supervisor and a secretary. On either side of the room doors led off into two separate offices – one for the company manager and another for the company owner. The secretary worked for all three men, she had a desk right next to that of the supervisor, who did not spend a lot of time in his office anyway, mainly being down on the printing floor. Clara and Tommy were quite lucky to find him in when they did. After introducing herself, Clara explained she wished to speak with Walter Stone.

"It is rather urgent. You may be aware that a woman has gone missing. Walter is not personally involved, but may be able to offer some insight into the situation, as he knew her."

The supervisor looked unhappy.

"We run a tight ship here. We expect people to work while on the company time, not fraternise."

The secretary, who had been doing some typing work, glanced at Clara and gave a roll of her eyes. Clearly this was a refrain she heard often.

"I would not normally disrupt you, but this situation is very serious, and every moment counts. If this woman is to be found alive…"

"Are you talking about Elaine Chase?" The secretary suddenly asked.

The supervisor cast a scowl at her, but she ignored him.

"I am," Clara admitted. "There is hope she might still be found safe and well."

"If you recall, Mr Keene, it was Mrs Chase who came in to place that order for personalised Christmas cards last November," the secretary had turned to the supervisor, speaking to him without any real hint of deference.

Clara had a feeling these two did not enjoy sharing a working space and annoyed each other.

"I remember well enough," Mr Keene grumbled. "She wanted her Christmas cards printed with a drawing she had executed. It was of a cottage, if I recall rightly, and she wanted a bespoke message printed inside. We don't get many orders like that and the cost was hardly cheap, considering we had to have an engraving made of the cottage. But she paid without hesitation and seemed pleased with the results. We let her keep the printing block of the engraving too."

Mr Keene sniffed noisily and then looked at the secretary beside him.

"She is missing then?"

"It was in the newspaper," the secretary explained to him patiently.

"Poor woman," Mr Keene said in a perfunctory fashion. "But what does that have to do with interrupting our work hours?"

"Walter Stone is one of the last people to see Mrs Chase before she vanished. I had hoped he might be able to offer some insight into her movements the day she disappeared," Clara was vague about her real motives for speaking to Walter, she didn't want his supervisor getting ideas about any impropriety. Especially when it might not be true.

"The printing works closes at six," Mr Keene said, meaning to end the discussion.

"That is seven hours away," Clara pointed out. "What might happen to Elaine in those seven hours? Who knows what she is going through or what the plans of her kidnappers might be?"

Mr Keene looked uneasy, but he was too stubborn to give in.

"This is all speculation. I mean, the woman is probably fine, maybe she got lost?"

Clara did not honour that nonsensical suggestion with a response.

"Mr Stone could be allowed an early lunch," the secretary remarked lightly.

Mr Keene snorted again.

"Or this young lady could wait until midday and speak to him them," he countered.

"She is right, however, that every hour waited is an hour wasted. This is a remarkable situation, by all accounts."

Mr Keene did not like being reminded of this by a mere secretary and he grumbled under his breath again. Then he sighed.

"Fine, Mr Stone can have an early lunch," he snapped. "But this will not become a habit. If you need to speak to him again it will have to be after he has finished work, understood?"

Clara remained mute. She was not going to respond to such a rude question. She did not work for this man, nor did he have any authority over her. Mr Keene seemed to accept her silence for an affirmative answer.

"I'll take you to Mr Stone," he rose from his chair. "I have to get back to the printing floor, anyway."

He guided Clara and Tommy out of the office and down the stairs. The main floor of the works was taken up by long rows of printing presses, which clattered and clanked rhythmically as they went about their business of printing books, papers, posters, flyers and anything else that needed type printed on paper. Clara noticed that one printing press was set up to produce colour plates for books or for posters. The process was tricky as each colour had to be added separately to the image. The workers attending to the machine were specialists.

The noise was deafening, made worse by the way it echoed about the walls of the building. Clara wanted to put her hands over her ears and wondered if the workers found themselves going deaf over time from the thudding clunking of the machines as they went through the motions of producing printed paper.

Mr Keene hustled them through the shop floor and to a door at the back. This led to a long room, where men sat at angled tables rather like drawing boards, mounting metal letters into blocks ready to send to the printers. This was a constant process; with so many projects ongoing at once the typesetters were kept permanently busy. Especially when a book was being printed, each page requiring to be typeset and mounted into a larger block that was then sent to the printing presses. Book pages could be printed in pairs, requiring an understanding of the layout of the book and the relevant page numbers. Though these were all pre-arranged for the typesetter, so they did not have to concern themselves with that complication. They still had to make up the blocks, however, and ensure there were no grammatical or spelling errors, and fix them ready to be used. All done with the letters back to front; if the letters were the correct way round, they would print backwards on the paper, like a page of text being held to a mirror. All the typesetters worked in this mirror-text and were masters of reading their work back-to-front.

Clara pondered whether, when asked to read normal text, they ever found it hard?

Walter Stone was working at a desk at the far end of the room. He was producing a four-page layout for a book on the waterways and lakes of Cumbria. His brow was knitted in a frown of deep concentration as he worked.

The last time Clara had see him was at the theatre. She recalled him as a bold, confident man giving a bracing performance as Macbeth. Now, sitting at his desk, he seemed less extraordinary. He wore a pair of spectacles and hunched a little as he worked. He had a charming face, though not as handsome as Clara had recalled when he stood on the stage. She supposed part of his glamour was his 'stage-presence', an indefinable thing that could turn the ordinary into the spectacular, could lift a reasonable, if unremarkable face, to the heights of Adonis good-looks. Could make a man who was otherwise no different to anyone else, suddenly unusual and incredibly attractive.

Away from that stage, Walter Stone seemed just like everyone else. You would probably have not noticed him if he walked by you in the street.

"Walter," Mr Keene snapped as they neared him.

Walter Stone jerked up from his work and blinked at Mr Keene with something that Clara felt looked akin to anxiety. That was another thing that was absent – his confidence.

"Mr Keene, is something the matter?" Walter Stone had not even noticed Clara and Tommy in his concern that there was an issue with his work.

"No," Mr Keene said sharply. "This lady needs to speak with you urgently, so you can take an early lunch break. Only Forty-five minutes, mind, I'm not paying you to eat."

Mr Keene gave Clara a reproachful look, rather as if he expected her to turn around and apologise for disrupting his employees. Clara certainly was not going to do that. She gave him a smile, that was all. Mr Keene huffed to himself and stalked off.

Walter looked at Clara and Tommy, his face had gone pale.

"You came to the theatre the other day," he observed of Clara. "This is about Elaine. My gosh, have they found her?"

The bleakness of his expression made Clara hasten to respond.

"No, that is not the reason I am here Mr Stone. I just want to ask you some questions about Elaine and her last day at the theatre."

Walter did not look appeased, still grimacing he rose from his seat.

"We best go to the lunch room, it will be quiet in there," he ran a hand over his face. His fingers were trembling. "I can't think what I can help you with, however. I last saw Elaine at the theatre."

"Don't underestimate yourself, Mr Stone. You may have information that can help me without realising it."

Walter looked unconvinced, though his grimace did finally disappear.

"I'll answer anything you ask to bring Elaine home," he said. "And, please, call me Walter."

Chapter Fourteen

The room set aside for the employees to have their lunch in was no bigger than a small box room. There was a round table in the middle, so battered with age that not a single leg was even with the floor and each had a wad of paper, of varying size and thickness, lodged beneath it. The chairs around it were equally bashed about. Walter pulled out one that looked reasonably steady and offered it to Clara.

"I apologise for the surroundings," he said shyly as he worked through the remaining chairs to find one that was not too wobbly for Tommy. "We are constantly being promised new furniture and a lick of whitewash to the walls, but you know how it is."

With the others seated, Walter took his own chair.

"Feel free to eat your lunch," Clara said to him. "As we are effectively interrupting your lunch break."

Walter shook his head.

"I only have a sandwich. To be honest, my appetite is not much at the moment," he pulled a face. "Since Elaine disappeared… well, its shaken me."

"You think a lot of Elaine," Clara said gently.

"She is a good friend," Walter said with haste. "I care about my friends, yes."

"Walter, this is a time to be honest. What you say will not go beyond these four walls without your say so, do you understand?"

"I understand, but there is nothing to say, really," Walter took a shaky breath. "Elaine loves her husband, I can swear to that."

"So, you have tried it on then, old chap?" Tommy spoke up. He had caught the inference in Walter's statement.

Walter was breathing faster, he looked a little spooked. Clara felt he was not a man who kept secrets well, not at all. A gentle prod would be all it took to have him confessing to anything.

So, she prodded him.

"Elaine turned you down?"

Walter cleared his throat, he was looking less and less like the confident Macbeth Clara had seen on the stage. Now he looked very worried, even scared.

"We had an understanding," Walter said somewhat desperately. "We could be friends, nothing more. Elaine would not betray her husband, not even with me. That is what she said. I thought, for a short time, there could be something between us. There never was, that is the truth."

Clara believed him. He might be a good actor, but he was not that good.

"Who… who told you?" Walter asked tentatively.

"Mary Worthing," Clara replied, seeing no reason to hide the fact that Elaine's fiercest enemy had been spreading talk.

Walter didn't seem surprised.

"She has a screw loose. She expected Elaine to keep the cottage as a shrine to her late mother. How extraordinary is that? She meant to call whenever she pleased to go into the cottage and absorb her late mother's presence. Elaine told me that shortly after she bought the cottage Mary turned up out of the blue and wanted to go into the living room. She sat on the old sofa and fell utterly silent. Elaine tried to offer her tea, and to talk to her, but nothing. She was like that for an hour," Walter's eyes widened as he recalled the strange episode. "Elaine said it was rather like Mary was communing with her departed mother. She found it disturbing and decided it was best to leave her alone and go to the kitchen. Eventually she heard the front door open and close. Mary had let herself out.

"Elaine thought that if she made the cottage her own it would make Mary aware that it was no longer her mother's house. I guess, as you have spoken to Mary, you know how that went."

"Mary thought Elaine should keep the cottage exactly as it was," Clara said.

"Disturbing, isn't it?" Walter gave a shudder. "The woman has a temper. I have wondered if she could be involved in Elaine's disappearance."

"She denies it, but I have not ruled her out," Clara admitted. "However, she would lose more than she would gain by making Elaine vanish. Unless it was a sudden act of violence."

"Mary is more than capable of those," Walter nodded. "But there was no sign of violence at the house. Everything seemed in order. I have been to Elaine's cottage often enough to know where everything should be. I saw no obvious signs that something bad had happened there.

"I told the police I was convinced she had been snatched on the road. They could find no evidence to support my statement, but I am still certain."

"Who else knew about your friendship with Elaine and that she visited your lodgings regularly?" Clara asked.

"It was not exactly secret. Elaine was very good friends with my landlady. None of us hid the fact."

Clara saw that this was a dead-end. In any case, the only person who might be angered by Elaine spending time with a young man was her husband, Captain Chase, and he had the army backing him up as to where he was at the time of her disappearance.

"Did Elaine have any enemies? Or anyone she did not get along with?"

"Wendy," Walter said without hesitation. "She is the stage manager at the company and a woman no one wants to cross. She has a mean streak. I keep my distance."

"Elaine was not afraid of her, though?"

"Elaine would not be bullied. She is tough like that," Walter paused a moment. Like many, he was unsure whether he should be talking about Elaine in the past or present tense. Both felt odd at that precise moment. At least the present tense offered the implied hope she was still alive. "Wendy would try to rule the roost and Elaine would not let her. There was hell to pay when Elaine was chosen to play Lady Macbeth. Wendy wanted the part to go to her niece. I suppose you saw that child acting?"

"I did," Clara said, without revealing her thoughts on the matter.

"I have never known such a person! She thinks she is the most remarkable actress, when quite plainly she is not. She wants to be a professional, heaven help us! And her aunt encourages her," Walter suddenly froze, as if a thought had struck him that made him hesitate. "Wendy would very much like Elaine out of the way."

"For the sake of a play?" Tommy asked incredulously.

"Oh, she would do far more than make Elaine disappear to get her niece on the stage," Walter was solemn. "She drinks too, and when she is nine sheets to the wind she comes up with some very odd ideas."

"Kidnapping Elaine for the duration of the play is hardly logical," Clara pointed out. "Eventually Elaine would need to be released and then she would go to the police and report what happened."

"Maybe Wendy doesn't intend to release her," Walter said darkly.

"You think she is capable of murder?" Clara asked. "That is a serious suggestion."

Walter frowned.

"I don't know. I can't imagine anyone hurting someone else, yet people do," he gave another long sigh. "I just can't think of anyone else who would be inclined to harm Elaine."

"Wendy doesn't have a car, does she?" Clara asked.

Walter shook his head.

"She has a bicycle."

They all fell quiet. For a moment no one could think what to say. Walter seemed as much a dead-end as everyone else who they had so far spoken to. Clara was beginning to think that either a complete stranger had kidnapped Elaine, or that she had thrown herself off the cliff as Patricia had suggested.

"Was Elaine worried or troubled about anything?" Clara asked Walter.

He had a faraway look in his eyes, as if he was thinking about another place and time. He blinked as the question registered with him and glanced at Clara.

"I…I'm not sure," Walter skirted the issue. "She did not talk a lot about her worries, she did not like to burden others."

"So, there was something?" Clara pressed.

"Her sister was very ill, and her parents had moved away to look after her and the children," Walter said quickly, a little too quickly.

Clara pounced.

"There is something Walter. This is very important, if there was something bothering Elaine…"

"She didn't jump off a cliff!" Walter snapped, his fists clenching and his face going bright red. He breathed hard and for a moment could not compose himself. Then his hands relaxed, though his face took on an expression of intense sorrow. "Elaine would not kill herself. I know that is what my landlady thinks, and what others think too. When Elaine could not be found, and no suspect was named by the police, well, everyone started to speak in whispers about the possibility that she…"

Walter hung his head. The thought clearly pained him

deeply.

"She would not do something like that. Elaine loved life, even when it was not going so well for her," Walter had gritted his teeth in an effort to maintain his composure and when he breathed in through them he seemed to whistle. "I won't believe that Elaine jumped. I won't believe that she is dead."

"You really do love her," Tommy spoke softly.

Walter looked at him, his eyes round and wet. He was not about to cry, but the strain of controlling himself was telling.

"I guess I do. I know she will never love me back, and I don't even mind. As long as we can be friends," Walter's hands were trembling again, he placed them on the table to try and stop it. "I should have walked her home that day. If only I had."

"Were you in the habit of walking her home?" Clara asked.

"No," Walter shook his head.

"Then why would you have done so that day?"

Walter was gazing at his hands, spread palm down on the table like he was part of some table-tipping session. He appeared to be trying to force them into the surface of the table, as if that would stop his anxiety.

"Elaine thought she was being followed," he finally managed to whisper.

Clara caught her breath. This was the first indication she had had that Elaine had suspicions of someone wanting to harm her.

"Why did she think that?" Clara asked.

Walter was still straining to keep his emotions in check. He was like some giant, coiled spring, desperate to explode all its energy across the room. He was clearly not coping well with Elaine's disappearance.

"Walter, what had made Elaine concerned she was being followed?" Clara repeated herself.

"There was some sadness in her past," Walter spoke so quietly Clara had to strain to hear him. "She would not speak of it, but it was this undercurrent about her. About a month ago Elaine arrived at my lodgings for Sunday tea and seemed unsettled. I asked her 'what was the matter' but she brushed it off, said she had smashed a favourite vase at home, or some such nonsense. I didn't push the matter, however.

"A little while into the evening, it was noticeable that she was upset about something and my landlady also asked her 'what was the matter?' Elaine started to make excuses again, then she paused. She seemed to stiffen a little and her voice trembled when she spoke. 'I've been a fool' she said, 'whatever will Dylan think of me?' Neither of us understood this, but what she said next was plain. 'Someone was following me tonight. I know it,' she declared. That was all I could get her to say. I wanted to walk her home, but she utterly refused. Told me she was just being silly and would not allow herself to be governed by nerves. She had to live alone in that cottage, after all, and she couldn't start being scared of the dark. I felt she was putting a brave face on things, rather like she was trying to convince herself. But I let her go.

"When I next saw her, she seemed calmer. She told me she had been very silly and I should not pay any heed to her ramblings. I asked if she still thought she was being followed, and she laughed. Said she was so embarrassed to think she had mentioned such a thing at all. She seemed more relaxed and I believed her. And then she went missing."

Clara glanced at Tommy. This had to be significant. Could it be someone had been plotting to kidnap Elaine for some time? Following her every move to pick just the right moment. Yet, she had climbed into a car willingly, according to the tramp. Who was the driver and why did Elaine trust her?

"Am I a suspect?" Walter suddenly said.

Clara was distracted. In truth, she had not considered him a suspect, though there was obviously the potential there. He might have kidnapped Elaine because of his unrequited love. She only had his word that he could live with Elaine not loving him back. Surely such strong emotion ate away at a man?

"You had opportunity," she mused. "Motive too."

"Because I love her?" Walter asked. "Doesn't that make it less likely I would harm her?"

"Love is a very complicated emotion," Clara pointed out.

Walter seemed to shrink in on himself.

"If only I was the culprit, at least then I would know where she was and would know she was safe," Walter shut his eyes. "When you walked in here and mentioned Elaine, I was convinced you had found her dead. That has been my biggest fear since the day we found her house empty. I know that is a possibility. I think most people are now of the opinion she is dead and the police have just failed to find her body. Sometimes I lay in my bed and I think of all the places she could be lying hidden. I want to go out and scour the countryside for her. One man alone can do so little."

Walter was becoming overwhelmed again. His grief and fears for Elaine were just as strong and palpable as those of Captain Chase.

"Walter, if Elaine is still alive then I will do all in my power to track her down. Time is of the essence and any clue to her location will be vital. I would ask you to encourage the other Brighton Players to speak to me if they know anything, anything at all."

Walter nodded his head.

"I understand."

"If you think of anything else, or learn anything new, please contact me at once," Clara took one of her business cards from her handbag and gave it to him.

Walter clutched it in his fingers so tightly it began to bend.

"Thank you for not giving up," he said, still choking on his own feelings.

"I can make no promises, but I am certainly going to

do my very best."

Walter managed a smile.

"Elaine used to say something similar before a performance," he said. "I always replied the same way."

He tilted his head.

"The best is all we can ask. The best is all we can expect."

Chapter Fifteen

A car drew up outside the Fitzgerald house. Annie looked at it suspiciously. At the opening of O'Harris' new convalescence home she had volunteered to assist with the arrival of the first patients. She liked Captain O'Harris, but she did not feel he had fully considered the practical needs of his patients. Oh yes, the bed linen was clean, and the rooms dusted within an inch of their lives, but where were the little homely touches that made a place feel comfortable and not institutional? Flowers in vases, for instance. Nice paintings on the wall. And, of course, home cooking. All that fancy food O'Harris had been serving at the opening was fine, but what people really appreciated with a bit of old fashioned fruit cake and some sandwiches. In fact, Annie had quickly suggested that a good way to settle the patients would be to have afternoon tea in the music room. There was nothing more relaxing and downright English. O'Harris had loved the idea; an informal way of welcoming everyone and letting them get to know each other. Before Annie knew what she was doing, she was volunteering to help with the arrangements and promising to provide her own fruit pound cake for the gathering.

Annie had regretted her decision about half-an-hour

later, when she realised the inconvenience it would cause her. The guests were arriving on her laundry day and she would have to put aside the washing to attend. Then there was all the strain of making sure things were right and coordinating with O'Harris' own cook (who happened to be the family cook, rehired when it was discovered O'Harris was alive after being missing for a year). There was also the matter of the cake contest; Annie had been intending to experiment with another sponge that afternoon. She wanted to see if there was an optimum time for creaming the butter and sugar together to produce the ideal spring to the finished cake. She was going to keep a record of her experiments, just like a scientist. Annie was taking her participation in the baking contest extremely seriously.

However, regrets would not change what she had done, and she could not back out of the arrangement and refuse to attend. That would be churlish. Anyway, O'Harris had sent his car to the house.

Annie looked at the car with narrowed eyes. She was not fond of cars. She could tolerate omnibuses because there were always lots of people on them, and she felt that if anything went wrong there were lots of hands at the ready to help. But in a car you were largely on your own.

Sighing, she collected the basket wherein her precious pound cake sat nestled beneath a cloth and headed out the door. She was greeted by Jones, O'Harris' driver.

"Miss," he tipped his hat and politely took her basket. "Would you like to sit in the front or back, as it is just you?"

Annie thought there was no good answer to that question, but she decided to sit in the front. Better to see doom coming her way. The basket was placed in the back and she took her seat. Jones closed her door and went back to the driver's side.

"The captain is rather anxious today, wants everything right," he confided to Annie as they drove off. "I think he is rather glad you are coming."

Annie felt a bit better, being needed was always good for the ego.

"He mustn't fret, this shall all go very smoothly," she replied. "I imagine the gentlemen who are arriving today are equally nervous."

"Captain O'Harris needs your confidence," Jones smiled. "You can keep him calm."

They headed slightly out of Brighton and towards the large house that was the O'Harris residence. Pulling up the drive, Annie noticed that members of the household staff were hurrying around like headless chickens. She tutted under her breath.

Jones grinned.

"No one knows quite how to behave. The old household staff are not used to all this excitement."

Jones pulled up and came around the car to open the door for Annie. She retrieved her basket without his assistance and headed inside hastily, feeling that there was an urgent need to stem the tide of this panic before the patients arrived. As she glanced about the hall, she noticed a group of well-dressed women in the library. They looked aimless and appeared to have been forgotten.

"Might you be the nurses?" Annie entered the room.

The women glanced up.

"We are," one said.

"Have you been shown about the house?"

The ladies shook their heads.

"We were told to wait in here half-an-hour ago."

Annie was appalled. Whoever was running the show on the staff side of things was clearly not on top of the matter. Never mind, she was here now and would get things under control.

"Well ladies, I can give you a tour, but first things first. We have patients arriving shortly and the place is only half ready. The house is very clean and presentable, but it has the hand of a man behind it, don't you think?"

The nurses glanced around them and seemed to agree. Annie soldiered on.

"I think what this place needs is a homely touch or two. For a start, flowers in the bedrooms and these main rooms would not go amiss and I know that the captain has a good store of paintings, some of which would be suitable to adore the bedrooms and give that extra touch of personalisation. Might I be able to persuade you to arrange this?"

The ladies looked uncertain.

"I have to get to the kitchens and see what is causing panic among the staff, and also to make sure afternoon tea is all in order," Annie stood up tall, addressing the nurses like a sergeant-major. "Your task ladies, from the moment you stepped through the door, is to make sure the patients are well-cared for and comfortable. An admirable task and one I can see you will undertake with efficiency and enthusiasm."

Smiles crept onto the nurses' faces at this praise.

"As such, I believe it your first responsibility, before the patients arrive, to make this place a home from home. This is not a hospital or, heaven forbid, an asylum. It is a healing hotel, a place to recover among friends. But, I ask you, is that how this room currently feels?" Annie waved a hand about the library which seemed very formal all of a sudden.

The women took another look at their surroundings and a unified 'no' was their response.

"Flowers, ladies, pictures on the walls, and any other soft touches you can think of that will make this place less… intimidating, that is what your patients need and what I am asking you to attend to. Are you willing?"

The nurses once more glanced at each other, then they seemed to come to a decision in unison. Their spokeswoman turned to Annie.

"We can do that. Better than standing here like lemons."

"We'll explore the house while we are at it," another nurse added. "Why wait for someone to show us the place?"

Annie was satisfied that the ladies had been rallied to action, and she offered them her thanks before heading towards the back of the house and the kitchen.

There was a smell of burning as she entered the servants' area and Annie started to pick up her pace. She was relieved to discover the cause of the aroma was just the gardener's wet boots which had been left too near the range. She was disappointed, however, to find the cook arguing with him over the matter instead of getting on with her work. The staff seemed to be flitting about aimlessly and there were a lot of raised voices and fraught faces. Enough was enough. Annie strode into the room and slammed her basket forcefully down on the kitchen table. Plates and cutlery on the table rattled as a result and the argument between the cook and the gardener came to a halt.

Annie marched to the range, picked up the slightly charred leather boots and threw them out into the back corridor.

"Attend to your shoes," she informed the gardener who, not knowing who the intruder was, scowled but hastened out the room. Annie turned on the cook. "Why are the staff flapping about all over the place?"

"Too much to do!" The woman threw up her hands and then collapsed into a chair. "I am too old for all this!"

The woman was in her fifties and had been the cook for the O'Harris family for many years. She was used to composing meals for a handful of people. In the past, when there had been grander dinner parties, O'Harris had arranged for an outside company to provide the food to take the burden off the cook. As was the case with the opening yesterday. But now, the responsibility for feeding patients and staff had fallen soundly on her shoulders and the cook looked fit to burst into tears at the scale of her task.

"It is merely a case of assigning work sensibly and efficiently to the staff," Annie told her, her voice softer now. "Have you prepared the scones and sandwiches for afternoon tea?"

"The scones are done, not the sandwiches," the cook took a handkerchief from her sleeve and dabbed at her eyes. "I asked the gardener if he had any cucumbers in the glasshouse, then I noticed his boots by my range and we started to argue. How am I supposed to make cucumber sandwiches now?"

"We shall send someone to the glasshouse to consult the gardener," Annie said calmly. "And there are other sandwiches we can make. Why are all these plates on the table?"

"I was making sure everything was spotless. This is the new dinnerware for the house."

Annie took a look at the smart white porcelain with an angular pattern of lines and squares in various colours running around the edges.

"Very modern," she nodded. "This needs to be removed to the cupboards in the dining room."

The cook nodded her head, but said nothing.

"Why were there staff out the front of the house?" Annie asked.

"They shouldn't be," the cook looked pained.

Annie resisted a sigh.

"Right, let's gather everyone together and get sorted," she declared, once more taking charge.

Annie sent the two kitchen maids out to find the rest of the staff and bring everyone to the kitchen. In the meantime, she made the cook a cup of tea and endeavoured to calm her down.

"You have made a good start," she reassured her. "Now we must continue the process. You might make a list of what we need to do and then we can go through it methodically."

The cook was recovering herself.

"There is a notepad on that counter."

Annie handed it to her and the woman started to write out her list. Meanwhile, Annie gathered up the plates and cutlery and stacked them into a neat pile. The staff slowly arrived in the kitchen as well.

"Is everyone here?" Annie looked up.

There was a chorus of 'yeses'.

"Good," Annie took the list off the cook and glanced through it. "Right, I need someone to take these plates to the dining room and see that the tables are set ready for afternoon tea."

One of the male servants volunteered and was sent off with the task.

"Next I need someone to persuade the gardener to give us some cucumbers," she glanced at another male servant, who accepted the task and disappeared out into the gardens.

That left three maids and the cook.

"The rooms are clean and the beds made?" Annie asked aloud.

One of the maids confirmed this.

"Then one of you will fetch the butter from the pantry and set about putting individual portions in those little butter dishes on the shelf. The rest of us can get on with making sandwiches and making sure the linen napkins are pressed and ready to go out."

The cook was looking more and more relieved.

"Oh dear, I did make life so complicated for myself," she breathed uneasily.

"No matter, we are getting there now," Annie smiled at her. "This will become second nature with time."

"I don't know about that," the cook grimaced. "O'Harris may need to find another cook. I think this is all too much for me."

"Nonsense, you are just out of practice," Annie patted her hand. "Are all the teapots washed and dried?"

"Yes, and the big kettles are filled with water and ready to be boiled."

"There you are then, you really are more organised than you give yourself credit for," Annie reassured her.

The cook sniffed one last time and put away her handkerchief.

"What is in the basket?" She asked, noticing at last the container Annie had brought in.

"Pound cake," Annie flicked back the cloth and showed off her baking.

"Lovely! I haven't made a pound cake in years. I have Bakewell tarts and rock cakes baked for the afternoon tea also. We will be well provided for."

"You see? All is sorted," Annie smiled.

The cook breathed deeply. Rising from her chair she appeared almost fully recovered. The kitchen maids were carefully cutting several fresh loaves of bread into neat slices and there were footsteps in the outside passage as the male servant returned with cucumbers straight from the glasshouse. The cook sighed again.

"When Captain O'Harris asked me if I would return to cook for him, I was delighted, you know. He told me his plans for the house, but I honestly did not take them all in. I was just so glad to be back in this old place, back in my lovely kitchen. I started here at the age of thirteen," the cook spoke wistfully, her words soft and directed at Annie. "I missed this place when I had to leave. I missed Captain O'Harris. I have cooked his meals since he came here as a young boy. I was heartbroken when I heard he was missing. I thought…"

The cook stopped herself.

"But that doesn't matter now. He is back and I am back. This place can once more be filled with the scents of good cooking."

"And you have new mouths to feed. The men coming here will need a good diet to restore them to full fitness," Annie was of the firm opinion that three hearty meals a day could solve all a person's ills.

"I can do that," the cook said with more confidence. "If that will help."

"It will," Annie reassured her. "Now, let us make sandwiches!"

Chapter Sixteen

Jones had been out again, this time to collect the first patients from the train station. Five men were in the car. Their faces peered through the windows with apprehension. For many of them this was a last hope to pull them out of the despair that had engulfed their lives. They were sceptical, unconvinced this new fashion for taking care of the mind to heal the body was anything more than quackery. Captain O'Harris was waiting to greet them. He was anxious too, though he was masking it behind a broad smile.

Annie stood just to one side. Her anxieties, such as they were, focused in a different direction to those of the men and O'Harris. She was doubting they had enough sandwiches to go around and was slightly concerned the cook might muddle up her scones and her rock cakes when serving afternoon tea.

O'Harris marched towards the car as Jones opened the back door. The men stepped out and looked around them. The house, refurbished as it was, was a sight to inspire awe and to intimidate a fraction. The men were of mixed ages, none older than thirty-five, however. Captain O'Harris had advertised his new home through various societies and papers. Those wishing to apply for treatment had to pay, as it was a private clinic and could not run on air and good intentions alone. The methods at the home were mildly unconventional, enough so that the applications had at first been slow to come in, and none had been from older men – men of a generation who did not believe in such things as depression and shell-shock. That was something only the weak-minded and insane developed.

O'Harris was aware that it was not just the officer-class who had suffered in the war. As such, he had decided that two of his patients would be subsidised for treatment at the home. These two would come from the many ranks of privates who had endured as much, sometimes more, than their wealthier superiors. These men would not have to pay for their care at the home and O'Harris hoped secretly that his work in Brighton would encourage others to help those who could not afford to pay for doctors and nurses.

His subsidised cases (he would not label them with the stigma of being charity cases) were nominated by doctors, who had treated them and thought they might benefit from the care. Spreading the word for these men had been even harder than the paid applications. O'Harris had relied on Dr Cutt and his network of contacts to find suitable candidates.

The first of these subsidised patients was a private, no older than twenty-four, he had been in and out of hospital since the war, often being confined to a mental ward because he was deemed a danger to himself and others. When O'Harris had been sent the details of his case as part of the application it had been bleak reading. Dr Cutt had been helping the captain go through the nominations and he grimaced as he read this particular one. The private suffered hallucinations when he thought himself back at the front, in these moments he could become dangerous, attacking others around him out of terror. These episodes were usually followed by deep depression which could last for weeks and then there would be a seeming recovery, only for a relapse to follow at some point. The pattern was plain and many had already given up on him and were hinting that he should be sent to a lunatic asylum, permanently. Only the strong determination of the private's family and his doctor had prevented that from happening.

Dr Cutt shook his head over the details. Too great a challenge to take on at the start of this venture, he felt. O'Harris disagreed. This was exactly the sort of fellow he wanted to help. He was a tough case, possibly incurable, but O'Harris would not be swayed. The private was accepted and became the first subsidised patient for the home.

Now, standing on his gravel drive, O'Harris was watching as a young man climbed out of the front passenger seat of the car. He had a surly look on his face; sceptical, determined to be unimpressed. He had been through the system and had not improved. He saw no hope ahead. Private Peterson, the man who was going to test O'Harris' new methods to the limit.

"Gentlemen!" O'Harris declared. "Do come inside and I shall show you your rooms. Then we can take a tour before settling down to afternoon tea where we can get to know each other. I wish to offer my wholehearted welcome to you all. I hope to offer you light at the end of the tunnel, a way out of the dark pits that are currently engulfing you. I have been deep in those pits myself, I have wondered whether it would be better to give up than to try and fight on. This is why I stand before you, and it is why you are here.

"But, there is plenty of time ahead for you to listen to my ramblings. Follow me indoors and we can progress from there."

O'Harris turned and the men followed, still casting suspicious glances about them. Annie stepped backwards on the front steps to let the guests through. The last to go past her was Private Peterson, who glanced at her, the only woman in the crowd, a fearful look in his eyes. She almost spoke up and told him everything would be alright, he looked so much like a scared little boy, but at that moment she was distracted by a stabbing pain in her side.

Annie managed not to wince visibly. She shot her hand to her waist, pressing it into the flesh were the pain hurt worst. As soon as the men were inside she retreated to the dining room and sat down on a chair, massaging her aching innards until the jabbing pain eased. She gave a long sigh. Annie had thought that nonsense was over and done with. No further twinges had attacked her since the episode the other day. She pressed tentatively at her flesh. Her side felt sore, but the worst was over.

A couple of servants had arrived in the room to begin laying out the tables for afternoon tea. They smiled at Annie and did not seem to notice that anything was wrong. Pushing aside what had just happened, Annie rose and set about supervising the arrangements of plates, napkins and food. The long table was set with enough places for all the staff and patients. Cake plates stacked with a selection of the delights the cook and Annie had prepared were stationed at intervals along the cloth and the teapots were set ready to receive hot water. The table was a sight that made Annie smile with delight; could anyone stay depressed with such glory before them?

The servants disappeared. They would return with the hot water kettles when summoned. Annie remained in the dining room, watching the spring sunshine lance through the windows and across the table. She sighed with happiness.

"Looks a fine spread."

Annie jumped and turned at the voice. She saw that the young man, Private Peterson, was standing in the doorway of the room.

"Sorry, didn't mean to startle you," he said quickly.

"I was lost in my thoughts," Annie said, feeling embarrassed she had reacted so foolishly. "Is the house tour over already?"

"No," Peterson walked towards the table and stared up its length. "But I was finding the whole thing… overwhelming. This is better. It's peaceful in here."

Annie observed him, trying to get a feel for the man. She knew none of his past; O'Harris kept such information private, only the doctors and himself privy to the details. She thought Peterson's skin looked rather grey, like a worn old photograph, and there was a feeling to him as if he had given up on being truly alive a long time ago.

"I don't much do crowds either," Annie said. "I like my private space. Sometimes, being too much with people makes my head feel foggy and my thoughts jumble together."

Peterson looked up and smiled.

"Are you Captain O'Harris' wife?"

"Oh no," Annie blushed. "I am a friend of the family. I just came over to help out. This is a daunting day for the Captain too. He has been wanting to see this place open for so long and he isn't sure how it will all turn out. He has to prove his methods, prove that he can help people get better."

"Then he picked the wrong man when he selected me to come here," Peterson said grimly. "There ain't no getting better for me."

Peterson looked solemnly along the table.

"Maybe I shouldn't have come."

"Why ever not?" Annie asked, taking a step nearer the young man.

"There is something not right with my head," Peterson pressed a finger to his temple. "Sometimes I don't know what is real and what is not. The doctors think I am mad."

"All the doctors?" Annie asked.

"Well, not my family doctor, but he has known me since I was a boy and I think he is blinded by that, and by my mum's insistence that I can get better."

"Maybe your mum is right."

Peterson shook his head.

"I've come here because she begged me to. I wish I could get better, for her sake, but every time I think I am right I get sick again," Peterson slipped his hands in his pockets. "Still, this is a nice enough place."

"You remind me of someone," Annie said softly.

Peterson turned to her, his brows knitted in uncertainty.

"My young man, he was like you. He was crippled during the war, the doctors said there was nothing physically wrong with him, that he should be able to walk, but he couldn't," Annie explained. "He had quite given up on himself. Then he met Dr Cutt, it took a lot of persuading to get him to see him, but he did. Dr Cutt believed he could not walk because of a mental block. His mind had shut down, it was very curious, and Thomas did not want to hear of it. What man wants to be told there is something wrong with his mind?"

Peterson gave a very slight nod of understanding.

"It took a great deal of persuading, but he agreed to try Dr Cutt's methods. He honestly had given up all hope of walking again. Well, that was over a year ago and this morning he walked out of the front door. Walked. No stick, no wheelchair. He was proved wrong and he is so very glad of it," Annie paused and smiled at Peterson. "Please do not give up hope. Especially when giving up means missing out on trying something that could be the answer. I can't say if your stay here will change your life, but I feel you ought to give it your best shot. If not for yourself, for you mother. She sounds like a very caring and loving woman."

"She is," Peterson mumbled.

"People like that don't come into our lives very often," Annie smiled sadly. "Do your best. For her."

Peterson shuffled his feet. There were voices in the corridor and O'Harris was arriving back with his other patients. He was looking pleased with himself, the tour had gone smoothly and everyone seemed satisfied with their rooms. He winked at Annie as he approached the dinner table.

"Was it you who arranged flowers in every room?" He asked with a twinkle in his eye.

"I might have had a hand in it," Annie replied shyly.

"And the table looks fit for the King," O'Harris grinned as he saw all the food laid out. "I take it all we need is the hot water for the teapots."

"I'll ring the bell," Annie told him, heading to the wall where a brass button connected electrically to the kitchens below.

She was reaching out to press it when the stabbing pain returned to her side. She hesitated and pressed her hand into her waist, taking a long deep breath. Whatever she had pulled was really playing up today, perhaps it was all the laundry she had done that morning? She had worked at double-pace to try to make sure she had a large chunk of it cleaned and on the line drying.

Annie tried to ignore the pain and reached out for the bell push once more. This time the stabbing sensation tripled in intensity and Annie doubled-over, unable to stop herself. She clutched both arms across her belly and closed her eyes as her insides seemed to writhe with agony. She had never known a pain so intense or inexplicable. The room went dim around her and she felt rather faint.

"Annie?" O'Harris had his hand on her shoulder. "What is wrong?"

Annie tried to stand up, but the process was unbearable. She clenched her teeth against the pain. It was not easing this time. One of the doctors had come over.

"Sit her down," he said, and Annie was helped back into a chair.

She still could not force herself upright.

"Where does it hurt?" The doctor asked her, despite being there to treat men's mental health, he was also a fully qualified traditional doctor.

"My side," Annie said. "But its spreading."

The doctor firmly pressed his fingers into Annie's side and she gasped sharply and jerked away from him.

"I would say it is the appendix," the doctor continued. "Needs to come out before it bursts. Have you had this pain before?"

"Years… ago…" Annie was trembling now. "Not… as… bad…"

"Definitely appendix," the doctor said. "We should call for an ambulance and have her taken straight to hospital."

"No!" Annie cried. "I have too much to do!"

"Young lady," the doctor told her sternly. "If you do not have that appendix removed, you will not be doing anything ever again, do you understand?"

Annie gulped.

"Is it serious?" She looked at Captain O'Harris for an answer.

"Annie, if your appendix bursts it will be very serious. You need to have it removed at once."

Annie gulped harder. O'Harris took her hand and clutched it.

"Someone call for an ambulance," he instructed and a nurse went to use the telephone.

"I am so sorry for spoiling your afternoon tea," Annie told O'Harris.

"Don't be silly," O'Harris grinned at her. "This is not your fault."

"What's going to happen to me?" Annie turned back to the doctor now.

"The hospital surgeons will operate as soon as they can," the doctor's tone had softened. "Then you will be fine."

"Can I live without an appendix?" Annie asked, for a moment wondering if the removal would result in her being unable to bake and cook.

"You can live just fine," the doctor promised.

Annie was in too much pain to argue further. She shut her eyes and braced herself to endure the next few hours.

She hated hospitals, but what had to be done, had to be done.

"I don't know where Tommy is," Annie said suddenly. "Can you find him and tell him?"

"Yes," O'Harris promised. "Of course."

He held her hand tightly and Annie squeezed it hard. This was far from how she had envisioned her afternoon going and she had certainly not intended to end up in hospital.

Chapter Seventeen

"Do you believe Walter Stone when he says there was nothing between him and Elaine?" Tommy asked as they caught the bus to head to the north of Brighton. They were going to attempt to track down the car that had given Elaine Chase a lift the day she disappeared.

"Not entirely," Clara sighed. "But that does not mean he is responsible for her disappearance. I mean, you don't run off with someone alone."

"No," Tommy agreed. "Unless you were being extremely careful and trying to make it look as though you weren't running off together."

"Why?" Clara asked him. "What would be the point?"

Tommy shrugged. He could not say.

"And this stuff about Elaine being followed," Clara pursed her lips together, thinking it all through. "That didn't sound made up."

"Who though?" Tommy said.

Clara found herself once more at a stop. She hated this stage in a case when there were more questions than answers.

The bus dropped them off near Mullender Road and they strolled along looking at the large villas that had recently been built on what were once fields. The houses were set back and substantial, enclosed in their own gardens and usually with high walls barricading them from the pavements outside. Plenty of Londoners with money liked to live in Brighton; some retired to the newly appearing suburbs about the seaside town, others were prepared to commute to the capital in exchange for waking up and going to sleep with the sea air in their lungs. The villas all looked magnificent and the sort of place where people could afford to own a car. In fact, several of the properties had what appeared to be garages adjoining them.

Tommy and Clara stopped at the address where Mrs Anderson lived with her husband. The iron gates were standing open, so they could walk up the drive to the front door. Clara noted a garage here too, but the doors were closed so she could not glimpse the Andersons' car. She stood before a honey-brown door that was pretending to be from a quaint, country cottage and rang the bell. It was only a moment before a maid answered.

"Is Mrs Anderson in?" Clara asked.

The maid was young, but not stupid. She hedged her bets, as she did not recognise the visitors.

"I shall see if my mistress is in, if you will tell me what it concerns?"

Clara had thought about this.

"Myself and my colleague work for the Rubber Regulatory Board. We are conducting a survey on car tyres and their reliability as part of a quality check on British rubber imports. We are speaking to all car owners in the area. It will only take a moment and would be of great assistance in improving the standard of tyre manufacture in this country," Clara spoke fast and the maid looked a little baffled, but she nodded and took the message inside. Closing the door on them for the moment.

"The Rubber Regulatory Board?" Tommy raised an eyebrow at Clara.

"You would be amazed at how people like to talk about

their cars," Clara told him. "Give them full opportunity to brag about their vehicles and they will most often oblige."

"About their tyre quality?"

"Tyres are a very personal choice," Clara said, though she really was only guessing. "They are the one part of a car where you have to make regular and repeated decisions. People like to justify their choice."

The maid opened the door again.

"Mrs Anderson will speak with you," she said, and then she led Clara through to a large morning room which overlooked the spacious gardens.

White sofas were situated in an arc before the windows, to provide the best view of the grounds. A gardener could be seen outside pushing a mower across the grass. Mrs Anderson sat in a loose white dress on one of the sofas, a cup of tea in her hand. She was an older woman and quite plump, the folds of the dress hiding a lot of extra pounds. She had a round face and curly hair, that had been cut short and seemed to stick out around her head like a comical wig. When she smiled her eyes disappeared into slits and she revealed that she had a gap between her front teeth.

"You want to talk about my tyres?" She said, waving a hand to the sofa for her guests to sit. She had a pronounced lisp. "I am very happy to talk about my car. It is mine you see, not my husband's. He won't drive. I absolutely love motoring."

Clara was already ruling her out as their suspect on the road. The tramp would surely have noted the woman's distinct voice and mentioned it.

"Thank you for seeing us," Clara said, feeling they ought to move on but knowing it would be rude to be hasty now they had gained entry.

"The Rubber Regulatory Board has to ensure that standards are met when it comes to rubber imports and, of course, the quality of the products being made from that rubber."

"I can precisely see that," Mrs Anderson continued.

"Our main concern is how the various tyres available in this country fare when being used on surfaces that are not tarmac-covered. For instance, were you to have to drive onto a grass verge."

"My car fares perfectly with those conditions," Mrs Anderson said, smiling and revealing her tooth-gap again. "Why, only the other day I had to cross a field in her and she was absolutely fine."

"You have had no issue with stones or other hard objects scarring or cutting into the tyres?" Clara was thinking of the marks in the tread of the tyre they had seen on the verge.

"Well, now you mention it, I did have a misfortune the other day," Mrs Anderson lost her smile. "I honestly don't know what caused the mark, but I had a piece of my tyre gouged out."

Clara could not believe her ears. Perhaps Mrs Anderson was their woman after all?

"Might we examine the gouge, for the sake of our records?" Clara asked.

Mrs Anderson was happy to agree. She put down her teacup and led them through the house and out the front again. Then she took them to the garage and showed them inside. Opening the doors wide she gave a contented sigh as she looked upon her prized vehicle. The car was a dark green colour, with black trim. Mrs Anderson placed a hand on the bonnet affectionately.

"I call her Betty," she said. "She was my birthday present last year. Arthur, that's my husband, asked what I wanted and I said a car. He was most unsure, but I was determined. I said it was safer than riding a horse these days, and he couldn't argue with that. I used to ride a lot, you see, until I fell badly."

Mrs Anderson seemed to glide around 'Betty' in her white afternoon gown. Her hand never disconnected from the chassis of the vehicle, following the line of the bonnet, then up and over the windscreen, before coming along the top of the doors.

"Which tyre was affected?" Clara asked to distract her. Mrs Anderson looked in danger of becoming so absorbed with her car that she would forget why they were there entirely.

"Oh, this one," she pointed to the front left.

Everything was adding up. It was the right tyre, on the correct side to have made the marks in the soft verge. Clara bent down, but the tyre was not spun round sufficiently to let her see the gouge.

"Wait a minute," Mrs Anderson said helpfully. "I'll push her out of the garage."

She lifted off the handbrake and would have merrily pushed the entire weight of the car out by herself. Tommy jumped into action to assist, but it was plain Mrs Anderson was fully capable of moving the car herself. She chuckled at him as he ran to get behind the car.

"Really!" She laughed. "Shout when you see the gouge!"

Clara was watching the tyre avidly. The wheel turned so slowly. Then a groove became noticeable in the rubber and she called for them to halt. Mrs Anderson, puffing from the exertion, pulled up the handbrake and looked delighted with herself.

"I say, is that useful?"

"Very," Clara assured her, but only because the mark on the tyre had solved one problem. The gouge was a long ragged groove in the rubber, like a sharp nail had been dragged deeply through it. It was completely different from the circular gouge they had noticed in the tyre impressions on the verge. Clara stood up.

"Thank you for showing us this, it has been most helpful."

"No problem, my dear," Mrs Anderson grinned. "You are contacting all car owners?"

"As far as we can," Clara said. "Not everyone will be available to see us when we call."

"Of course," Mrs Anderson was understanding. "If you have any more questions, please call again."

She waved them goodbye as they headed down the drive and back onto the road. Clara glanced at her watch when they were stood on the pavement.

"Miss Erskine lives about half-an-hour's walk from here," she calculated. "I think we should pay her a call before we go home."

They began to walk.

"You know," Tommy mused. "I don't think I would buy Squires tyres, they seem rather prone to damage."

Clara smiled at him.

"Luckily for us, at least they are easily identifiable."

Clara had a rough idea of where they were heading to and it was a nice day to stretch their legs. They talked about nothing in particular until they reached Elm Lane, a turning off the neatly paved roads that led to an older area of Brighton. The lane was unpaved and had once stretched from a small series of homes on the outskirts of the town, right to the harbour. The building of the new suburbs had encroached on the land between the homes and Brighton, changing their location from a rural idyll, to a mere remnant of nature.

However, once upon the lane the world changed yet again. The bricks and mortar and tarmac of Mullender Road and those around it fell into the background. Trees grew up over the lane and shaded it with their leafy boughs. Elms, of course, earning the small path its name. The lane was only just wide enough for a car to come down. Ruts in the dry earth indicated that something with wheels came along it quite regularly. Clara imagined that Miss Erskine must drive down this lane all the time.

The lane eventually widened and became a large road. Older cottages stood on either side, with a large Victorian manor house set back some way and almost masked by leafy trees. Miss Erskine's address was Sandy Hall and this proved to be a timber-framed property of reasonable size, set on the right of the lane. There was no drive, the property being nearly on top of the road, and Clara assumed Miss Erskine's car was kept at the back of the house.

She lifted the old iron knocker and rapped on the door. No one answered.

"Perhaps she is out?" Tommy suggested.

Clara was disappointed. She knocked again, but there was still no response. After a moment she decided to glance around the back of the house, to see if her surmise about the location of the car was correct.

That was easier said than done. The house extended to the limits of the plot and there was no path from the front garden to the back. They had to go back into the lane and walk along a footpath that went beside the road and then peer over the hedge into the back garden.

Tommy was ahead and was tall enough to see over the hedge easily, while Clara had to stand on her tiptoes.

"Oh dear," he declared.

"Oh dear?" Clara asked, trying to stand as tall as she could. The top of the car was just visible to her. "What have you seen?"

Tommy frowned apologetically at her.

"Miss Erskine appears to have been in quite a dramatic accident," he said. "The car is a mess."

Clara could hardly believe her ears. She caught the top of the hedge, which was a mix of hawthorn and dogwood, and heaved herself up.

Before her sat a forlorn blue sports car. Its front was completely buckled in. One wheel was laid on its side in the grass. The windscreen was smashed and a fender ripped off. The fact that the grass had grown up around the car and the discarded tyre suggested it had been stood there some time.

Clara was aghast. She had heard no news about a serious car accident – and this one was clearly serious.

"Poor Miss Erskine!" She said, looking at the state of the car and thinking that whoever had been in it must have been badly hurt.

"There is an old man coming along the footpath," Tommy said. "Maybe he knows something."

Clara was about to stop him, but he had already dashed off. She glumly looked at the wreckage of the car. Another dead-end. She hoped Miss Erskine was alright.

Tommy reappeared.

"The old man is a neighbour. Says no one is quite sure what happened, but Miss Erskine has been in the hospital ever since."

"That's a shame," Clara said glumly.

The wreck of the car suggested a collision with something solid, maybe a tree? If it had been another vehicle then very likely someone would have been available to explain what happened.

"Will Miss Erskine recover?" Clara asked, thinking that here was a very good reason why she avoided travelling in cars. The twisted metal was giving her goosebumps as she looked at it.

"Too early to say for sure, but she is apparently better than she was. Took a bad bump to the head, by all accounts. Has been having trouble with her memory. But that isn't the really interesting bit," Tommy's eyes flashed with excitement. "When this all happened, Miss Erskine was driving along a country lane. It was a Saturday – the Saturday!"

"The Saturday Elaine vanished?"

"Yes!" Tommy said in delight.

Clara turned back to the car, her mouth open in surprise.

Could it be?

She hardly dared hope!

Chapter Eighteen

Miss Erskine's nearest neighbour was an older couple who lived in a smaller cottage further along the lane. Their side windows looked over into Miss Erskine's garden. The older man who had been walking down the footpath indicated that if anyone knew about the accident, it would be this couple. They were the sort of people who liked to be involved in their neighbours' lives, whether that was agreeable to the neighbour or not. The implication was that they were interfering busy-bodies. Clara liked interfering busy-bodies, they usually knew a lot of information, and a lot more gossip, and they were never afraid to speak about it.

The old man was less accommodating. He disliked others involving themselves in his life, thank you very much, and would be sticking clear of those people. Those people had a name; Mr and Mrs Woodcock.

Clara and Tommy headed for the Woodcock's cottage. Clara was hopeful the couple would provide some vital details about the accident Miss Erskine was involved in. Someone, after all, had brought the car back to her cottage and that was just the sort of thing an interfering busy-body would gladly do – to be helpful, of course.

The Woodcocks' cottage was smaller than Miss

Erskine's and looked a good deal older. The timbers had faded to a pale grey and the whitewash of the plaster had turned yellow with age. The garden was mildly unkempt, but in a rather artistic fashion that suited the landscape. Roses grew over the porch, but it was too early in the year for them to have bloomed. Clara knocked on the door and waited. There was no knowing if the Woodcocks were in.

An older man appeared, not from the door, but from around the side of the cottage. He had his hands full of weeds and a battered hat tilted precariously to one-side on his head. He looked surprised to have someone knocking at the front door.

"Would you be Mr Woodcock?" Clara asked him.

"Indeed," the older man replied. He was about seventy, though it was hard to age him as his face was so tanned by the sun and the many years working beneath it. He had also lost all his hair, which made him look older. He was only as tall as Clara and made himself even smaller by an unfortunate habit of hunching. After talking to him for a while, Clara surmised this was due to a bad back which forced him to bend forward to ease it.

"I am trying to find out about Miss Erskine and her unfortunate accident," Clara explained. "I am concerned that a friend might have been involved and may have been hurt. She is missing, you see."

Mr Woodcock scratched at his head and the worn hat fell to the ground. He looked at it, but seemed to find the effort to reach down and retrieve it too great for the moment.

"I can tell you a bit," he said. "My wife will know more, she has been visiting Miss Erskine at the hospital."

"Could we interrupt your day for a while to chat?" Clara asked politely.

Mr Woodcock was still observing his hat with a look that suggested it had offended him by falling from his head.

"I suppose it is nearly time for tea. The wife likes me

to stop for a little something around about now. Would you come this way? We never use the front door."

Mr Woodcock turned and led them along a narrow path around the cottage. It was a thatched house, and the eaves bulged over the walls providing a run-off for rain water. The path around the walls was covered with gravel and was just about wide enough for a person. Tall hollyhocks and other rustic bushes grew up alongside it and filled the space between the path and the far hedges that bordered the garden.

Mr Woodcock took them around another corner so they were at the back of the cottage. Here the garden consisted of pristine lawn, the shrubs and flowers confined to narrow borders along the boundary of the grass. A vegetable patch had been dug out near the back door and it appeared this was what Mr Woodcock had been weeding when they interrupted him. He stopped them outside a dark brown door and dropped the weeds he still carried into a metal bucket. Then he made a great effort to stretch his back out, arching his belly and hips forward, while pulling his shoulders back until there was an almighty crack and he sighed with pleasure.

"I seize up after a while," he told them. "The wife gets cross if I work until my back gives, so I have to make sure she doesn't know."

With a wink, he opened the back door and led them into a spacious kitchen. The room was nearly the width of the cottage and had a large range set in a deep hearth. An oak table, recently scrubbed, filled the centre of the room and there was still space for a large dresser opposite it. Clara's heels clicked on red earthen tiles, while her head nearly touched bunches of herbs hanging from the rafters and scenting the air with their delicate aroma.

"Esther?" Mr Woodcock called out. "Visitors!"

A plump woman in a brown and cream dress appeared from a doorway. She wore an apron and had her hair swept up into a bun. She glanced at Clara and Tommy with a similar look of surprise to that which her husband had given them earlier.

"This is unexpected," she said.

"They want to talk about Miss Erskine," Mr Woodcock elaborated. "They are worried a friend of theirs might have been involved in the accident. Did you say the person was missing?"

"Yes, and no one knows what befell them," Clara said. "They vanished the same day as the accident and I have wondered if perhaps they were knocked down into a ditch. If they were badly hurt, they might not be able to tell anyone who they are."

"Oh dear," Mrs Woodcock clasped soft, fat hands together and looked grim. "I don't like to think someone else was involved in that dreadful thing."

"Can you tell me what happened?" Clara asked.

"As best as we know ourselves," Mrs Woodcock nodded. "Miss Erskine lives alone at the cottage down the lane and we have become friendly. She is some sort of writer, and spends a lot of hours locked in that cottage by herself working on whatever it is she does. Anyway, I like to invite her around for dinner at least three times a week. She doesn't employ a cook, and I dread to think what she subsists on. I doubt she does much cooking for herself."

"I help her with her garden," Mr Woodcock added. "It's no bother. I don't work these days. When my father died I inherited a little money, enough to let us get by without me having to continue on the farm. I was a stockman, but it isn't an old man's job."

"His back isn't good," Mrs Woodcock intervened. "He has terrible pains in the wet weather."

"I get by, on a day like this I hardly think of it. But you can't pick and choose which days you go to look after cattle. Anyway, I have plenty of free time and I like to keep busy. I told Miss Erskine I would keep her garden neat for her, and so I do," Mr Woodcock looked pleased with himself. "She is a nice young lady. Writes romances, I believe? Anyway, seems to pay well enough. As you can see from her car."

"Not cheap," Tommy agreed solemnly, memories of his recent experience at the garage coming back to him. "Is she a keen driver?"

"Went all over the place in that car," Mr Woodcock replied. "Loves to drive. She gave me a lift once or twice, just into Brighton for the odd thing. She seemed very sensible about it all. Never would have expected her to be in a crash."

"Do you know what happened on that day?" Clara asked.

Mr Woodcock glanced at his wife, nudging the responsibility of continuing the story over to her. Mrs Woodcock looked forlorn, rather like it hurt to speak about what had happened, or maybe it just stirred up bad emotions.

"I go to see Miss Erskine every day, if I can," she said. "I have to ride the bicycle there and back, but I know she appreciates it. She doesn't remember a lot of what occurred that day. She hurt her head quite badly."

Mrs Woodcock started to become choked with emotion.

"The doctors fear she might be permanently blinded," she said tearfully. "We haven't told her that yet. There is still a possibility…"

Mrs Woodcock dragged a handkerchief from out of her sleeve and quickly wiped at her eyes. Clara felt that the old man on the footpath had been wrong about these two. They were friendly neighbours, perhaps a little overwhelming, but not for any harmful reason. She could see that they genuinely cared about Miss Erskine.

"I am so sorry," Clara said softly.

"Miss Erskine is putting on a brave face. I admire her for that," Mrs Woodcock recovered herself. "She can only recall that she was driving along and everything was fine, and then there is this gap in her memory. Something happened. The police thought she might have tried to swerve to avoid something and ran up a bank, before clipping a tree and going nose first into a ditch. It was fortunate that a lady on a bicycle happened past and saw the wreck."

"A terrible thing to occur," Clara said honestly. "No one likes to think of accidents happening, especially when it appears there was nothing Miss Erskine could have done to prevent it."

"We will never know," Mr Woodcock answered. "Unless Miss Erskine regains her memory of those events, and the doctors think that unlikely, we shall have to just guess as to what caused that incident."

"Who brought the car back to the cottage?" Tommy asked. "We saw it in the garden as we came along."

"I called in a favour with a friend," Mr Woodcock answered. "I couldn't have afforded to pay for it to be brought back, but I know someone who has a tractor and they towed it here. It took some effort to push her into the garden, I might add. Minus a wheel and all bent about as she was, she didn't want to move at all. I thought Miss Erskine might want to do something with her. Couldn't just leave her in that ditch for anyone to take."

"Miss Erskine adored that car. She saved up for over a year to buy it," Mrs Woodcock was tearful again. "Sometimes, when I think she might never be able to look upon it again, I feel quite ill."

"Do you know where she was going that day?" Clara hoped to distract Mrs Woodcock with questions.

The woman shook her head, however.

"She was off to drop some papers to someone," she shrugged. "I remember her saying that when I asked if she wanted to pop in for a cup of tea. I don't know what she had been working on. A new project, she told me. Anyway, she said she would pop round after she had run her errand. Of course, she never did.

"The first I knew that something was wrong was when a policeman came to the door. He said Miss Erskine had been in an accident and was in the hospital. When she had been asked about next of kin, she had mumbled our names and the address. I suppose she really was alone here, apart from us. Oh dear, it really upsets me."

"She's alive, my dear," Mr Woodcock reminded his wife. "We must be grateful for that."

Mrs Woodcock nodded her head, but she did not have the power to say more. Clara felt they had interrupted the lives of the couple for long enough. They would gain no more.

"Thank you for speaking to us," she said. "I hope the doctors are wrong and that Miss Erskine regains her sight."

Mr Woodcock showed her back to the front of the cottage, picking up his hat as they passed it.

"The wife has taken this hard," he said with a pained look. "I suppose we both have."

With those parting words he wandered off, turning the corner of the cottage and going out of sight.

Clara and Tommy headed for home. It was necessary to walk a way before catching a bus. Clara looked fretfully at her watch.

"Annie will not be amused. We are going to be late for dinner."

Tommy pulled a face. It was never good to be late for dinner. Annie would be in a mood for the rest of the evening. She took dinnertime tardiness as a personal affront.

"We have achieved something, however," Clara remarked as the bus rumbled along. "I have this feeling that Miss Erskine's accident and the disappearance of Elaine Chase are connected. Two major things like that occurring on the same day is just too much of a coincidence. The police will have all the details, including where the accident happened. If it is along the road Elaine was walking then we will really be onto something."

The bus deposited them a few roads from their house and they set off on foot. Tommy was growing a little stiff from all the walking they had done and was beginning to limp. Clara slowed her pace to match his.

"I am wondering if Elaine might have been in Miss

Erskine's car. What if she was thrown out during the accident and slipped down into a ditch?" Clara grimaced. "People can be swallowed up in the muddy water of ditches."

"Before you know more about Miss Erskine and whether she would have offered Elaine a lift, perhaps it is best not to think such unhappy thoughts," Tommy suggested.

Clara could not help it. The unhappy thought was already there, impressed upon her mind.

"Ah, look!" Tommy pointed up the road. "Annie can only just be home herself, that is O'Harris' car."

The car was parked outside the house and Jones was in the driver's seat. As they approached he climbed out.

"There you are, thank goodness! I have been all over Brighton, in the end all I could think to do was wait outside your house," Jones spoke in a rush.

His tone brought Clara and Tommy to an abrupt halt. Clara felt her stomach flip over. Jones was outside the house, with no sign of Annie. She felt a glimmer of dread creeping over her.

"What has happened?" She asked.

Chapter Nineteen

They arrived at the Brighton Hospital. Tommy was fraught, feeling guilty that he had not been around when Annie needed him the most. No consoling words from Clara could ease his mind. It was too early for the visiting hour and the receptionist would not tell them which ward Annie was on, or whether she had been in surgery yet.

Tommy almost screamed at her in frustration. Clara rarely saw him in such a temper, he paced and raged, and pointed a finger at the receptionist, informing her she was evil for preventing him from seeing Annie. Clara took his arm and attempted to calm him, but he shook her off.

"I'll search this whole damn hospital for her!" He yelled at the top of his voice.

His activities had already aroused the attention of other people in the reception area of the hospital. Now an orderly who had been coming down a back corridor arrived and took an interest.

"Thomas Fitzgerald!" Clara told him sternly, one eye on the orderly. "You are not helping Annie this way! You will be banished from the hospital and not be able to see her at all."

Tommy's face was a picture of distress as he turned to Clara. His temper was a result of terrible fear and anxiety, the dread of losing something extremely precious to him. But he was also spent, his rage had boiled over and now was gone. He blinked, as if becoming aware of where he was. He took a long breath and steadied himself.

"I very much apologise for my behaviour," he said to the receptionist, who was an older woman of equally fierce demeanour. She had dealt with more than one irate visitor in her time and had endured Tommy's rant with the same expression of stubborn disinterest.

"Go sit down," she commanded Tommy.

Tommy looked fit to fall down now his fury had left him. Clara took his arm and settled him in a chair. Tommy trembled and she reached out to clutch his hand.

"It's only a half hour until visiting time," Clara reassured him. "And Jones said that Captain O'Harris was with Annie."

"I should have been with her," Tommy said bleakly.

"You had no reason to suspect she would become unwell," Clara reminded him. "You can hardly be her shadow forever more."

Tommy shook his head.

"I should have been with her," he said quietly, in a tone that broached no argument.

Clara pursed her lips but said nothing. She did not think there was any way she could change his mind on the matter. Tommy would lash himself with his own guilt whatever she said. Instead, Clara remained silent and tried to quell her own inner fears. Jones had explained what had happened earlier that afternoon and the doctor's opinion that it was an acute attack of appendicitis. When Annie had been brought to the hospital the doctors had agreed with the diagnosis and she had been prepared for immediate surgery.

Clara could only imagine what her friend had been feeling at that moment. She had no doubt that Captain O'Harris would be a stalwart aide to her, and would have done his best to keep her calm and distracted from what was about to happen, but Annie must have been scared –

wouldn't any of them be scared? Clara felt bad too that she had not been there to comfort her friend. However, she was more pragmatic than Tommy and realised that it was not her fault she was not around, just a fluke of chance.

The hands of the clock finally reached half-past and a bell rang indicating visiting hours were to commence. Clara went up to the receptionist as meekly as she could, and politely asked which ward Annie would be on. The receptionist scowled at her and it was plain that she was not forgiven for her association with Tommy. Luckily the receptionist was not so spiteful as to refuse to tell her. She quickly went through her book of in-patients and found Annie's name.

"Ward ten," she informed Clara. "Unless she is still in surgery."

Clara hoped that was not the case. She thanked the receptionist and shuttled Tommy upstairs and to the ward. Clara had worked in the hospital during the war as a volunteer nurse and she knew its layout well enough to not have to ask directions for ward ten. That was a recovery ward for post-surgery female patients. Clara was optimistic that this meant Annie had come through her operation successfully and was now recuperating.

As they came down the final corridor, Clara recognised Captain O'Harris leaning against a wall outside the door of the ward. He looked up at their footsteps and gave a visible sigh of relief.

"I have been waiting for you," he said as they came up to him. "I hoped Jones would find you. She is doing good, old man."

He directed this last to Tommy.

"The surgery went smoothly. They were able to remove her appendix without it bursting and it was a relatively quick procedure," O'Harris continued. "They brought her back a little while ago, but she is still drowsy from the anaesthetic."

Tommy glanced past him and to the doors of the ward.

They had large glass windows in them and he was attempting to peer through in the hopes of seeing Annie.

"You can go in," O'Harris told him. "I was waiting outside to catch you. She probably won't say much, she is mainly sleeping off the drugs."

"Thank you," Tommy told O'Harris earnestly. "I owe you so much for taking care of her."

"Nonsense!" O'Harris frowned. "She is a friend of mine too."

Tommy gave them a last look and went through the doors. Clara did not follow. O'Harris glanced a questioning look at her.

"My presence will only be an interruption to them," Clara explained. "This is their time. In any case, you know the hospital's rule about one visitor per patient."

"Not like you to obey rules," O'Harris teased her. "You have something else on your mind."

He was right. Now Clara knew that Annie was fine, and she had Tommy watching over her, she could relax and continue with her own investigations. After all, Miss Erskine was in the same hospital…

"I do have something in mind," Clara admitted. "There is another patient here I would like to speak to. I just have to find her."

O'Harris nodded. He looked tired.

"Why don't you go home?" Clara said to him. "We are both extremely grateful for what you have done. I am most glad Annie had such a good friend at her side when this occurred."

O'Harris gave a wan smile, a little embarrassed by the praise. Clara touched his arm, pressing her fingers gently into him to express what words could not.

"Go get some rest, and some supper. I shall make sure Tommy behaves himself and doesn't outstay his welcome," she winked.

O'Harris grinned.

"He loves that girl something rotten. About time he made his feelings plain."

"Sometimes that is harder said than done," Clara replied wistfully. Their eyes briefly met and an unspoken 'something' lingered in their gaze. Clara finally took a breath and moved away. "You must be famished."

"She you later Clara," O'Harris moved away from the wall and then he bent down and kissed Clara's cheek. He squeezed her shoulder then departed with a smile.

Clara stood very still until he was gone around a corner. She wanted the moment to last as long as possible. She was not quite ready to admit to herself what she truly felt for Captain O'Harris but, in moments like this, her feelings defied her and she was engulfed by them. It took a good deal of effort to not go after him, to race to him and return that kiss.

Clara had to take several small breaths to bring herself under control. There was a job to do, she told herself. Emotions would have to wait.

Heading along the corridor, Clara located another orderly and asked him where Miss Erskine was resting. He was able to direct her to another female ward and the matron within pointed out Miss Erskine's bed. The young woman was situated in the far corner with a screen partly pulled around her. Clara approached a little apprehensively. She had not been invited, nor had she been introduced to Miss Erskine. She was a complete stranger intruding on the woman's time. She had to hope that Miss Erskine would understand the urgency of her visit.

The screen squeaked on its wheels as Clara slipped around it to be near the bed. The woman lying under the blankets was pretty, even if her face was bruised and cut. She had a white bandage wrapped around her eyes, perhaps the final pretence made by the doctors to fool themselves and her into thinking she was not actually permanently blind. She was painfully thin; Clara now saw why Mrs Woodcock had been concerned she did not eat well. Clara guessed she had lost more weight in the hospital during her recovery. The stress of her ordeal and the onerous nature of her recuperation was enough to make anyone lose their appetite.

"Who is there?" Miss Erksine asked, and Clara realised she had been standing in silence staring at the woman.

"Clara Fitzgerald," she said quickly to mask her embarrassment. "I hope you don't mind me visiting, but I had wondered if you could assist me."

"Assist you?" Miss Erskine obviously thought that a laughable request considering her condition. "I hope you do not want me to look at anything!"

Miss Erskine's dry wit about her situation was not what Clara had expected and she almost hesitated. She gave a cough, to indicate she was still there and listening, before speaking.

"I wanted to ask you about your accident, if you wouldn't mind? I was wondering if it was somehow connected with the disappearance of a friend of mine."

"How so?" Miss Erskine asked uneasily.

"My friend disappeared the same day you had your accident. No one knows what became of her. I wondered if you might have seen her that day?"

It was a white lie, but Clara was laying the groundwork. She did not want to make Miss Erskine think she was accusing her of anything, such as running down Elaine.

"Who is your friend?" Miss Erskine asked, her brow furrowed in confusion.

"Elaine Chase," Clara answered and Miss Erskine's whole expression lifted.

"Elaine!"

"You know her?"

"Of course, Elaine is one of the Brighton Players," Miss Erskine explained. "We have been meeting quite often these last few weeks. I am writing a play, my first endeavour in the genre. Elaine was guiding me with the protocols of stage directions and so forth. She is going to take the lead in my play."

Miss Erskine paused.

"She is missing?"

"Yes. Since the Saturday of your accident," Clara was trying to nudge her memory. "Maybe you saw her that day?"

Miss Erskine was frowning again.

"My memory of that day is hazy at best. The doctors say I took a bad bang to my head and may never recall what occurred," Miss Erskine gently sighed. "Sometimes I lay here and try to piece together the fragments of it all. Maybe if you help me I shall recall something?"

"How can I help?" Clara asked.

"Sometimes when people talk about that day it jogs a memory. I don't know, little things, like the weather and so forth. I can't say what will trigger a memory, sometimes it is a very random thing."

Clara decided it was worth a go; what else did she have to go on?

"That particular day Elaine had been at the Brighton Players theatre, rehearsing for Macbeth. I was told it was her best performance and there was great excitement for when the play was performed for the public."

"I went to the theatre that day too," Miss Erskine said. "I got up in the morning and decided I would take the latest version of my script to the Players and see what they thought."

"Mrs Woodcock asked you in for a cup of tea before you left, but you declined as you were busy," Clara added.

"Yes!" Miss Erskine said in delight. "I can remember that, picture it even in my head. I said I would pop in for a cup of tea when I returned. Then I got in my car with my manuscript on the passenger seat. That is as clear as day!"

"And you went to the Players? Did you see Elaine there?"

Miss Erskine paused and considered carefully.

"My memories are sometimes false," she admitted to Clara. "I am pretty certain I did not see Elaine there. I spoke to the director and handed him my manuscript. He said he would read it and let me know his thoughts. He hasn't, of course, but I suppose me being in here has stopped him."

"It was a dull day, slightly rainy," Clara continued, painting a picture for Miss Erskine. "I noticed your car had its roof up."

"You saw her?" Miss Erskine smiled sadly. "Poor girl. She took a pounding from what Mrs Woodcock told me. Yes, now you mention it, I expected rain so I put up the roof. The sky was very grey as I began to drive home."

"Which route did you take?" Clara asked.

"Always the same one," Miss Erskine replied. "I cut across country, heading west before I turn north for my cottage."

Miss Erskine suddenly paused. She had remembered something.

"That's the same route Elaine takes to walk home, though she will walk across fields rather than on the road."

Clara said nothing, allowing Miss Erskine to figure things out for herself. The woman was paused with her mouth slightly open, recalling that day. Somewhere in her mind the information was contained and now it was coming back. She just had to unlock the right mental door to reveal it.

"Wait," she held up a hand. "Don't talk, I just need to think."

She was sitting upright, staring at nothing through the bandages, but nonetheless staring. She was watching an internal scene play out.

"I remember that when I got out to my car the sky looked so grim and I thought we must surely have rain. I hate driving in rain, it makes seeing out of the windscreen so difficult. I have wipers, of course, but I wouldn't describe them as very good, more a case of moving the rain about…"

Miss Erskine's fingers played on the blanket as she dredged up the scene from that Saturday.

"I drove along, hoping to get home before it started to

rain," she continued. "Then…"

Miss Erskine's fingers stopped moving. She remained perfectly still for several seconds.

"Why, I had completely forgotten," she mumbled. "I saw her. I saw Elaine climbing over a stile.

"Oh my, I offered her a lift!"

Chapter Twenty

Miss Erskine's revelation, as much as Clara had hoped for it, made her feel a little unwell. There was a chair next to Miss Erskine's bed and Clara sat down in it, her legs had gone rather shaky. After all this time, it looked as though the answer to the mystery was that Elaine had been in the same car accident as Miss Erskine, that she had been thrown from the vehicle and had yet to be found. Which surely meant she was dead. Clara closed her eyes. She might have been thrown into dense bushes or into the deep mud of the ditch. No one had been looking for her at the site of the car crash, the only person imagined to be in the car was Miss Erskine.

"You've gone very quiet," Miss Erskine said, her own voice soft.

"I was just thinking," Clara replied.

"They haven't found Elaine," Miss Erskine said in a hush. "After all this time…"

Both women were sensible enough to know what the implication of that was.

"If only I could remember what happened," Miss Erskine chastened herself. "My damn brain! Why won't the fog clear?"

"It's not your fault," Clara told her. "Don't feel angry

with yourself."

"But I do, especially now…" Miss Erskine bit her lip. "I always considered myself a careful driver, maybe even prided myself on it a little. I can't believe I crashed and I feel awful now knowing that Elaine was with me and that because of me…"

Miss Erskine gulped, the reality of what she was saying was creeping over her. Because of her a woman was dead. And she could not say if the accident was completely out of her control or something that she could have altered. That made it all the worse and compacted her guilt.

"If I hadn't offered her a lift…"

"Don't do that to yourself. You weren't to know."

Miss Erskine touched the bandages over her eyes.

"It is bad enough thinking what has happened to me. But to think someone else was involved breaks my heart. All these days I have been sitting here, wishing I could remember what happened. Now I have remembered a little bit and I wish I had not."

"I am sorry," Clara said, feeling awful that she had raised these memories in Miss Erskine.

"Why did you have to come talk to me? Why?" Miss Erskine demanded of her suddenly, her voice choked.

"I am sorry," Clara rose and began to leave. "I only hoped you might be able to say what had become of my friend."

"Well it looks as though she is dead, because of me!" Miss Erskine was becoming hysterical. "Are you satisfied?"

The matron was heading in their direction, a look of consternation on her face. Clara began to retreat. Miss Erskine was sobbing now and Clara apologised to the matron as she aimed to disappear as fast as she could. Other patients and their visitors were looking over as Clara fled. She was almost at the ward door when she heard Miss Erskine screaming out;

"I didn't want to remember! I didn't want to remember

that!"

Clara hurried back to ward ten feeling as though she was a terrible person for pursuing the truth. Worse, she now feared she was on the trail of a corpse rather than a live person. What had she done to Miss Erskine by insisting on asking her questions? Surely that made her a truly horrible person?

Clara slumped against the wall outside the ward doors and attempted to calm herself. Miss Erskine's hysteria had upset her more than she had initially thought. It wasn't just guilt that made her tremble but looking upon the blinded woman and thinking how suddenly fate could take your life off-course in a terrible fashion. A simple thing as a lift in a car because rain threatened had resulted in the disappearance of one woman – perhaps her death – and the permanent disabling of another. Clara placed a hand on her chest and realised her heart was racing.

The conversation with Miss Erskine had not alone caused the fluttering, it was also due to the sudden thought that a twist of fate had nearly taken Annie from them. Annie seemed such a permanent thing in Clara's life, a fixture that was always there, and then, quite abruptly, there had been a risk she would not be there. Clara took a deep breath. She understood how awful Captain Chase must feel, how anyone must feel when a person they loved was suddenly and unexpectedly snatched from them. Clara had lost loved ones before, but that was in a time of war and seemed many years ago. It was not the sort of thing that was supposed to happen when the world was at peace, and yet it could happen. Clara's foundations, her daily world, had been shaken.

Steadying herself, she pushed open the door to the ward and looked for Tommy and Annie. A nurse came over to her and asked who she was looking for. When Clara said, the nurse explained that patients were only allowed one visitor at a time. Clara promised she would wait outside, but first she caught Annie's eye and smiled at her. Annie smiled back, looking a little pale and sleepy, but otherwise well. Clara kept her promise to the nurse and returned to the corridor. A short time later the bell rang to say that visiting hours were over, and Tommy appeared.

He looked relieved.

"She is fine. The doctors are very pleased with her progress."

Clara relaxed. That was something, at least.

"Good! I'll tell you what I learned from Miss Erskine as we head home."

"I wondered what you did to while away the time while I saw Annie," Tommy said.

"Patients are only allowed a single visitor, so I thought I might as well make the most of my free time. Miss Erskine would probably say she would rather I had not."

Clara told her brother the information she had gathered from Miss Erskine in snatches as they left the hospital and caught the bus home. By the time they were back in their own kitchen and eating cooked ham sandwiches, Tommy was up-to-speed with the details.

"What a shame for Miss Erskine," he mused sadly. "I know how it is to have your life change in an instant. Do you think Elaine is dead?"

"I am inclining that way," Clara sighed. "She was in the car when the accident occurred, at least I assume she was. Miss Erskine's crash happened before she had an opportunity to drop Elaine at home. Anyway, if she had gotten out of the car then surely she would still be around? No, it seems the solution to this mystery is quite simple. She accepted a lift with Miss Erskine, the car crashed, and she was thrown from it. Whether she was dead at once, or died later, I can't say. If she had been found injured she would be at the hospital."

"I suppose," Tommy mumbled.

Clara glanced up.

"What do you mean?"

"Well," Tommy paused over his sandwich, "life can be odd. Supposing someone did find her and took her to their home to nurse her rather than to the hospital? If she has suffered memory loss, like Miss Erskine, possibly she has been unable to say who she is. Just think of O'Harris. Everyone assumed he was dead, it seemed impossible he could be alive, and then a year later he reappears."

Clara hesitated too. She had been so inclined to think the worst that it had not occurred to her that there were other possibilities.

"Until you find Elaine Chase's body, I don't think you should rule out the possibility, how ever slim, of her being alive," Tommy added.

Clara was about to reply when there was a loud knocking on the front door. Both Fitzgeralds glanced up.

"Now what?" Tommy asked, trying to sound nonchalant but actually somewhat uneasy.

They both feared bad news arriving from the hospital, even though that was unlikely. Clara pushed her chair out from the table and went to see who it was. She did not say a word, but her stomach was knotted. Supposing Annie had taken a turn for the worse?

Upon her doorstep was Agnes.

"Clara, the Inspector wants you," the policewoman said. "Been a spot of bother with that Captain Chase fellow."

"Oh dear," Clara said, though in fact she was feeling relieved that the emergency had nothing to do with Annie.

Behind her Tommy was loitering and listening in.

"Captain Chase has been drinking and it don't suit him," Agnes said in her practical fashion. "He got himself into a fight with some Irish lads and made a right nuisance of himself. After he was arrested he tried to do away with himself. He is in a terrible state, never seen a man so broken. The Inspector thought you might be able to calm the lad."

"I'll come at once," Clara agreed, even though she was

utterly exhausted and did not want to set a foot outside her door. She glanced back at Tommy. "Looks like I'm off to the police station."

"Do you want me to come?" He asked.

Clara shook her head.

"Hopefully I won't be long."

It was dark now and they walked along beneath the street lamps.

"Agnes, were you at the scene of a car accident involving a woman called Miss Erskine?" Clara asked as they walked.

"I do recall a nasty smash involving a woman," Agnes nodded. "Was a couple of weeks ago now. Along the western road. Car went into a ditch after hitting a tree."

"Could you tell me where, precisely?"

"Do you know where Paston Field lies?"

"Yes," Clara nodded. "Just over Middling Bridge."

"That's it," Agnes said. "The car crash was a little further on from there. Next to where this big oak stands close to the road. You can easy see the tree as the car gouged it. Why are you interested?"

"I think Elaine Chase was in the car," Clara said sadly. "Actually, I know she was in that car, so the odds are she was involved in that crash."

Agnes whistled through her teeth.

"We saw no sign of the missy."

"That's what concerns me. I'm going to take another look along that road."

Agnes became solemn.

"If she is still there she will be dead as anything," she said. "If we missed her – and I ain't saying we did, but we weren't looking for two women in that there car – so if we did miss her, she must be lying someone and it won't be a pretty sight."

Agnes tutted to herself.

"I ought to come with you."

"I am sure I can manage."

"And I am sure the Inspector would like a police

person on the site, just in case you do find her. Won't look good on us if we missed her, remember."

Clara could see that. She thanked Agnes, though she felt the woman was being overly concerned about her. Clara doubted Agnes had seen a decomposing dead body anymore than she had – though she had seen a mummy. Still, it would be good to have an extra pair of eyes and, if she did find Elaine, she would need to summon the police anyway, so Agnes might as well already be there.

They arrived at the police station and Agnes escorted Clara inside. The desk sergeant, never fond of Clara even at the best of times, eyed them both with equal contempt as they walked past and to the holding cells at the back of the building. Inspector Park-Coombs was talking to a constable in the corridor, given specific instructions about keeping an eye on a prisoner in their care. Clara could guess which prisoner that was.

"Inspector."

"Clara," Inspector Park-Coombs frowned at her. "Have you been told about our situation?"

"The gist," Clara nodded.

"Not what I wanted right at this moment. I was meaning to be off home. Had terrible gut ache since that rich food the other day," Park-Coombs placed a hand to his stomach. "I wanted to be home having a nice cup of cocoa, instead I have this Captain Chase upsetting the Irish dock workers by accusing them of snatching his wife."

"Oh dear," Clara said seriously.

"He has apparently convinced himself that the disappearance of his wife is a plot against him concocted by Irish rebels. He muttered about that when he first reported her missing, said there was always some malcontent wanting to get revenge on a British officer, and he is Anglo-Irish," Park-Coombs paused as a burp threatened, he rubbed at his chest as if it burned. "I have been trying to persuade him there is no evidence for that, but clearly he did not believe me. He went drinking and ended up accosting some Irish lads and demanding to know where his wife was. It descended into a brawl pretty quickly. We brought them all here to sober up, and then Captain Chase tries to hang himself from the window bars. It has been quite an evening so far!"

"You want me to talk to him?" Clara asked.

"He doesn't trust anything I say," Park-Coombs shrugged. "I don't want him finishing himself off in one of my cells. If you could reason with him and calm him down, I would be most grateful."

"I'll do what I can," Clara was not optimistic of her chances of making Chase feel better.

"Don't suppose you have any new leads on the matter of his wife?" The inspector asked in a quiet voice.

"I now know she was offered a lift in the car of Miss Erskine the day she died. That car was involved in a bad crash."

"The one near Paston field," Agnes interjected.

Park-Coombs' face fell.

"Don't tell me we missed her?"

"I can't say for sure," Clara replied. "I have also learned that Elaine thought she was being followed, but the two events do not appear connected."

Park-Coombs winced, but it was not to do with his indigestion.

"If she has been lying in that field since the crash what will everyone say?" He looked miserable. "Shoddy police work. I can't believe we missed her!"

"I haven't found her yet," Clara tried to reassure him. "It may be that she is not there."

"What are the odds?" Park-Coombs groaned. "Damn! What bloody fools we have been! I'll never forgive myself if that is where she has been all this time!"

Clara didn't think there was anything she could say to make him feel better, so she remained quiet. Park-Coombs rubbed at his chest again.

"You best go see Captain Chase," he said.

"I'm sorry, Inspector," Clara said honestly.

"Damn!" Park-Coombs muttered to himself. "Damn!"

Chapter Twenty-one

Captain Chase was sitting on the bench in the cell, his head resting forward in his hands. He looked like a man who was utterly defeated. The crisp, upright army officer was gone, replaced by a scruffy red-eyed vagabond, still slightly drunk and most definitely emotional. Chase's hands were red on the knuckles, showing where he had been fighting. There were cuts and bruises on his face and where his open shirt cuffs had fallen back there were similar marks on his forearms. His clothes were smeared with dirt and blood, and there were rips at the seams. Clara didn't think that Captain Chase had been doing so well in the brawl before the police intervened.

"Good evening."

Captain Chase looked up, then he winced to see who it was. He was sober enough to feel ashamed of himself. He took his hands from his face and folded his arms to hide them, but nothing could hide the cuts and bruises on his cheeks and forehead.

"Looks like you were lucky not to get your nose smashed in," Clara observed.

Chase's right eye was badly swollen, and cuts close to the bridge of his nose showed where a punch had nearly connected with bone and smashed it. Chase rubbed his nose with a finger, perhaps only now realising how fortunate he had been. He was a handsome man, and not one who would like to spend the rest of his days with a deformed nose.

"I made a misjudgement," he said, his words hoarse.

"I can see that," Clara sat down on the bench beside him. "I thought I was investigating this case for you?"

"I have no doubt of your abilities," Chase said hastily. "That is not what this is about."

"Then, what was it about?" Clara asked patiently. "I don't think you are a man who gets into serious fights ordinarily."

Chase sighed. He flexed the fingers of his hands; the joints had swollen a little and tightened up after the fighting.

"I don't know how aware you are of what has been going on in Ireland," Chase said. "The last few years have been… complicated."

"I have read the papers, as much as they can be relied on," Clara knew the last statement would hit a chord with Chase.

He nodded solemnly.

"Newspapers report what suits them. Ireland has been a bubbling pot of troubles for many years, long before I or you, or most of today's politicians were born. There are those in Ireland who feel that being governed by the English makes them dependent and weak, and means they are always being done-down in favour of Englishmen. When you consider the famines that have happened in Ireland in the last century, perhaps that is understandable," Chase smiled sadly, though the movement hurt. "The problem is that not all Irishmen want to be independent from the English. Some believe that great strength comes to Ireland from being connected and governed by politicians in London. The politics are deeply complicated. On the one hand you have the emotive voices of the rebels who wish for Irish independence as a way of restoring the country to her former glory, and then, on the other hand, you have the powerful men of Ireland – politicians, noblemen, businessmen – who fear the financial and political impact of independence and will fight for all they are worth to remain united with England.

"Then consider those who have a toe in both waters, half-Irish and half-English, like myself. Many of the lords and gentry in Ireland have land and interests in England. Some share their time between the two countries. These Anglo-Irish not only fear the loss of their assets should Ireland gain full independence, but also whether their own lives and those of their family might be at risk. Some perceive the Anglo-Irish nobles as really just Englishmen and might like to revenge a few wrongs, either personal or political, against them. Fear for their safety leads many Anglo-Irish to be aggressive in their attempts to keep Ireland with England."

"But Southern Ireland has gained independence," Clara pointed out.

"Southern, but not Northern. It is a very bad compromise, and no one is really happy. The rebels want the whole country independent, the Anglo-Irish are scared to remain in Southern Ireland. Freedom has not ended the turmoil, only changed its appearance."

"And the British army sits in Northern Ireland trying to keep some sort of peace?" Clara surmised.

"The country is on the edge of civil war," Chase explained. "Among those whose reasons for wanting Ireland free are very genuine, there are also those who just like any excuse to cause trouble. The Irish problem has not ended, it never will while some Irishmen scream for freedom and others scream for unity."

Clara let this sink in. The Irish problem was not something that occupied much of her time, if at all. She had read reports in the papers and felt sorry for those innocents caught up in such a political mire and that was very much that. Ireland was a long way away, or so it felt.

"What does this have to do with your wife?"

"As an Anglo-Irish army officer, I have received a lot of threats. I am deemed a traitor by the rebels. An Irishman who sides with the English. I am compromised by my heritage and by my career choices," Chase gave a sarcastic snort. "Anglo-Irish officers get more threats made against them than English officers. We are villains to so many people. I have received more than one anonymous letter which has threatened to harm my family."

"Are these taken seriously by your superiors?"

Chase shook his head.

"Most of them are the work of malcontents wanting to stir up fear. The official line is that our families are safe as houses while in England."

"And then Elaine disappeared."

"Yes."

They both became silent. The question still loomed over Clara – what had caused the crash of Miss Erskine's car? Was it possible that there was an Irish connection? But then, how would any Irish rebels intent on hurting Captain Chase know that Elaine would get in Miss Erskine's car?

"Have you any reason, other than these threats, to imagine Elaine has been taken by Irish rebels?" Clara asked.

"Not really," Chase admitted. "No one has claimed responsibility, but that makes it all the worse. What if this is just the start? That other relatives of army officers in Ireland will now be kidnapped?"

"Then the solution is to resolve Elaine's disappearance, that we might prevent others, if needs be," Clara said. "What of these men you fought with? Could they have been involved?"

"I don't know," Chase rubbed at his forehead, there was a big bruise on his temple. "I've been roaming the docks looking for Irish workers, asking them questions…"

"You were not content to leave things to me," Clara

pointed out. Not particularly offended, she knew in a situation like this it was hard to sit still and wait for someone else to come back with news.

"I apologise," Captain Chase looked genuinely regretful. "I should have been more patient, but I couldn't be in the house alone any longer. I have walked the roads for hours, looking for a sign of Elaine. I felt I was letting her down by not trying to do more."

"You don't need to apologise. I understand," Clara promised him. "What happened today?"

"I had been poking around the docks, hoping to find something that would lead me to Elaine. The Irish connection is perhaps a little slim, but what else have I got? I had seen these fellows at the docks and been told they were prone to talking rot about the English and kept going on about Irish independence. They were local lads, born in Brighton to Irish parents, who thought they had the right to slag off those around them because of their ancestry," Captain Chase could not mask the sneer that slipped into his words. "I had the impression more than one of the English dock workers would have been glad to have seen them knocked for six, if they dared. These fellows roamed in a pack and were said to be mean and quick to fight. I already had a few drinks in me, and I had enough of my own arrogance to decide I could handle them."

Chase managed a strained laugh.

"I caught up with four of them drinking together. The other two were absent, which was perhaps my saving grace in what happened next," Chase examined his grazed knuckles. "I wanted to fight, I won't lie. I have been bursting with this… anger, since Elaine vanished. I started accusing them of being involved in my wife's disappearance. They started to laugh at me, taunt me. Called me a stupid Tommy and indicated that everyone would have been better off if the Germans had won the war."

Captain Chase had to pause as his anger flared up and

almost choked off his words again. He closed his eyes for a moment and attempted to compose himself.

"They are fools," Clara said softly. "But that does not make them kidnappers."

"No," Chase said, his voice so quiet Clara barely heard him.

"I can't recall who started the fight or even why. It wasn't so much about Elaine anymore, as it was about my pride and my guilt that I was not around to protect her," Chase breathed hard. "I've lost her because I was careless."

"You were serving your country," Clara pointed out.

"I was still careless. I didn't listen."

"Listen to what?" Clara asked, suddenly curious. "Is there something more I should know?"

Captain Chase did not immediately reply. He licked his lips and seemed to be trying to moisten his dry mouth.

"I have been spending a lot of my evenings going through my letters from Elaine. I was doing it just as a way to stay connected with her, but, I started to sense a pattern."

Clara was growing concerned. Was this similar to Walter Stone's idea that Elaine was fearful of being followed?

"What sort of pattern?"

"Elaine seemed uncertain. I don't know how to describe it. Little things, like she mentioned feeling uneasy in the cottage alone and would be glad when I was back. I put that down to the problems we had had with Mary Worthing, now I am starting to wonder. There was an undercurrent of anxiety to her letters these last weeks. Something I can't quite place, but there nonetheless."

"Might you be reading more into them than what is there?" Clara asked.

Chase sighed.

"Always possible, I suppose. But…" Chase glared at the door to the cell. "No, I think there was something there. I think Elaine was hinting at something bothering her. I just don't know quite what."

Clara did not know what to say. She had convinced herself that Elaine had died in a car crash that was just pure bad luck. Her body had been flung into some hiding place where, so far, she had not been found. What if she was wrong? What if there was a conspiracy behind this all that she had yet to tap into? Walter Stone had hinted at it, now Captain Chase was saying the same thing. Could two men who loved Elaine both be desperately reading more into her words and actions than was really there?

"Do you think Elaine is dead?" Clara asked Captain Chase.

He started with the question, but she felt the reaction was somewhat forced.

"Why would you ask that?" He said defensively.

"Because you tried to kill yourself," Clara replied calmly. "That strikes me as the action of a man who has given up hope."

Captain Chase turned to her with grieving eyes. The emotion within them was so palpable it made Clara want to shudder. Everything was so raw and so real for Chase at that moment in time. He looked broken.

"For a moment..." he hesitated and placed a hand around his throat. "For a moment I lost my belief in Elaine's capability for survival. It won't happen again. Until I see an actual body, I shall cling to the certainty my wife lives."

Clara was not sure if that was a good thing or not. Hope was a marvellous tool for survival, but sometimes blindly hoping for what was likely impossible had the potential to be devastating to the person when the truth was revealed. A little seed of doubt, might be best sown now.

"I don't know if they will press any charges against you," Clara said, working up to destroying his hopes. "I have a few leads to work away at. Elaine..."

Clara's tongue seemed to go numb; she couldn't tell

him to brace himself for the worst.

"You know where my wife might be?" Chase asked, a brightness returning to his eyes.

Clara could not bring herself to say what she really should. Could he not last a few more days on this hope? Surely better to have a little more time with the idea of Elaine being found safe and well? Clara knew no option was perfect, or very consoling. They were just options.

"I have an idea or two," Clara admitted. "I should be able to pursue them in the morning."

"Then we may have the answer soon?" Chase's eyes lit up. "I will be forever grateful if you can bring Elaine back to me."

Clara could not continue deluding him any longer. She rose, feeling she had to leave before her guilt at continuing this masquerade overwhelmed her. She had told Tommy she was still working on the premise that Elaine was alive. That was no longer true. She was working on the premise that Elaine was most likely dead, with a very slim outside chance that she was alive and that something beyond the obvious had happened to her. Watching the hope returning to Chase's eyes because of her words was heart-breaking. She felt both a fraud and a crook for allowing him to keep clinging to that notion, and yet she could not bring herself to tell him otherwise.

"I'll do my very best," she promised instead, angry at herself for those words.

Then she left the cell, feeling ashamed of her empty vows.

Chapter Twenty-two

When morning came Clara went with Inspector Park-Coombs to the scene of Miss Erskine's car accident. A team of constables had been given the task of searching the immediate area to look for any sign of Elaine Chase. Bushes, ditches, even tall trees had to be searched in case she had been flung into them. The hushed undercurrent was that they were looking for a body. Clara volunteered to assist, she felt as responsible for Elaine as the police did, and as concerned that her corpse had been lying undiscovered in the countryside for days. Park-Coombs was reluctant at first and then conceded as long as they searched together. Clara guessed he did not want her coming across a decomposing body alone. She didn't have the energy to explain that she had seen some terrible sights during her time as a nurse during the war, and a decomposing corpse was unlikely to send her into hysterics.

The search parties began at the place the car had crashed and then fanned out in a circle to cover the area all around. Someone in the police laboratory who was clever with mathematics, had been tasked with determining how far a person could be thrown from a car at a given speed (Miss Erskine rarely did more than twenty miles an hour, so they had taken that as their upper limit). An equation had been devised and a search area composed. Park-Coombs now had a rough perimeter within which to scour the ground closely. He had determined that if Elaine Chase was there, he would find her.

Clara looked at the gash in the old oak tree where Miss Erskine had collided with it. The tree grew on the bank of a ditch, on the side nearest the road its gnarled trunk was missing a sizeable section of bark where the car had swiped it with its front wing. The wound still looked fresh and raw, even as the tree acted to heal itself and the exposed wood began to weather into a new outer layer. There were still deep tracks on the bank where Miss Erskine had driven up it, hit the tree and then fallen forward into the ditch. The muddy ditch, however, did not show any signs that it had recently been housing a car.

"Have you any idea of what happened to cause this crash?" Clara asked the inspector.

Park-Coombs was staring up at the sky, which was clouding over. He took a deep breath and then brought himself back to present events.

"It's all a puzzle. Miss Erskine remembers nothing and there was no sign of another vehicle of any description being involved. We speculated that she had swerved to avoid something, since the road shows no evidence of anything untoward. We had the car examined and there was no damage found that could not be ascribed to the accident. Our mechanics did not think it was a fault in the car that caused the crash."

Clara looked alone the road, which was relatively wide for a country lane and smooth. Though not covered with tarmacadam, its sandy surface was even and unrutted. There was no hint of why someone might suddenly lose control on it.

"There were cows in that field," Park-Coombs pointed to the meadow opposite them. "We wondered if one might have come out and walked into the road. Livestock cause a lot of car accidents. You see this part of the road bends around the edge of the fields and the hedges are high. You wouldn't see a cow on the road until it was too late."

The field Park-Coombs had pointed out was now empty. There was a gate set into the hedge, but it was shut.

"Any reason to suppose the cows had been out?" Clara asked.

"The farmer said they were all fine, none showed signs of being hit by a car. Of course, Miss Erskine might have swerved in time to avoid the animals. The gate was closed, as it is now. If the cows had been out, they had put themselves back into the field and closed the gate behind them."

"In other words, that seems an unlikely cause of the accident."

Park-Coombs shrugged. Clara turned her attention back to the ditch. The water at the bottom was shallow and looked black as tar. She wondered what would happen if a body fell into it, how far and how fast would the body sink? Would it disappear entirely?

There was a fallen bough near the oak, presumably swiped off during the crash. Clara picked it up and used the end to prod the murky water. The end of the branch did not go very far before it hit relatively firm ground. She pulled it out and calculated that the end had sunk about six inches. Not enough room to hide a corpse. Clara continued to explore the ditch, nonetheless. She was hoping to find something small that would prove for definite that Elaine had been here. It seemed unlikely that she had gotten out of the car before the accident and then disappeared, but it was not always possible to predict just what people would do. She scraped around in the mud for a while without success.

"Might have been something else, like a bird, that made her swerve," Park-Coombs continued thoughtfully.

"Or could have been a wild animal, like a deer. People react fast when they fear they are going to hit something and not always in their best interests."

Clara was only half-listening as she stirred up the waters in the ditch. A small frog suddenly darted from where it had been hidden in the mud and fled up the bank. There was something slightly accusing in the way it sprang away, as if it was not just annoyed, but hurt that Clara had interrupted its sleep.

"No one has come forward to report being involved in an accident. I know not everyone likes speaking to the police, but you would think they would report a person running off the road in a car, even if they did not want to say they had been the cause," Park-Coombs was grumbling to himself. He kicked at a stone. "If only we had known Elaine Chase was in that car."

Clara was not listening. Her stirring activities had dislodged something from the muddy side of the ditch. It had briefly surfaced and caught her eye as it glimmered for a fraction of a second, before slipping back under the water. She prodded about with her branch a little more and the shiny thing surfaced again. This time she was able to hook the tip of her branch underneath it and shuffle it to the side of the ditch where it could no longer slip away into the brackish water. It was small and she nearly lost it a couple of times.

To reach it with her hand required Clara to lay on the ground and stretch her arm into the ditch as far as she could. Even so her fingers could not quite touch the object. She pushed herself a little further forward, stretching down as much as she could.

"Clara!" Park-Coombs had suddenly noticed his companion disappearing into a ditch head-first. He took hold of her around the waist before she slipped away. "What are you doing?"

"I can almost reach it," Clara answered him. "If you could just keep hold of me?"

Before Park-Coombs could agree Clara was stretching

out to her full extent, her middle now over the edge of the bank so she was nearly toppled into the mud. The inspector held onto her as best he could, as she reached out her fingers and finally was able to grab the glimmering thing that had attracted her attention. It proved to be a fine chain, and once it was in Clara's closed fist she used her other hand to push herself back up and onto the bank. Park-Coombs caught hold of her upper arms and helped. Soon she was sitting on the bank, her arms and hands covered in black mud. She opened her fist and displayed in her palm the object that had caught her eye.

It was a silver bracelet. Its relative plainness was misleading, it was a well crafted piece of jewellery. A small oval of silver was inset into the chain and displayed tiny hallmarks on one side, and the initials E.C. on the other.

"Elaine Chase," Park-Coombs noted the initials.

"Then she was here and may have been in this ditch," Clara indicated where the clasp of the silver chain had snapped. The metal had worn thin in that area and the impact of the crash had broken it. Only, if the bracelet had ended up in the ditch, surely that meant Elaine should be there too? Or had the silver chain been thrown from her wrist in one direction while she went the other?

"This makes no sense," Park-Coombs iterated what Clara was already thinking. "If her bracelet is here, then Elaine should be here, and yet we cannot locate her."

Park-Coombs spread out his hand and indicated the landscape around them. It was fairly open and there were not that many places a person could be hidden.

"Where did you find Miss Erskine?" Clara asked, thinking that the position of Miss Erskine might provide a hint as to where Elaine might have been thrown.

"She was still in the car, thrust forward and compressed against the steering wheel. The car had plunged into the ditch nose-first and prevented Miss Erskine from being flung out," Park-Coombs explained.

"Miss Erskine was unconscious. Her door was closed, but the passenger door was swung open and the window was down. We did not consider that of importance at the time, just assumed the door had sprung open by itself. Now, it makes me wonder if it was the weight of Elaine falling on it that forced the door open."

"In which case she should be here, in the ditch," Clara pointed out. "Could she have been thrown through the open window?"

"Size-wise it would be possible. But a body does not fly around neatly. It would be quite a fluke."

"More likely she fell out when the door opened?" Clara suggested.

They both looked down at the shallow mud.

"I had wondered if the water could have drowned her and covered her body," Clara said. "I know animals can drown that way and not be found for some time."

"We have had a lot of rain to flood the ditch," Park-Coombs agreed. "And it rained the day of the crash. But, that leaves us with a problem, because Elaine is clearly not here now."

They both looked into the murky water.

"This doesn't make sense," Clara scowled at the water. "If Elaine was thrown into this ditch, which seems likely, then she either got up and walked away herself before Miss Erskine was found or someone removed her. Either way, no one bothered to seek help for Miss Erskine and if Elaine was found why has no one come forward to say where she is?"

Park-Coombs had an odd look in his eye.

"I can only think of one scenario where Elaine would be removed and the accident not reported," he said solemnly.

"Me too," Clara groaned. "Elaine had to be still alive and someone helped her from the car or from this ditch for the sole purpose of kidnapping her. I mean, maybe they would have taken her even if she was dead if they were doing it to spite Captain Chase, but why has there been no ransom note or any other indication that this is an act of retaliation against him?"

"I don't know," Park-Coombs answered. "I thought we would find Elaine Chase's corpse this morning, but now I am not so sure. It looks as though we are once more back to the assumption that Elaine is still alive."

"Elaine thought she was being followed. Captain Chase thought she seemed nervous. What if these were not idle anxieties? What if someone was really after Elaine and took this opportunity to snatch her?"

"We are still no way closer to discovering who that person might be," Park-Coombs was more frustrated than ever by the situation. "Whoever this person is, they are covering their tracks well."

Clara did not reply. She was gazing at the muddy ditch water, imagining Elaine being pulled from it by someone she imagined was rescuing her, only to discover a new nightmare was about to begin.

"Are you the police?"

They both turned to see an old man leaning over the hedge behind them. He had a tall crook in one hand and a dirty-looking sheepdog lying beside him.

"I'm the shepherd up on the water meadows," the old man continued. "I've heard someone has been stealing stuff from farms."

Park-Coombs shifted a mental gear as he returned to a problem he had almost forgotten about.

"Yes," he said, "there have been thefts of fuel and tools."

"I have a little shepherd's hut on the top meadow. I only use it when the sheep have lambs. I moved my flock up to that meadow this morning and went to open my hut and air it. Looks like someone has been in it. Reckon it could be your thieves."

"I'll send a man up to look," Park-Coombs assured him.

The shepherd was turning away, calling his dog to him when Clara stopped him.

"Wait, how do you know someone has used the hut?" She asked him.

The shepherd looked at her as if that ought to be obvious, then he spoke.

"There was a blanket on the bed, I didn't leave that there, and mud on the floor. Fresh mud. My kettle had water in it, though I left it empty and my stove had hardly any oil left in it," the shepherd looked hurt that someone would be so inconsiderate to him.

Clara was thinking fast, connecting the two scenarios.

"How far is it from here?"

The shepherd shrugged.

"Couple of miles across the fields," he answered.

Clara looked at Park-Coombs.

"She had to be taken somewhere," she pointed out to him. "Somewhere close and out-of-sight. Just for a little while."

"You think…" Park-Coombs paused and his eyes lit up.

"We need to investigate this at once!"

The shepherd was smiling, feeling that at last his problem was being given the due consideration it deserved.

"I can lead you up there now," he said.

Clara did not reply to him, her eyes were on Park-Coombs, a new excitement was growing inside. At last, here was a lead – could it be she would find Elaine Chase alive after all? She could only hope so.

Chapter Twenty-three

The shepherd did not seem to notice the urgency in the inspector's or Clara's manner as he headed at a steady amble up the hillside. He appeared to not have a speed above sauntering, certainly he did not rush and once or twice even stopped to pause and observe a sheep that had caught his eye. The sheep were happily grazing with several lambs milling about among them. The sheepdog continually circled the shepherd's legs waiting to be told what to do. Once or twice the dog nearly managed to trip up Clara or the inspector as he herded his master. The inspector grumbled under his breath.

Eventually they reached the crest of the hill, roughly two thirds up the field, and there was the shepherd's hut. It looked rather like a garden shed raised up on wheels and with a short set of wooden steps leading up to the door. It was painted a dark green, though it would need another coat before the winter came again. The shepherd leaned his crook against a wheel and then walked up the steps and opened the door. He revealed a compact living space. On the left side was a folding bed, hinged so that it could swing up flat to the wall when not in use. The bed was currently fitted with a thin straw mattress and a rumpled blanket. Beneath the bed was a bucket; Clara preferred not to speculate on its uses. There was also a large old trunk marked rather crudely in white paint with the word 'medicine'. At the back right corner of the hut was a small stove, with its chimney flue going up through the roof. Sitting on it was a battered copper kettle. A wooden crate had been turned on its side to form a rudimentary cupboard, with no door, and in this was sat a frying pan, several battered mugs, a plate, bowl and some mismatched knives and forks. A teapot perched on the top of the cupboard and looked fit to fall at any moment.

There was a window on the right wall and a shelf running over it, which contained a range of assorted items. Clara could see a box of safety matches and a ball of string from where she was stood.

"What has been moved or touched, as far as you can tell?" Clara asked the shepherd.

"Bed wasn't down when I left it. I never leave a mattress and blankets in here, they go damp," the shepherd motioned to the folding bed. "Bucket might have been used. Its been rinsed out recently, still had water in it. Same with the kettle. Also, there are tea leaves in the teapot. That was washed and empty when I left here last autumn. I take the tea with me.

"Matchbox looks emptier than I remember, and the stove is very low on oil, which it wasn't before. Apart from that, mostly it is clean and tidy."

Clara stepped up on the stairs beside him and looked inside the hut.

"Do you lock it when you leave?"

"Yes," the shepherd shrugged. "Tramps would get in otherwise. I don't mind a fellow taking shelter from the rain, but in the past they have taken advantage of me. I end up with no fuel for the stove, or all my matches gone. Not to mention the mess they leave."

The shepherd huffed to himself.

"I ain't a rich man. I can't afford to lose stuff like that."

"The padlock had been broken then?" Inspector Park-Coombs asked.

"That's just the thing," the shepherd said, his eyes widening. "The padlock was still there. Admittedly the key didn't want to fit, but otherwise it seemed as good as when I left it. That is why I was so surprised when I saw this."

Clara took another step into the hut. The wood on the inside had been white-washed to reflect the light from the small window and make everything seem brighter. An old lamp hung from the central rafter of the pitched roof.

"Had the lamp been used?" She asked.

"As far as I can tell," the shepherd nodded. "There was oil in it. It seems to me as if someone had topped it up."

"Whoever was in here was no tramp," Inspector Park-Coombs politely moved the shepherd off the steps so he could join Clara. "Tramps don't carry oil for lamps."

"Do you smell that Inspector?" Clara turned to him.

The inspector sniffed the air and then hesitated.

"Perfume?"

"Rather like oil of roses," Clara agreed. "No tramp goes around wearing perfume."

"We need to take a good look at your hut," the inspector spoke to the shepherd who was looking rather peeved now they had taken over his small domain. He seemed to be regretting involving them as they kept asking questions and poking around. "We won't take anything, but we may need you to look at things to confirm they are yours."

The shepherd sighed and whistled to his dog. Together they walked off towards the sheep and stood a few yards from the hut. The shepherd leaned on his crook and watched his flock. Park-Coombs turned back to Clara.

"If Elaine was here, let's hope she left us a clue."

Clara set to work in the far-right corner, while the inspector looked at the folding bed. It appeared that while the person responsible for breaking into the hut had not been bothered about people knowing they had done so, they had gone to the effort of keeping everything clean and tidy. As if they did not want to be disrespectful to their unsuspecting host. As the shepherd had said, his kettle still contained water, but it did not smell stale, which implied it had not been in there for long. The stove was cold and there was no way to tell when it was last used. It could be fuelled by wood or oil, and there were ashes in the grate. Clara felt those too, but they were also stone cold.

The rudimentary cupboard was no more revealing. The crockery was old but clean. If it had been used it had been washed up again with care. The teapot was the only thing that had been forgotten; when Clara lifted its lid she saw that tea leaves were stuck to the inside walls. Who had made this final cup of tea?

The inspector was rummaging under the bed. He had pushed aside the trunk marked 'medicine' and was exploring the dust and cobwebs that had gathered where the walls and floor met. He stopped after a moment and emerged. The arms of his jacket were covered in dust, and the knees of his trousers would be no better when he rose up, but in his hand was something small and metal. He showed it to Clara.

"That's a button," he told her.

Clara took the small object. It was less than half-an-inch in diameter. A metal button with a loop on the back for sewing onto fabric. The button was domed and a small ivy leaf appeared to be embossed onto the top. Strands of black cotton still clung to the back loop. Clara studied it thoughtfully.

"I would say it is the button from a lady's jacket," she said at last. "A nice jacket too."

"Maybe Captain Chase can identify it as belonging to his wife?" The inspector suggested.

Clara almost laughed, though the situation was not really funny.

"Inspector, if I brought you a button from one of your wife's jackets would you be able to tell me if it belonged to her?"

Park-Coombs paused and then shook his head.

"I take your point. But it suggests a woman has been in here, does it not?"

"It does indeed," that Clara was certain of.

A thought crossed her mind. She moved passed the inspector, which was not easy in the cramped space, and opened the medicine trunk. Inside was an array of glass bottles and cardboard boxes, each bearing handwritten labels with long names. Beneath the names was a description of what the medicine was used for. She saw that one was a bottle of disinfectant. It was nearly empty.

"Excuse me!" She called out to the shepherd. "When did you last inventory your trunk of medicines?"

The shepherd turned at the mention of his trunk and almost ran back to the hut. Until that moment he had not seemed to be fazed by anything that had occurred – put out, perhaps, but not unduly concerned – now he was agitated. He came up the steps of the hut and glanced in his trunk. Then he bent down and started pulling out the contents; boxes and bottles began to pile up in the small space. A frown came onto his brow.

"I had a full bottle of disinfectant," he took the bottle from Clara. "I can't believe this! I made sure it was full before I locked up the hut. I go through so much of the stuff during lambing."

"Is anything else missing?" Clara asked.

The shepherd looked forlorn as he took stock of his box.

"There should be a roll of bandages in here and some gauze pads," he said.

"The sort of thing you would use to dress a wound," Inspector Park-Coombs pointed out, though Clara had already guessed as much.

"I'll have to restock at once," the shepherd was crestfallen. "Someone has even used the laudanum."

"You keep an opiate in here?" Clara was surprised.

"Occasionally I need a sedative for the animals. It calms them, can help a ewe that is becoming distressed by a bad birth. I don't use a lot and it has a milder effect on them than on people."

The shepherd returned the bottles to the trunk looking miserable.

"It's thoughtless to use up someone else's stuff like that, thoughtless."

Clara had other notions on her mind. She was imagining that Elaine had been hurt in the crash, just like Miss Erskine had been hurt. Someone had dragged her from the car, that is if she had not been thrown out, and they brought her to this hut. Why? Perhaps because Elaine was so badly injured that taking her further was impossible. This was a quick and easy alternative. Once in the hut the medicine trunk was found, and Elaine's wounds could be treated. She must have been badly banged up, so much disinfectant had been used. The laudanum would not only dull the pain, but sedate Elaine and make her more biddable. How long was she here for? Long enough that someone had to bring her bedding and for her, or her kidnapper, to use the kettle and make tea. The only question left was where had she been taken to next?

"Where is the nearest farm to here?" Inspector Park-Coombs asked.

"John Nuggins has the farm six miles north of here," the shepherd said without looking up.

Park-Coombs considered this.

"Are there any buildings nearer here?"

"Nothing anyone lives in," the shepherd shrugged.

"What about places that are standing empty?" The inspector persisted.

The shepherd seemed to be finding the questions annoying, he was more concerned with his missing supplies.

"There is a barn a mile from here. Used to be used to store fodder, but it was never looked after and the roof leaks too badly to make it any good now," he rose up and gave them a stern glare. "I have to go into town and buy supplies. If you want to keep looking in my hut, do so, but when you leave close the door and put on the padlock."

With that he stormed off, calling to his dog who quickly came to his heel.

"Charming fellow," Park-Coombs snorted.

Clara was not really listening, she had picked up the blanket and was looking at it. It was made from thick wool with a distinctive herringbone pattern. The mattress was rougher, not a modern mattress, but something that you would have found in a cottage during her grandmother's day. It was made of striped cotton and appeared hand sewn. It had been stuffed unevenly with straw.

"Why was this left behind?" Clara said to the inspector. "Had these been removed, the shepherd would not have noticed for a long time that his hut had been used."

"Maybe our kidnapper meant to come back but didn't get the chance. Events crop up and if by the time they could get back the shepherd had turned up, well, that was their chance gone."

"There are elements to this that feel carefully planned," Clara continued. "And other elements that feel as though they were done in haste. Like breaking into this hut. That would seem to have been a spontaneous thing, as the kidnapper could not be sure when it would next be used."

"And this is the right time of year for a shepherd to be using his hut, yes, I see what you mean. This was handy in a pinch."

Clara surveyed the hut one last time, willing some clue, some hint as to what had gone on there to slip from the walls. Nothing.

"You think Elaine may have been taken to this abandoned barn?" She said to the inspector as they left the hut.

"Well, if we assume this all points to Elaine being here, then she had to be moved somewhere else. And it would need to be remote from people, but not too far away. I don't think Elaine would be in much of a state to walk a great distance. An empty barn would be ideal."

Clara's excitement was building. If they were correct, if this was a sign that Elaine was alive and being held somewhere, then it could be they were nearly on top of finding her. She could be at the barn this very moment – surely she would be there? They might find her waiting for them and this would all be over.

Clara was almost breathless with anticipation.

"We must go at once, Inspector!"

"I agree," Park-Coombs grinned. "But not before I have my constables. We have no idea what will greet us. Whoever stole away Elaine, I don't intend to underestimate them."

"Please hurry," Clara begged him, unable to bear the suspense any longer. "If Elaine is there…"

She didn't need to finish that statement. They both knew what relief it would bring if they could just find Elaine. She had to be there and she had to be alive and well, didn't she?

Clara felt the small metal button in her hand as she clutched it firm in her palm. It was almost as if Elaine was signalling to them. They would find her and rescue her. Clara just knew it.

Chapter Twenty-four

The old barn was clearly abandoned. There was a large hole in the roof, near one of the ends, and a pigeon fluttered through it as Clara and the inspector approached. The building had an aura of something forgotten, the neglect seeming to hang over it like a shroud. Clara felt a little sad as she approached. Surrounded by fields and a few trees, the barn seemed like a peaceful place, but its abandonment made it eerie.

The pigeon fluttered out of the hole in the roof again as they neared and disappeared over the trees. Clara guessed it was nesting.

"Foot prints," Park-Coombs pointed to the ground nearest to a large pair of double doors. The recent wet weather had made the earth soft and there were faint impressions in the ground. Clara crouched and looked over the marks.

"This is a woman's high heel," she indicated the print she had spotted. There was the outline of a pointed toe and behind it a hole where the narrow heel of a woman's shoe had dug into the soft ground. "Elaine."

"Certainly not a farmer," Park-Coombs nodded. "But the place seems very quiet."

Clara did not want to hear that, but she had to agree.

The prints were old and the place had an aura of emptiness. Her heart was starting to sink.

The inspector walked to the old double-doors, large enough to enable a cart of hay to go through with ease. There was a metal latch on them, it slipped over a loop of iron and could be secured with a padlock, however, it was currently folded back on itself. Clara felt her hope droop further. If Elaine was being held here, then surely the door would be locked? Even so, they both paused at the door. What was to be expected on the other side? Would there be someone watching over the unfortunate woman, who could be a danger to them?

The barn had no windows and there was no way to peer inside and get an idea of who might be about. The inspector put his ear to the door and listened. His forehead wrinkled into a frown. He shook his head at Clara, indicating he could hear nothing. There was no choice but to enter and hope for the best.

Park-Coombs pulled back the door. He did it sharply, hoping that anyone inside would react by making a sound of surprise and indicate their presence. All they actually got was the sound of a startled pigeon launching off its nest and out of the roof hole.

Clara stepped through the door. The barn was dark, the only light coming through the big doors and where the lapped wood of the walls had rotted away to leave gaps. Thin beams of light streamed in at varying angles and collided with each other to make a criss-cross pattern of white haze. The main space of the barn was empty. Leftover piles of hay, too wet with damp to be any good now, stood at the corners and edges. Forgotten like the barn, unwanted, unneeded. A broken plough was nestled against the back wall, right under the hole in the roof, so the rain had hammered down on it and rusted the exposed metal. It looked like the skeleton of some monster that had died in the dusty barn.

Clara took another pace forward. There was no one in the barn, that was plain. The pigeon, deciding the intruders were not dangerous, had returned to its nest and was cooing contentedly to itself. The space was quiet, almost serene.

"We should look for signs that she was here," Park-Coombs said, having stepped into the barn behind Clara.

They spread out, each taking one side of the barn. Clara was nearest the decaying plough and found her eyes drawn to the old, rusty chains and the curving metal. There was something unnerving about the machine, as if it was able to watch her. She shook off the sensation and took a closer look among the leftover bundles of hay. She was reminded that someone had made up a straw mattress to use in the shepherd's hut, perhaps the stuffing materials had come from the barn?

Two of the piles of hay seemed to have been crudely raked up in right angles to each other, creating a small square with the corner of the barn forming the far side. It was a little alcove and as Clara stepped through a narrow gap where the hay piles did not quite meet, she saw that this little space had been lived in.

"Over here!" She called to the inspector. He joined her in a matter of moments.

The square room had been constructed to provide a modicum of warmth in the draughty barn. It was far enough away from the hole in the roof to not get wet when it rained, but light could still stream down into the space. The hay formed walls and insulated from the biting wind which whipped through the ruined wood lapping. The barn walls in this corner were in relatively better condition and did not let in the wind. On the ground were two lengths of old cardboard. Their position and width suggested they had been used as base layer for a bed, keeping the sleeper off the earthen floor. Possibly there had been straw mattresses here too and blankets. They were gone.

The floor area had been compressed by feet and there were more marks of a woman's heeled shoe in the ground. Clara also spotted a length of rope, frayed badly at one end and partly cut through. She could not say for certain, but she had a hunch this had been used to keep someone tied up.

"Someone was here," Park-Coombs agreed. "Two people, it would seem."

The space was surprisingly clean. There was no trace of food waste or any other rubbish that might be expected if this was the sleeping place for a tramp. The area had almost been stripped bare apart from the pieces of cardboard which were probably not deemed worth the effort of dragging from the ground. They would have shed dust and straw on the person doing so, in any case. However, overall it felt as if the little shelter had been meticulously scoured before being left behind. As if someone was trying to hide all trace of their presence.

Clara paced around the area, hoping to see something that would hint at where the people had gone next. Could it really be a coincidence that Elaine had been in the shepherd's hut and that someone had spent time in this barn and then attempted to erase the signs? And whoever was here had worn ladies' heels – no tramp would do that. This had to be where Elaine was taken after the shepherd's hut became too dangerous. But who had brought her here and why?

"I think this all points to her still being alive," Park-Coombs said thoughtfully. "Whoever has her is taking great care of her and moving her from place to place. If they just wanted her dead, why tend her wounds after the car crash?"

"But what is the motive?" Clara raised the question that was bugging her the most. "If this is a kidnapping to get revenge against Captain Chase, or to demand a ransom, then why has no note been sent or any contact been made?"

"The reason for the kidnapping revolves around Elaine and no one else," Park-Coombs replied. "She is who they want. They are not interested in ransoms. Their revenge is aimed at Elaine and Elaine alone."

"And yet they keep her alive," Clara groaned at the confusing nature of it all. "They keep moving her to mask what they are doing."

They both stared at the tiny shelter, lost in their own thoughts. Clara felt sure that this space had been abandoned at least a couple of nights before. The place felt settled, the traces of the occupants already fading. She could not smell the perfume here as she had in the shepherd's hut, but then Elaine had not been able to reapply it and strengthen the scent. Clara dragged a hand across her face, feeling tension building in her temples as the puzzle grew and solutions eluded her.

"Whoever has done this, they keep one step ahead all the time."

"They won't forever," Park-Coombs replied to her, his words firm but gentle. "I shall have my men keeping their eyes peeled. Elaine has to have been moved to somewhere else remote. I'll have all the empty barns and houses we can find searched for any clue. We shall find her, now we know she is out there to find."

Clara glanced at him. A few days ago Park-Coombs had thought Elaine had run away, that she was just another unhappy wife who had disappeared to start again. Now he was regretting that assumption and his guilt would spur him on to renewed efforts to find her. He had the resources at his disposal to equip a large manhunt, Clara did not. She would have to leave the searching to him and his men. On the other hand, she could do something he did not have the time for. She could continue prying into Elaine's life, trying to discover who might have a grudge against her strong enough to warrant this crime. So far, she had ruled out her main suspects; she did not think either the Players' stage manager Wendy, or Mary Worthing clever enough to have orchestrated such a cunning plan. Walter Stone seemed an unlikely culprit too, besides, his work kept him firmly in Brighton and he could not have made regular trips to this remote barn. No, there was someone else in the equation, someone that Clara had so far missed.

She made up her mind. She knew what path she must take.

"I am going to go back to Elaine's cottage and search for a clue as to who did this," she told the inspector. "I shall leave you to the hunt and wish you the very best."

"My men will begin at once," Park-Coombs frowned. "Why must everything always come at once? I have to keep some men back to continue patrolling the lanes for these farm thieves who keep striking. If not, I could put more bobbies onto the job of tracing Elaine."

"The thieves are still about?" Clara asked idly, it was nice to consider something other than the disappearance of Elaine Chase. The farm thefts, though unpleasant and inconvenient for the farmers involved, were remote enough from Clara to be distracting rather than worrisome.

"Potters' farm was raided last night," Park-Coombs sighed. "Half an hour after my lads went past to check it was all right the thieves broke in and took a large amount of fuel, several smaller tools and the labourers' wages which old Potter rather foolishly keeps locked in a cashbox in an outbuilding he uses for an office. The wages had just been placed there as they were to be given out the next day. Someone knew that."

"You think these are local thieves with insider knowledge?"

"At least one of them has spent time scoping out the farms. They always strike right at the moment they can gain the most. It is very frustrating. I just don't have the men to guard all the farms. The patrols are the best we can do and, as has been proved, it is not enough."

Clara felt sorry for the inspector, but there was nothing she could do to help.

"Hopefully you will catch them soon," she said, trying to sound confident.

Park-Coombs merely grimaced. He obviously did not hold out much hope of that.

"At least I now know to search for Elaine Chase," Park-Coombs said. "Thanks for that Clara. If you had not discovered Elaine was with Miss Erskine, we would not have known to keep looking."

Clara shrugged off the compliment.

"It was just luck," she said modestly.

They walked out the barn leaving the pigeons to their peace and quiet. Park-Coombs pulled the doors closed and looked at the flimsy latch. It hung loose and was clearly badly worn. Even if it had been locked it would not have taken great effort to break it open.

"Who would do this," he mumbled to himself.

"I'll find out," Clara said, even though the question was not particularly aimed at her.

Park-Coombs smiled.

"You find the culprit while I find Elaine, sounds like a reasonable suggestion."

Clara knew his smile was forced, so was hers, but there was hope in them too. They set off walking back to the road, not saying a word, each lost in their thoughts.

~~~*~~~

"Have you remembered to put the milk in the pantry to keep cool?"

"It arrived yesterday, and yes, I did," Tommy tried not to get irked by Annie's constant questions regarding the standard of care being given to her kitchen.

"I hate thinking of milk spoiling. Did the tea towels get washed?"

"Not yet, but I put them to one side."

"Well, that's something," Annie pursed her lips. "The doctors say I must be here another night at least Tommy."

"They have to be sure you are all healed up before you come home," Tommy consoled her. "It won't be long. Just hang in there."

Tears welled up in Annie's eyes.

"And they say I must take it easy when I am allowed out. No hard work, just bed rest. It's awful!" Annie cried softly to herself.

"It's not so bad," Tommy clutched her hand. "You deserve a rest."

"But the baking contest!" Annie burst out, no longer able to hold her tongue. "I'll miss it!"

Tommy was thrown.

"What baking contest?"

"It happens in less than two weeks and I was going to enter my Victoria sponge and now I can't and Jane Jenkins will win and lord it over me forever and ever!"

Tommy opened his mouth, but didn't really know what to say. He started to form the sentence 'it's only a baking contest' and then realised how that would sound and how much it would upset Annie, so he stopped.

"I didn't realise," he said instead.

"I know it is not the end of the world, but I was so looking forward to showing off my sponge," Annie wiped at her eyes, the emotion spent. "My mother would say this is what comes of being proud."

"I don't think appendicitis is caused by pride," Tommy promised her.

Annie let out a shaky breath.

"I meant to win it, I would have won it. Now I cannot. The one thing I could excel at and now I can do nothing, nothing!"

Annie fell silent, her disappointment palpable. Tommy didn't know what to say. He ran a few sentences through his head and each sounded either dismissive of Annie's feelings or rather like platitudes. He wished Clara was there to help out.

"Maybe you will be better by then?" He suggested, which was really no better than any of the other sentences he had played through his mind.

"Tommy, you just don't understand," Annie said miserably. "You have your war service and your heroism and your triumph over your injuries. You were in the

Brighton cricket team and were one of their best players. You have something that you can look back on and feel proud of. Something people will remember you for. Clara has her detective work, which she is so good at. Again, it will be the thing that people recall in years to come. And then there is me…"

Annie dabbed at her eyes.

"I am just so very ordinary. No one remembers a person who cleans the house well and always has supper cooked on time. Though they remember you if you neglect to do so."

"Sorry Annie," Tommy frowned.

"I didn't mean you, never you," Annie reached out for his hand. "It's just that this was something I could do really well, something I could make a statement with. I could demonstrate that while I might not be all that clever, or all that athletic, there was something I was good at. I wanted… I wanted people to go away talking about my sponge. I supposed I wanted people to be impressed."

Annie started to sob.

"Oh Annie," Tommy squeezed her hand. "Lots of people fought in the war and lots of people play county cricket, that is not really very special. But to be able to cook like you do, that, that is something many people would crave. Many husbands would wish their wives had your knack for cakes and pies and, well, everything. I would be lost without you, you know. And not just for your divine cooking. I couldn't live without you."

Annie's tears eased a little.

"When I heard you had been rushed here I was so very scared, Annie," Tommy continued, leaning closer to her. "I couldn't bear the thought of something happening to you. I would give my legs all over again if it meant keeping you in my life."

Annie's eyes met his. Her tears had stopped and she was taking trembling breaths as her emotions came under control.

"You are the most important thing in this world to me, and I would like to think that my opinion matters a whole lot more than the opinion or approval of strangers. I don't tell you often enough that I love you."

Annie's eyes glistened, but this time with happiness rather than sadness. She gave a long sigh and the tension slipped from her.

"You are right, what do I want the approval of strangers for? The people whose opinion I value the most live in the same house as me," Annie smiled. "I love you too, Tommy Fitzgerald. I was scared to death at the thought of dying and leaving you."

Tommy laughed and Annie looked at him oddly. She had not picked up the contradiction in her statement.

"You know you will have to put up with my and Clara's cooking while you recover?" He chuckled.

Annie grimaced.

"Aren't I suffering enough with this hospital food?" She groaned.

Tommy laughed harder, glad to see the humour returning to Annie's eyes. Distantly the visitor's bell rang and it was time to leave. He squeezed her hand once more.

"I'll be back this evening."

"If Clara is cooking supper, please don't let her attempt to fry eggs again. It took so much scrubbing to get the mess off my pan the last time. And don't let her boil the potatoes dry and don't let her use my best casserole dish, I couldn't bear to think of it getting broken."

"Maybe I will cook," Tommy replied, pretending to be offended. "I am sure I could whip up something simple."

Annie's grimace became more exaggerated.

"If you plan on doing that messy omelette business you picked up in France you can buy your own pans!"

Tommy grinned.

"I'll report on my cooking later."

Annie groaned.

"Just don't break any of my plates!"

Chapter Twenty-five

Clara knocked on the door of the Chases' cottage. Captain Chase had been released from the police cell first thing that morning, deemed sober enough to go home. There had been a brief discussion about his suicide attempt, but it was agreed this was an aberration brought on by a sudden moment of despair. Now he had renewed hope of Elaine being found it was thought he would not try something so foolish again. At least for the moment. Chase's fellow brawlers had not been inclined to press charges. Chase had come off worst in the fight and they were satisfied with that. The less they had to do with the police the better.

Dylan Chase opened the door to Clara.

"Is there news?" He asked her with sudden excitement.

"There is," Clara admitted. "Whoever took Elaine kept her for a time in a shepherd's hut nearby, before moving her to an abandoned barn. She has been moved on again and the police are searching the area to try and locate her."

That was the bare bones of the story, there was far more to it, but Captain Chase need only know those facts. He breathed in sharply and looked relieved for a moment, before frowning.

"She is still alive?"

"I think so. At least, whoever took her seems to have taken care of her. We are still stumped as to why, however. This does not seem to have been an act of revenge against you, Captain Chase, as no contact has been made with you about the situation. Nor does it seem to have been for a ransom attempt. I think this is about Elaine."

"Mary Worthing?" Chase said sharply, his face darkening.

"She is not clever enough for this," Clara shook her head. "I came here in the hopes of finding some clue. May I come in?"

"Of course," Chase stood back from the door and let her inside. "Search where you please, but I can't think of anything that might hint at what is going on."

"Did Elaine keep a diary?" Clara asked as she stood in the hallway.

Chase shook his head.

"Only the basic sort for keeping track of appointments."

"Did she have any private place she liked to keep letters and such? Like a writing desk?

Chase shrugged this time.

"I can't say I know of one. We don't have a writing desk."

Clara saw this was taking her nowhere.

"Thank you, I think I will start in the bedroom, if you don't mind?"

Captain Chase motioned for her to go ahead. Clara went into the bedroom and cast her eyes around, trying to imagine where Elaine kept her private things. Everyone had something they liked to keep to themselves, some private memory they wanted no one else to see. Most of these memories were innocuous, some were a little bit silly or embarrassing, like a baby photograph or a collection of childhood letters that contained a lot of nonsense but were too precious to destroy. Things you could not bear someone else to look at.

But Elaine had a secret. She had told Walter Stone that she had been foolish and that she thought she had been followed. What did that mean? When he had pressed her, she had brushed the matter aside, and then she was gone. There had to be something in that. And if Elaine had a secret, she would keep all physical evidence of it locked away from her husband's eyes. At least, that is what Clara hoped. She also hoped that if she could find that evidence she would have some idea of who was behind Elaine's kidnapping.

She started in the mundane places; the chest of drawers, the vanity table, the bedside cabinet. She did not expect them to reveal anything as they were too easily accessible and anything in them would be too easy for someone else to discover. But she needed to be thorough, now was not the time to overlook the obvious. When those places failed to reveal anything, Clara got creative. She examined the top of the wardrobe, requiring a chair to reach and found a suitcase. It felt heavy and she brought it down and opened it. Inside was a large collection of theatre programmes dating back nearly two decades. Elaine was clearly a theatre lover and had been attending plays since she was a child. She had kept the programmes from every performance she had ever been to, and some were even autographed by the main actors. Clara removed all the programmes in case there was something there, but nothing struck her as significant. She replaced the suitcase on top of the wardrobe.

Next, she examined a jewellery box on the vanity table. It was locked, which intrigued her. She recalled seeing a key in the top drawer of the beside cabinet. She retrieved this and tried it in the lock which sprung open. The lid cracked open, its latch broken so that it only remained closed when locked. Inside was jewellery, as to be expected. Clara moved the necklaces and earrings about in their tray with one finger until something caught her eye. She took out a thin silver chain, a bracelet identical to the one she had found in the ditch. Clara was puzzled; why would Elaine have two matching chains?

The box revealed nothing else and Clara closed it and locked it, before returning the key to where she had found it. Now she paused and considered where to look next. The room had proved unenlightening. Clara had felt that the bedroom, which is typically the most private room in anyone's home, would be the likeliest place for Elaine to have kept her most personal possessions. But nothing struck her as providing a clue to why Elaine had to disappear.

Clara started to think about trying another room, when she recalled she had not looked under the bed. The space beneath a bed was a prime place for tucking things out of sight, usually just belongings that needed to be out of the way but still easily accessible. Clara dropped to her hands and knees and looked under the bed, lifting up the edge of the quilt that hung down over it. In the dark space beneath she noted a hat box, another suitcase and a wickerwork case that proved to be a sewing box. She shoved things around to get a better look. There was a cardboard box marked Christmas, which proved to contain old Christmas cards and decorations for the house. There was a roll of parcel paper next to it and another box that contained photo albums. Clara was beginning to feel this was another dead end when she noticed, squeezed into a corner, a small pasteboard box. It was painted red, though had clearly once stood in sunlight as areas had faded. The way it was pushed up into the corner formed by the leg of the bed resting against the wall intrigued Clara. It looked as though it was being hidden away as much as possible.

She retrieved it and found that it was locked. She almost cursed. Events were proving so frustrating. Clara had not come across any other small keys in her search, just the one for the jewellery box. Hoping that Captain Chase might know where other keys were kept she took the box through to the living room.

"Do you know what is in this box?" She asked him.

Captain Chase looked surprised, then he narrowed his eyes at the box in Clara's hands.

"I've never seen that before," he said, somewhat surprised.

"Do you know of any small keys that might fit its lock?"

Chase stared at the box, then shook his head. Clara sighed and placed the small container on the sofa beside the captain. She sat down next to it, so the box was sandwiched between them.

"I would like to look inside, but it is locked," she explained.

Chase touched the latch with his finger and looked puzzled.

"I don't recall this box at all," he said. "Do you think there could be something important inside?"

Clara shrugged, she really did not know, but when you were hunting for a motive for a kidnapping, any locked box was worth searching. Chase turned the box around and looked at the back, before spinning it around once more.

"If we need to look in it, there is no choice," he put a hand in his pocket and pulled out a Swiss army knife. Using the blade of the knife, he wedged it under the lock and wriggled it until there was a ripping sound. The blade slipped under further and he levered it up, gradually pulling the flimsy lock from where it was clued to the cardboard of the box. The pretty red paintwork cracked and crumbled as the lock gave way and Clara only hoped the contents were worth the destruction. She was feeling guilty at wrecking one of Elaine's possessions.

Suddenly the lock plate sprung loose and the lid was free. Chase lifted it up to reveal more photographs. They were stacked in a bundle and held together by a rubber band. Clara took them out and glanced at the top one – a grainy family portrait – wondering why these photos had not made the family albums. Why were they locked away and kept secret?

Clara studied the picture. There was an older couple, presumably Elaine's parents, and three young girls in the photo. The girls were all under the age of eight and Clara could not say which one was Elaine, as she had only glimpsed her in modern photographs. She removed the elastic band and started working through the images, what struck her at once was that in each there were three little girls. Clara had thought the third girl in the first image might have been a friend or cousin, but she was in all the others too, and over the span of many years. There were a number of shots of the three girls posing for the camera and they were too similar in appearance to be anything but sisters. Yet, Elaine only had one sister, or so she had been told.

Clara showed the pictures to Captain Chase.

"Did Elaine have a sister who died?" She asked him.

Chase shook his head.

"No, her only sister is alive. I told you about her. There was never another."

Clara pointed to the picture in his hand.

"Then who is this girl?"

Captain Chase thumbed through the photos, in each one the third girl was there smiling at the camera. Chase looked bemused.

"I don't know," he said in astonishment. "I really don't know."

Chapter Twenty-six

The picture that caught Clara's eye the most was a close-up shot of the three little girls. They were all dressed in the same white outfit with large ribbons in their hair. They smiled at the photographer as they held hands. Hanging around the wrists of all the girls was a thin chain – a silver bracelet. Clara could not make out a lot of the detail, but she would hazard a guess that the chain was the same as the one she had found in the ditch and subsequently in the jewellery box in Elaine's room. The sisters had each been given a bracelet with their initials on it.

Clara pulled out the chain she had recovered from the ditch, from her pocket.

"I need to check something," she excused herself and returned to the bedroom, retrieving the second bracelet from the jewellery box. The first had the initials E.C., which Clara had assumed meant Elaine Chase, but if the bracelet was given to Elaine as a child that could not be. The bracelet from the jewellery box had the initials E.M. Clara returned to Captain Chase.

"Does your wife have a middle name?"

Chase looked up from the photographs which he was still studying in confusion.

"Yes," he said. "Maud."

Elaine Maud. The bracelets did not feature the girls' surname, only their first names. Which meant the bracelet in the ditch belonged to another sister.

"What is the name of Elaine's sister?"

"Julia Anne Neven," Chase said. "I don't understand. Elaine never spoke about a third sister and these pictures were locked away, as if it was a secret."

"I need to talk to Elaine's parents," Clara answered. "It is urgent I get them on the telephone."

"They are not connected," Chase shook his head, his confusion making him pessimistic.

"Then we send a telegram and ask them to come to the Post Office to use the telephone there. You must do this for me Captain Chase. I might be wrong, but I think this third girl could be the key to Elaine's disappearance."

Chase started to brighten.

"You do?"

"I found this bracelet where Elaine disappeared," Clara showed him the silver chain. "I thought it was something you had given Elaine."

"I never gave her that," Chase said quickly.

"I see that now. These chains were given to Elaine and her sisters when they were children. Elaine's was in her jewellery box, which means this second chain with E.C. belongs to another of those girls in the picture. And it cannot be Julia."

Chase's eyes went wide.

"What do you need me to do?" He asked.

~~~*~~~

Three hours later Clara was at home awaiting the call of Elaine's parents. The telegram had been sent from the Brighton Post Office, explaining its urgency and that Elaine's parents needed to ring Clara at once. Now she just had to wait and hope they did. Captain Chase was aware that Elaine's parents were living on a pittance, trying to support the ailing Julia and her children, he therefore explained in the telegram that he would pay for the phone call. He hoped this would assuage any financial concerns Elaine's parents might have about making the call.

That seemed a long time ago, however, and Clara was still waiting. She was growing impatient, thinking that either the telegram had not been delivered or Elaine's parents had, for some reason, decided they could not ring Clara. She had told Chase not to mention the photographs and their suspicions of a third sister in the telegram, just in case that put off Elaine's parents from making contact. There seemed to be a family secret at the bottom of all this, a dark one.

Down the hall Tommy was fussing about in the kitchen. Clara had already told him that they would go out and buy fish and chips for their supper, to save cooking. Clara could not think about preparing a meal with all this going on. Despite Tommy agreeing to the arrangement he was still up to something in the kitchen and it was beginning to annoy Clara.

"What are you doing?" She demanded.

"Putting up father's old camp bed. It's a bit stiff and rusty in places," Tommy replied.

"Whatever for?" Clara asked in bafflement.

Tommy popped his head around the open kitchen door.

"Just concentrate on your telephone call," he told her, then he vanished again.

Clara pulled a face, twisting her lips together in frustration. She was about to rise and see what Tommy was doing when the telephone rang.

The shrill ring nearly made her jump from her skin and she rose so fast from the chair she was sitting on she banged her leg on the telephone stand. She grabbed up the receiver and answered.

"Clara Fitzgerald speaking."

There was a gasp down the line and someone uneasily

said;

"Oh. Hello? Can you hear me all right?"

"Yes, you need not shout," Clara informed the person, who sounded male and was clearly not used to telephones. "Just talk as you normally would."

"Like this?" The gentleman said, his voice returning to a normal tone.

"Perfect," Clara replied. "Might you be Elaine's father?"

"I am," the man said. "John Denis. I had a telegram from Captain Chase saying I ought to ring you urgently. Have you found my daughter?"

"We are close," Clara told him. "But I have a few questions I hope you can answer."

"Anything," John said hastily.

"Good," Clara relaxed a little. "I need you to tell me about your third daughter."

The silence that followed this statement almost made Clara think John had hung up. She tentatively asked if he was still there.

"I am," he said, though he sounded distant. "I have never had a third daughter."

"Mr Denis, I do not believe you. Elaine had a locked box of photographs in her bedroom. In every single one of the pictures there were three young girls. Sisters, I would say, from how alike they looked."

"She kept them!" John gasped to himself, then his voice came back firmer. "That is a matter of the past, something from long ago and not relevant to today."

"I disagree," Clara told him, firmly but gently. She did not want to alienate the man, after all. "This third girl, I believe she had the initials E.C.?"

"How did you know that?" John was sounding more rattled.

Clara heard a woman's voice in the background and wondered if it was Elaine's mother.

"I found a silver bracelet at the place where Elaine was kidnapped. It had the initials E.C. I thought at first it was

Elaine's, until I discovered her bracelet in her jewellery box. Then I saw the photographs and realised that the bracelets had been given to Elaine and her sisters as children. Who was your third daughter, the one with the initials E.C.?"

"Her bracelet," John hissed down the line. "Can it be? You really found it? A small link silver chain bracelet with a half-inch rectangular plate engraved with initials?"

"Yes, that is it," Clara told him, sensing he could hardly believe all this. "I am right in saying they were given to your daughters?"

"By their late aunt," John answered, too stunned to continue to protest. "It was the girls' Christmas present for 1906. My late sister had married well and liked to treat her nieces. She had no children of her own."

Clara heard a voice in the background again, and John excused himself to talk to someone else. There was a hushed conversation that Clara could only hear in tiny snippets. She gathered he was explaining himself to another person and why he was talking about the girls' bracelets. When he came back on the line he sounded upset.

"This is a very private family matter," he stated. "I can't really talk about it."

"Mr Denis, your daughter is missing. I believe she is still alive and being held a prisoner, every hour wasted is an hour she has lost. I don't know what her kidnappers intend to do with her, so we must hurry. Now is not the time for secrecy when it could cost your daughter her life," Clara did not think that was too harsh, she needed John Denis to appreciate the seriousness of the matter. "I am trying to make sense of this all, so I can rescue Elaine. So far the only lead I have is this bracelet and the photo of a mystery girl."

John Denis said nothing, but she could hear him breathing down the line.

"Is family pride worth your daughter's life?" Clara pressed him. "Whatever this secret, you have my promise of discretion, if only you will speak with my candidly."

"You don't understand," John said softly.

"That is true," Clara replied. "I do not understand why Elaine has been kidnapped and why what appears to be the bracelet of her secret sister was at the place she was taken from. Because I do not understand I am handicapped in finding your daughter and bringing her to safety."

There was talking in the background again and Clara was sure she heard someone say 'for heavens sake, tell her!' But she might have been hearing what she wanted to. The voice was faint, and it could have been saying anything really.

"Mr Denis? Are you still there?" Clara asked.

"I am," John answered softly.

"Will you tell me what this is all about?" Clara softened her tone, she was desperate, she felt that without understanding the situation fully she could not save Elaine.

"I suppose..." John hesitated as once again a voice spoke behind him. "My wife insists I tell you. She thinks it will help."

"It will," Clara promised him.

John let out a deep breath, when his words came he had dropped his voice to a whisper. Clara listened keenly, not daring to ask him to speak louder.

"You are right, I had three daughters."

"Had?" Clara pressed.

John paused for a long moment before saying;

"Have."

He coughed to clear his throat, a nervous little croak of a cough.

"Julia, Elizabeth and Elaine," he continued. "Obviously you know about Elaine and we live with my eldest daughter Julia who is very unwell. Elizabeth is the third girl, the daughter we never talk about."

He stopped again, but Clara did not speak. She knew he needed to take this at his own pace.

"Elizabeth Caroline. You have her bracelet," John gave that cough again. "She was a wild girl, always up to some sort of mischief. We put it down to enthusiasm and high energy when she was younger, but the older she became the more dangerous the mischief she was involved in. By the time she was fifteen she was in trouble with the police.

"Her friends, if you can call them that, were common thieves. We did what we could to keep her away from them, but she was wily and, I hate to say it, but she was sometimes very violent. She tried to stab my wife with a pair of scissors when she went to stop her going out one night. Another time she threw Julia across a room in an argument over a dress pattern. She… she scared us."

John Denis had to pause again and catch his breath. Clara could hear the rattle of emotion in his voice.

"We hoped she would settle down, fools that we were. Then, at the age of sixteen, she robbed a gentleman. She had lured him into an alley with a false promise of…" John Denis could not bring himself to say the words. "She had lured him, anyway, and then when he was distracted she robbed him. He chased her and grabbed her, but she had a knife. She nearly killed him. The police said the savagery of the attack was frightening.

"We agreed there and then that she had to be sent away. It was either prison or an institution of some sort. The police detectives concurred, they felt she was unstable and would be better in an asylum. I thought at the time it would help her. She cursed me when they took her away, the things she said…"

John Denis' breathing had become ragged. Clara feared he would put down the phone.

"She has been in an asylum ever since?"

"As far as we knew," John answered. "We could not afford to visit her, it was such a long way away, and then we moved to look after Julia. So many years have passed. We decided it would be better to erase her from our memories. We burned all the pictures with Elizabeth in them, ridding ourselves of her once and for all. It seemed for the best."

"Not all the pictures," Clara pointed out. "Elaine kept some."

"Unbeknown to us," John sighed. "There was only a year's difference between Elaine and Elizabeth. They were very close as little girls and even when Elizabeth turned wild in her older years, Elaine still clung to her. That was another reason for sending Elizabeth away, to save her sister from following her blindly down the path of criminality. Elaine is a good girl, but she would do anything for Elizabeth."

Clara remembered the phrase that had haunted her since Walter Stone had mentioned it – 'I have been such a fool', Elaine had muttered. A fool over what? Over a sister she had idolised?

"They would have told us if she was to be released from the asylum," John Denis said, his tone frantic now. "They promised they would. In case…"

"Did you fear your daughter would seek revenge against you?" Clara suggested steadily.

John took several breaths.

"She was so angry with us, so very angry. They said they would only release her when she was no longer a danger to anyone," John sounded terrified and Clara was beginning to appreciate just how frightened he had been of his daughter. "They would have warned us."

Clara did not like to say that promises made years ago were often forgotten. Directors of asylums changed and informal arrangements were not passed along. Probably there was an official system in place for informing the families of inmates when they were due to be let out, but then again there might not be. Whatever the case, Clara finally had a suspect in her kidnapping. The motive for taking Elaine was not altogether clear; Elaine had been good to Elizabeth by all accounts. Yet she did not doubt that Elizabeth was involved, the bracelet was proof enough, but also the personal aspect to this kidnapping. Clara had always suspected this was about Elaine and her family, no one else.

What she really needed to know was just how dangerous Elizabeth was these days.

"I'm going to need the name of that asylum," she told John Denis.

Chapter Twenty-Seven

The name of the asylum was Greenviews. John Denis did not know much about it, other than that it was a very secure establishment and that the director was called Dr Knole. After saying goodbye to John Denis, Clara spoke to the girl at the telephone directory and asked if she could help find a number for Greenviews Asylum. It took about fifteen minutes for the girl to track down the number and then connect Clara. The line rang several times before a woman answered.

"Greenviews Lunatic Asylum."

"I need to speak to Dr Knole urgently, concerning one of his patients," Clara explained.

"Dr Knole can only be reached by appointment. I can make one for you for next week."

Clara was not having that. She had been prepared for resistance.

"I must speak to Dr Knole at once concerning Elizabeth Denis. This is a police matter. A young woman has gone missing and Miss Denis is implicated in the matter. I need to know how dangerous she is and why she has been released from Greenviews without the family being told."

The woman on the other end of the line gave a

strangled groan. There was a pause.

"A police matter?" She repeated carefully.

"Yes. The police are conducting a search as we speak, while I try to get what information I can about their suspect."

"Has she hurt anyone?" The woman asked uneasily.

Clara's mind flicked back to Miss Erskine. How had she come off the road? There was no sign of what had driven her into that ditch and so conveniently put Elaine Chase at her sister's disposal.

"I think we can say her actions have caused harm to people," Clara replied.

The woman gave that strange noise again, then she grunted.

"I shall see if Dr Knole is busy."

With that the line went quiet, rather as if the receiver had been placed in a bag or a drawer. Clara wondered what excitement she had caused at the asylum, she was also beginning to question whether Elizabeth had been deliberately released. There was something about the tone of the woman she had spoken to that seemed to imply they had been dreading something like this.

Clara watched the hall clock tick down the minutes. She was thinking of her telephone bill. She could accept the cost when she was actually talking to someone, but when all she had was silence she seemed to feel the pennies trickling away. She started to tap her fingers on the telephone table.

There was a rustling sound down the line, like paper being crumpled.

"Hello?"

It was an older man's voice.

"Dr Knole?"

"Speaking. I have been told you have information regarding one of our patients?"

"Actually, I was hoping you could give me information. There is every reason to believe that Elizabeth Denis is here in Brighton and is involved in the kidnapping of her sister Elaine Chase. I hoped you could tell me more about Elizabeth and why she was released from the asylum."

Dr Knole coughed. It was a nervous sound.

"I find myself in a rather awkward position," he said unhappily. "I had hoped things would not come to this. I suppose there is no point beating about the bush. We did not release Elizabeth Denis. She escaped just over a month ago."

Clara was not entirely surprised, she had begun to suspect that was the case.

"How did she escape?" She asked.

"She seduced one of our younger doctors," Dr Knole was having to force out the words. "He has been dismissed, naturally. Through him she was able to get what we call 'freedom permits'. Basically, a doctor can grant one of these permits to a patient who has proven themselves reliable. The permit enables them to do things such as travel into the nearby town for an hour or two. It is only granted to those patients who are close to being released anyway, as a means of reintegrating them into normal life.

"Elizabeth Denis was not someone who should ever have been entitled to a freedom permit. Her behaviour did not inspire trust at all. But, as I say, she used her charms to persuade one of our doctors to grant her the permit."

"And then she escaped," Clara surmised.

"I was alerted to the situation by a gate porter who had been shown the permit by Elizabeth. He had been a little surprised, but he recognised the signature and porters are not expected to question doctors' orders. It was only after he had let her out that he started to have doubts," Dr Knole sighed. "By then it was all too late. Elizabeth is wily and cunning."

"And dangerous?" Clara asked.

"Distinctly," Dr Knole did not bandy his words. "There is no simple diagnosis for the condition Elizabeth suffers from, at least not one that has as yet been recognised. At first glance she seems an intelligent and perfectly normal young lady, however, it soon becomes apparent that she has no concern for anyone else, all that matters to her are her own desires. She cannot empathise with anyone, though she can make a good pretence at it when she wants. But, actually understanding how another person feels is impossible for her. She has no compassion, she does not even see the need for it.

"She might still function as a normal individual, if it was not for the way she deals with situations that are not going her way. Her behaviour is always extreme and unnecessary. Take, for instance, the occasion that another patient was sitting in the chair Elizabeth deemed hers. She asked them to move and when they did not, she took up a pencil from another table where patients were taking a drawing class and stabbed the person who offended her in the leg with it. She struck them so hard the pencil dug into the flesh."

Clara grimaced at the thought. She could understand John Denis' fears about his daughter being released.

"You say she has kidnapped her sister?" Dr Knole asked.

"We believe so," Clara explained. "But we are not sure why. From all accounts Elizabeth and Elaine were close."

"Elizabeth does not get close to people," Dr Knole corrected her solemnly. "Never for a moment think that she is capable of caring for another. If it suits her she will hurt her sister just as easily and without guilt as she would hurt a stranger. We are not dealing with a rational human being, nor one who is curable."

"Then there were no plans to release her?"

"She was as much a danger to the general public when she escaped as she was the day she arrived her," Dr Knole said candidly. "Which is why we have put our full resources into tracking her down."

"Does that include informing the police of the situation?"

Dr Knole huffed under his breath.

"I thought as much," Clara sighed. "Had the police been informed, then Elaine Chase's disappearance would have rung alarm bells sooner."

"I regret that," Dr Knole said and he sounded genuine. "We were trying to deal with the problem discreetly. In hindsight, we ought to have considered the possibility of Elizabeth seeking revenge on her family. She has a deep hatred for her parents who she blames for being placed in the asylum. She might be intending to punish them by harming her sister."

"Only she has made no effort to announce her intentions," Clara replied. "If you intend revenge on someone by harming a person they care about, you would usually tell them."

"There is that," Dr Knole agreed.

"Could I speak with the doctor who granted Elizabeth her freedom permit, he might be able to offer me more insight into her plans."

Dr Knole huffed.

"We dismissed him, as I said, as soon as we discovered what he had done. I believe Elizabeth convinced him that she had been maliciously confined to the asylum by heartless parents. Or some such rot. I know that Dr Vaugh has recently taken on a new position at a hospital in London, one that didn't require a reference."

"Could you give me the name and a telephone number?" Clara asked.

Dr Knole huffed again.

~~~*~~~

Half-an-hour later Clara was asking another receptionist if she could speak to Dr Vaugh on a very urgent matter concerning a former patient. The receptionist was less obstructive than her counterpart at Greenviews and made no fuss about locating the doctor. He was doing his afternoon rounds, but she was able to summon him and get him on the telephone.

"Dr Vaugh?"

"Speaking."

Clara took a deep breath, the next few moments would be key to getting Vaugh to talk to her. She feared he would dismiss her if she was not careful.

"I apologise for interrupting your work, but I had to speak with you urgently concerning a former patient of yours," Clara said, trying not to pause to let him interrupt. "It is a delicate matter concerning Elizabeth Denis, who is implicated in the kidnapping of her sister."

"Oh," Dr Vaugh gave no further reply.

"I appreciate this is a difficult situation, but I must ask you some questions concerning Elizabeth's escape. Let me assure you I do not intend to attach any blame to you or to condemn you. I merely need your help."

Silence fell on the phone line and Clara felt a brief moment of panic coming over her. Had Vaugh walked away from the telephone?

"What has she done?" Vaugh's voice calmly broke the quiet and Clara relaxed.

"As I said, she is implicated in the kidnapping of her sister," Clara repeated herself. "Do you have any knowledge of her plans after she left the asylum?"

Dr Vaugh gave a strange laugh.

"I guess you must think I am a pretty big fool? Did Knole paint me as a gullible idiot who was charmed by a pretty face? Well, it is a fair point," Vaugh sounded disappointed in himself. "Elizabeth made me believe she had been confined in the asylum unfairly, that her parents had lied to have her put there because she was intending to marry a man they disapproved of. He had then abandoned her when she was declared insane. She spun a good tale."

Clara was careful when she spoke, she did not want to imply that she thought Vaughn had been damn stupid, infatuated, in fact, and as a result had allowed a very dangerous woman to escape. She needed him to talk to her and putting his back up would not help. She did think he was damn stupid, but he didn't need to know that.

"I understand Elizabeth can be extremely persuasive," Clara said. "I was hoping you might have some idea of what she planned to do when she left the asylum?"

"She didn't talk about revenge, if that is what you mean. I would have reacted to that, so I don't suppose she would have mentioned it. No, if anything she talked about leaving England altogether and starting a new life somewhere else. She fancied going to Australia. She thought it would provide her with more opportunities and no one would be looking for her. She felt she needed a fresh start."

That made sense. Elizabeth knew her time free would be limited unless she went into permanent hiding or left the country completely.

"How did she plan on getting to Australia?" Clara asked the obvious question.

Dr Vaughn was silent again, clearly he had considered this only after the event.

"Look, I did not give her the permit thinking she was going to escape. She said she was depressed, that being confined was taking its toll and she just wanted to see something outside the four walls of the asylum. She was only meant to be gone a couple of hours, do a bit of shopping, that sort of thing. The Australia talk was just idle chat. We used to discuss what would happen when she was officially released, that's all. I was under the impression that might happen in the near future. I guess I got that wrong. Call me naïve, if you will, but Elizabeth never struck me as harmful or secretive. I thought she genuinely wanted to start anew when they released her."

"She was never going to be released," Clara told him calmly. "You must have known that."

"That was up to Dr Knole and, no, he did not tell me. He was always too busy to speak with me. I had her files and I made my own assessment. I thought she was improving and I reported as much. The Australia think was just an idea, a notion we mulled over. Daydreaming is not a sign of lunacy."

Vaughn was becoming irritated. He had been played and he knew it. Clara suspected there had been more to the talk between him and Elizabeth. Probably there had been promises made about a future together once she was no longer a patient. They could both go to Australia to escape the scandal of a doctor becoming involved with his patient, especially a patient who had been considered insane and a criminal. Dr Vaughn was smarting from the sting of Elizabeth's betrayal; only now did he see how gullible he had been. That made him defensive and he was putting a good spin on everything.

"Dr Vaughn, did Elizabeth ever talk about her sister Elaine?"

Vaughn grumbled something under his breath.

"She rarely talked about her family, but she did mention she had sisters. I believe Elaine sent her birthday and Christmas cards. She was the only member of the family who had any contact with her. Patients aren't supposed to receive letters without official approval, but the cards were allowed. They were always opened by a staff member first and examined."

Elaine had made the effort to keep in contact. She had kept the photographs of her sister when the rest of her family wanted to eradicate the memory of Elizabeth from their lives. Clara now sorely hoped that Elizabeth had not completely betrayed that love by harming Elaine.

"Thank you for your time, Dr Vaughn," Clara told him. She wanted to say that she hoped he was exerting better judgement in his new position, but she bit her tongue. If Elaine had been harmed by her sister then Dr Vaughn was just as responsible as Elizabeth – it might even be argued he was more responsible as he was sane and could rationalise right and wrong, unlike his patient. Miss Erskine certainly seemed a victim of his negligence. She didn't say anything, however.

Vaughn gave another mutter, then he put the telephone down without saying goodbye.

"Charming," Clara put down her receiver.

She was just going to make herself a cup of tea when there was a thud at her front door. It sounded more like someone falling against it than knocking. Clara hesitated for just a moment, then she opened the door. On her step was a young man with blood trickling down his temple.

"Are you Miss Fitzgerald?" He asked, swaying on his feet.

Clara frowned.

"I am."

"Thank goodness!" The young man groaned, then he fainted into Clara's hallway.

Chapter Twenty-eight

The young man lay at Clara's feet. She grumbled under her breath. In the street outside Mrs Kipling strolled past and glanced at Clara's open front door to wave. She stopped as she saw the prone man before Clara, her hand frozen in the act of waving, her mouth emitting a shocked gasp. Clara wished her a breezy 'good afternoon' and closed her front door, having to shove the young man's feet to one side in the process.

"Well," Clara said to herself, still looking down at her unconscious visitor.

She managed to get her hands under his arms and dragged him a couple of feet towards the door of the parlour. Tommy appeared from the kitchen, curious at the noise.

"Clara?"

"He collapsed at my feet," Clara grunted.

"You know how to charm a young man," Tommy sniggered.

Clara glowered at him.

"Would you care to help?"

Together they were able to haul the man into the parlour and heft him onto the sofa. Clara went to the window and pulled the curtains until they only let in a slither of light. Mrs Kipling was a gossip and she didn't want the whole street trying to see in her front window.

"He has left a trail of blood," Tommy observed grimly, pointing to a streak of red that ran from the hallway, across the floor and to the sofa.

Clara was torn between feeling bad for the young man and dreading what Annie would say at the mess. It was just as well she was in hospital.

Tommy crouched by their visitor and pulled open his jacket, he pointed out a dark patch on the shirt beneath. When he opened the shirt it was obvious the man had been stabbed, though fortunately the injury did not look deep. Along with that was the gash to his head, which was bleeding profusely and was probably more to blame for the blood trail than the stab wound. Tommy felt for a pulse and went through the rudiments of field medicine he could remember from the war.

"Any idea who he is?" He said.

"None," Clara replied, taking a better look at the young man in the hope she might recognise him. "I don't think I have ever seen him before in my life."

"I guess we clean him up, then, and wait until he rouses. I don't think either wound is life threatening."

They set to work tending the patient. Tommy stripped off the man's jacket and shirt, while Clara boiled water and found clean rags to wash him with. She reappeared with a basin of water and several thick towels that they could place beneath him to avoid getting the sofa wet.

"Not the cleanest of individuals to begin with," Tommy observed, holding up the shirt which was severely stained by sweat beneath the arms and on the back and chest. The jacket was also dirty. It was brown in colour, which masked much of the dirt, the cuffs were clearly dark from filth and it had a stale smell. As Clara washed blood from the young man's torso, she noticed she was also washing away a layer of filth to reveal white skin.

It was too much work to wash the unconscious man's

entire body, and there were parts which Clara did not wish to venture near, despite having washed more than one male patient during her time as a nurse in the war. She satisfied herself with cleaning the area where he had been stabbed and then wrapping it with bandages. Tommy fetched more boiled water and Clara washed the young man's face, (which at least appeared to have been regularly scrubbed) and the gash at his temple. When everything was done, they threw a blanket over him to keep him warm and settled to wait for him to come around.

Towards half-four, the young man opened his eyes and groaned. He peered about the room, somewhat dazed and clearly baffled as to where he was. Then his eyes fell on Clara and Tommy and he seemed to remember what had happened.

"Ah…"

"Good, you are awake. Now we can make you some tea and something to eat," Clara told him before he could say anything. "Once that is done and you are feeling more restored we can properly talk."

The man looked a little shell-shocked by everything. Clara and Tommy began to act as good hosts, providing fresh tea with sugar and fetching sandwiches that had been prepared earlier in anticipation of their guest waking. Then they sat by as their guest tucked in, he was a little self-conscious at being watched.

He was aged in his twenties. Neither handsome, nor ugly. An ordinary looking sort of lad who you would probably not give a second thought to if you passed in the street. He had straw-blond hair, that was a little too long and fell in his eyes as he ate and drank. He was lean, but not under-fed, and muscular in the wiry way people who have worked hard all their lives are. His skin was tanned beneath the dirt and it seemed likely he spent his days working outside. His fingernails were grimy, the filth entrenched beneath them. His hands were as brown as buttons and roughened despite his youth. Clara guessed he was a farm labourer or something similar.

When he had eaten his sandwiches and drunk his tea, the young man looked up at his hosts with a sheepish expression.

"Richard Munford," he introduced himself. "Everyone calls me Dickie. Thanks for the food and for sorting me out."

Dickie touched the bandages around his waist thoughtfully.

"Perhaps you can explain what you were doing on my doorstep?" Clara asked him.

Dickie blushed red, realising he had not explained himself very well at all, and also contemplating how he had fainted on a stranger's doorstep.

"You are Miss Clara Fitzgerald?" He clarified.

"I am," Clara said. "And this is my brother Tommy."

"And you are the lady who is the private detective?" Dickie pressed.

Clara agreed that she was. Dickie gave a sigh of relief.

"I didn't know what to do, you see. I couldn't go to the police, but I had to find someone to help. I remembered hearing about you and thought you were better than nothing."

Clara was not sure whether to be offended or complimented by that statement.

"Let's start from the beginning," she said. "Who hurt you?"

Dickie pulled a face and touched his bandaged waist again. Then he lifted his hand and very tentatively touched his temple.

"If you are half the detective she fears you are, you will have already worked it out," Dickie said. "And you will know her name. She was watching you when you went to the shepherd's hut and then to the abandoned barn."

"Elizabeth Denis," Clara stated.

Dickie nodded and his eyes sparkled with pleasure. He had obviously not been certain he had picked the right place to go in his desperation and wanted Clara to prove her abilities to him before he was prepared to say more. Now he spoke with greater confidence.

"Liz has been fretting ever since she learned you were investigating her sister's disappearance on behalf of Captain Chase. She had slipped into town to buy supplies and she spotted that woman from the theatre who doesn't like Elaine. Can't remember her name?"

"Wendy," Clara said.

"Yes," Dickie grinned again. "Elaine told us about her one night. She said this woman Wendy would be delighted she was missing and how she had been so awful to her. Liz was thinking of dealing with the woman herself."

"Wait up," Tommy raised a hand to slow the conversation. "You are saying that you have been working with the person who has kidnapped Elaine Chase?"

Dickie nodded, looking a little worried.

"You won't hand me in to the police, will you?" He said.

Tommy looked about to say something along the lines of 'what else would you expect me to do' and Clara quickly interjected.

"We need to get this clear," she said to Dickie. "Elizabeth Denis is responsible for the kidnapping of her sister Elaine Chase and you are working with her, but for what purpose?"

Dickie scratched at his head, pouting his lips as he realised he was not explaining himself very well at all.

"Let me start again," he said. "Just about a month ago I met Liz for the first time. She was looking for a group of people to help her with some work and my name was mentioned. I do casual labour on the local farms from time-to-time. Nothing regular, just helping out when I am needed. But that means I know where the farmers' keep all their valuable stuff and also how secure the farm is."

Dickie shrugged as if this was really unimportant and

that he had not done anything wrong by passing this information along.

"Liz wanted to earn some money quickly and she had this idea of raiding the local farms for stuff we could sell on easily. She knew people in London who would happily buy any fuel we could siphon off the machines without asking questions. Liz said she had been locked up for a while, but that had not stopped her making friends in the right places."

Somehow it didn't surprise Clara that Liz had been keeping her connections with the criminal world while being stuck in a lunatic asylum. She was resourceful enough, for sure, and her form of mental aberration was not the sort that made people avoid her – not like someone who talked to themselves or had fits. No, Liz could function in the world and get the world to function for her. It was just a shame that she was so incredibly dangerous.

"Elizabeth asked you to help her organise these farm robberies," Clara prompted Dickie.

"Yes, she did, and I was not really uptight about it or anything. I don't owe any of them farmers a thing," Dickie's tone had darkened, suggesting he had a grudge against more than one farmer. "Anyway, we started doing these raids and then Liz said we had a problem. Her sister had learned what she was up to and had said she would go to the police if Liz did not leave off. So, Liz planned on kidnapping her sister and holding her somewhere until she had finished the raids."

"How did Elaine learn about all this?" Clara asked.

"Liz was staying with her," Dickie seemed to think that was obvious. "Liz needed a place to lie low and knew Elaine would take her in."

"But, it was rather rash to start committing these crimes when she was living with her sister," Tommy pointed out. "She must have realised it was so risky. Elaine would put two and two together eventually."

Dickie shrugged again. The thought had never

occurred to him, and presumably it had never occurred to Elizabeth either. Clara suspected that Elizabeth was arrogant enough to think she could keep her criminal activities a secret from her sister while residing in her home. She had sought out the one person who she believed would shield her from the world. What lies she had told her Clara could not say. Presumably she had convinced Elaine she had been released from the asylum, but would have insisted she not tell their parents, perhaps protesting that she wanted nothing to do with them. In any case, the hush-up at Greenviews meant that neither Elaine nor her parents knew that Elizabeth had escaped. How much sooner might they have realised that Elizabeth was involved in her sister's disappearance if only those responsible at Greenviews had been honest!

"Elaine figured out what her sister was doing," Clara prompted Dickie again.

"Yeah, she did," Dickie shifted on the sofa and winced, the wound in his side hurting. "Liz liked being in a proper house, rather than dossing down somewhere. She didn't have any money at first. Couldn't rent a room, or anything."

"Which meant seeking out her loyal sister was a good plan," Clara understood. Elizabeth had needed somewhere she could hide which would not cost her a penny, and Elaine had written all those birthday and Christmas cards to her.

"Did Elaine threaten to go to the police?" Clara asked.

"No, she just told Liz she had to stop," Dickie answered. "Liz couldn't stop, though. She needed the money. She wants to buy a ticket to Australia."

That was one thing Elizabeth had not lied about to Dr Vaughn, apparently.

"Which meant she had to keep Elaine from talking," Clara understood. "She kidnapped her and has been holding her ever since. And when she is done she plans on releasing her?"

"I think so," Dickie looked uncertain suddenly. "That

seemed the plan at first, but lately Elaine and Liz have been arguing a lot, and Liz has said some things that scare me."

Dickie's eyes widened and his fear was palpable.

"The police have been conducting all these patrols and I thought people were getting suspicious of me, because I always worked on a farm to scope it out before it was robbed. Also, the thing with her sister was getting unpleasant. I wanted out before something bad occurred," Dickie screwed up his mouth, grimacing at the memory of what had happened. "I said I was done, that I was leaving. Liz blew her top, never seen anyone so furious before. She told me I could not leave. I was not allowed. And when I insisted, she came at me. First, she hit me over the head with a hammer she had picked up from this barn we were in. I managed to duck and it just grazed me," Dickie lifted his hand, almost touching his wound, but then stopping himself. "I started to run, but she got in front of the door. I went to rush past her and I never even saw the knife, but I felt it."

Dickie looked miserable.

"I ran as fast as I could, even though I was bleeding and hurt. Liz followed me for a bit, but then I got onto a road and there was a group of horses and riders coming along. I stayed close to them and she abandoned the chase."

"I remembered her muttering about you, Miss Fitzgerald, and I couldn't think who else to go to for help. She'll come after me, I am sure, unless I do something first."

Dickie frowned.

"I think she will kill her sister, in fact I am certain of it," he said. "I don't want to be a part of that. I'm not a murderer."

Chapter Twenty-nine

Time was critical. Dickie's flight would make Elizabeth start to consider moving her sister again. She might be confident that Dickie would not approach the police and get himself into trouble, but she could not be sure he would not speak to someone else. They had already lost several hours; Clara did not think they could waste any more by trying to locate the police. If Dickie was right and Elizabeth was considering killing her sister, then she might do away with her rather than attempt to move her to a new hiding place. Elaine's presence was holding Liz back, and she would not tolerate that for long.

Dickie could tell them of the location of Liz's last hideout.

"There is this old barn near Peterwood farm. The farmer at Peterwood is very old and he just keeps a small herd of cows these days. The barn has not been used for some time, though it was not ideal, as occasionally labourers helping out on the farm will go there looking for spare tools," Dickie groaned. "The other barn, the one you searched, that was perfect. Liz was in such a temper when she had to move out of there. She is running out of places local to the farms we have been raiding to hide."

Another reason, Clara mused darkly, for doing away

with Elaine and being free to run.

"Is Elizabeth alone with her sister?" She asked.

Dickie nodded.

"We have been helped by Les Martin, but he doesn't stay at the hideout. He has his own farm to run. He takes a cut of the fuel as his payment and I think he has enjoyed getting back at a few of his neighbours."

Clara was satisfied. She informed Dickie that he could rest in her house until they returned. It was probably the safest place for him if Elizabeth was out for his blood. Dickie glanced at his wounds miserably again. He was not in a fit state to do much, any movement caused pain and he had a pounding headache.

Clara left him to rest and took Tommy to one side.

"We need to act fast. I have no idea where Park-Coombs is and it will take too long to find him. We may already be too late."

Tommy could only agree.

"Just us then?"

"I'll ring O'Harris and see if he can offer assistance, along with the provision of his car."

~~~*~~~

A short time later Clara and Tommy were sitting in O'Harris' red Bentley, with Jones driving and O'Harris at his side perusing a map. Peterwood farm was marked on it, like most of the farms in the area, but there was no indication of where the barn was. The best they could do was head for the farm itself and ask for directions once there.

"How dangerous is this woman?" O'Harris asked as Jones drove.

"From what the doctor at Greenviews told me, highly," Clara was not about to lie to them. "She is extremely violent with no thought for the consequences of her actions. Mercy does not enter into her head. She is without compassion and, as far as I can tell, without remorse for anything she has done. If a person poses a threat to her, however minor, she will dispatch them rather than waste time finding a gentler solution."

O'Harris let out a long sigh.

"I've brought my revolver, Jones has one too. I wasn't sure whether we would need it, but now…"

"Guns are not my favourite thing, but on this occasion I don't think we can take any chances," Clara looked out of the window of the car and felt a cold, wave of dread slip over her. She was not sure what was about to confront them, but she doubted it was good.

"Hold up, isn't that Captain Chase?" Tommy had been looking out of the other window when he spotted a man riding a bicycle along the road.

Clara leaned over him to get a better look.

"It is," she said, hesitating for a moment before adding. "Jones, please pull over."

The car drove past Chase and pulled up a few feet away. Clara opened her door and waved to the captain who came to a halt.

"Miss Fitzgerald, have you news? I have been cycling everywhere to try and catch up with the police search."

"I know where Elaine is being held," Clara told him quickly. "We are heading there this instant. If you wish to join us…"

She did not need to finish the sentence. Chase dumped his bicycle at the side of the road and hurried to the car. Tommy budged up to the middle of the seat as Chase clambered in. Jones set off once more and Clara explained what she had learned to Chase. He was silent for a while after she was finished. It was a lot to take in, that his wife had a sister who was both insane and highly dangerous. That this deadly secret had been kept from him, kept from everyone, until it was too late.

"My word," he said at last.

"Takes some absorbing," Tommy sympathised.

"And this woman may kill Elaine?"

"The possibility is there," Clara replied. "We must act

in haste."

There was not a lot to say as they continued the journey. Mostly they all sank into their own thoughts. Clara was becoming more and more anxious about everything as the roads slipped by. She was starting to wonder what they would find at the barn. In her mind she kept picturing rushing into the building to find Elaine dead and her sister long gone. What was holding back Liz from killing her sister? Was it just a vague sense of loyalty due to Elaine's support all these years? Was that enough? Clara didn't think that Liz wasted much energy concerning herself with such considerations. She was keeping Elaine alive because it suited her. It suited her to have someone with her who had known her before. They could share memories and talk about old times. How long that would last was debatable. Possibility Liz had already grown bored with the novelty.

"I think this is it," O'Harris turned his head to look into the back seat. They were driving towards an old farmhouse flanked on two sides by outbuildings. A cluster of chickens ambled in front of the car and Jones had to almost slow to a stop to avoid hitting them.

There was no sign to indicate the name of the farm, but it seemed very quiet and looked rather neglected, like the property of an elderly farmer who was letting the place run itself down in his final years. They were in the right location, at least; O'Harris had followed the map diligently.

Clara pushed open her door and hurried out. She ran across the yard and scattered the chickens. Behind her the men were also exiting the vehicle. She heard the ominous click of revolvers being checked.

Clara hammered on the door of the farmhouse and hoped that its owner was in. She did not know his name, Dickie had not revealed it, and she knew what she was about to say would sound preposterous, but what else could she do? She hammered again, but no one was answering.

"Maybe he is tending his herd?" Tommy suggested. "It can't be far, he won't want to walk a long way to reach them."

As he spoke, there was the distant low bellow of a cow. Clara turned towards the sound and then glanced at her watch.

"We are being bloody stupid. It is about that time in the afternoon when cows are milked, of course that will be where he is."

She hurried back into the yard and in the direction of the moos. She heard the others following, but did not look back. The glance at her watch had informed her that yet another hour had disappeared, and she doubted that poor Elaine could afford the loss. Her only consolation was that Liz might have opted to go after Dickie first, fuelled by rage and fears of him betraying her, he would be the priority. A sensible soul would simply move on, abandon their plans here and head for somewhere else to continue their raiding. Clara was hoping that Elizabeth was not sensible and that her passion for revenge would overrule her common sense. Dickie had crossed her and he had to pay for that. With luck she was attempting to hunt him down at that moment and Elaine was merely an afterthought.

A field came into view. Cows were clustered at a gate where an old man was taking his time with a lever latch. The sound of people running towards him made him look up in surprise.

"Sorry to disturb you," Clara rushed up to him and blurted out. "But you have an old barn on your property that is not used?"

The old man was so astonished by the question that he just immediately answered.

"Yes, up in top field."

"How do we reach it?" Clara continued.

"Just through that gate," the old man said. "It's easy to see once you are past the trees. What is this about?"

Clara had no time to explain and was hurrying for the

gate he had indicated. Her companions followed and the old man scampered behind them as best he could. The cows mooed in protest at his abandonment.

"What is this all about?" The old man kept asking.

He was falling behind and growing breathless. On another occasion Clara would have stopped and explained, but there was simply no time. Every minute that slipped away was one less Elaine might have. She stumbled as she passed through a small corpse of trees, a clear path running through them. As she emerged on the other side an old barn came into sight at the top of a hill. Clara would have given a sigh of relief if she was not having to catch her breath. Her chest was tight, but it was not from the run, but rather from the anxiety that was snagging at her heart and making all her muscles tense. In her panic she almost raced straight to the doors of the barn, but her sense overrode her urgency and she stopped a few feet away. Here they could regroup and decide what to do.

The others clustered around her and looked at the barn. Like the previous one it had no windows, as they were unnecessary. There was, however, a hatch close to the roof-line, with a winch projecting from it, so that goods could be lifted up into the space easily. Clara could only see one set of doors ahead, but that was not to say there were no others. She turned to her comrades and raised her concerns.

"We need to know if there is any other means of exiting the building."

Jones nodded and, without waiting to be asked, headed off around the barn to look for more doors or similar entryways.

"Wait…what…what…are doing…"

Clara at last turned to see that the farmer was still pursuing them. He had fallen behind and now he was shouting at them. That was the last thing they needed. Clara hurried back down the hill to him and took his arm.

"You have heard about the kidnapping of Elaine

Chase?" She asked him.

The old farmer looked puzzled for a brief moment, then nodded his head. He was too winded to actually speak.

"We have been told that Elaine is being held in your barn," Clara told him. "And her life might be in peril."

"My barn!" The old man gasped loudly and Clara hushed him.

"We must be quiet. Please, go back down the hill and wait there. This is a dangerous business."

The old man was blinking his eyes rapidly, trying to take in how his peaceful little world could suddenly have been overtaken by this drama.

"The barn is empty," he said, as if that would counter Clara's assertions.

Clara endeavoured not to sigh.

"That is why it has been chosen as a hideout for the kidnapper and her victim," she said.

"Her?"

The old man might be out-of-breath, but he was capable of picking up Clara's slip-of-the-tongue.

"We believe a woman has taken Elaine Chase and she is very dangerous. Now, I really don't have time to explain more. You ought to go back to your cows where it is safe."

"I'm staying right here!" The old man declared sternly. "You could be anyone, thieves or some such! There have been robberies about the farms and your sort prey on old people! I won't be thought of as vulnerable! I shall remain right here and keep an eye on what you are doing!"

Clara did not intend to argue with him further.

"You are welcome to do that," she said, "but, please, keep quiet."

The old man huffed, but was silent. Clara re-joined the others. Jones was reappearing, running softly as he had been trained to do in the war. Four years of being acutely aware of enemy snipers tended to engrain stealth into you. He closed to the others before speaking.

"There is a small door on the opposite side. I tried it carefully and it does not appear locked. I suggest that it is a better entry point than those main doors," he said.

"I was wondering about that loft hatch," Tommy interjected. "There is still a rope on that winch and if we could climb up to it we could sneak in without being seen."

Clara looked up at the winch and saw what he meant. Her heart sank; she had never been good at climbing ropes.

"We should cover all the doors," Captain Chase interrupted. "There are enough of us. Two of us on these main doors, two on the side doors and one to climb into the loft and scope the area. On the signal of the scout in the loft we should all dash in and corner our suspect."

After another moment of discussion, this seemed a reasonable plan, the only point of argument was who would scramble up into the loft hatch. Chase was keen, but Clara felt he was too emotionally engaged in the situation to be a reliable scout. He might react too soon or with undue passion. When Jones volunteered to be their scout she felt that was a much better idea. Jones admitted to being a good climber and he felt he could scale the wooden planks at the side of the barn, which were overlapped and had a number of cross-beams that could provide footholds. The decision was made. Tommy and Chase were positioned on the front door, while Clara and O'Harris went around the back.

Chapter Thirty

Everything was quiet. Clara was holding her breath, scared the slightest noise would alert anyone inside the barn to their presence – If there was anyone inside the barn. O'Harris was right beside the door, ready to burst in as soon as Jones cried out. His face was tense, his mouth thinned to a line of deep concentration. Clara could not help but think that this was what it must have been like during the war, when there were operations to raid an enemy trench or fortification. Men screwed up tight to await the moment to strike. Waiting for a cry…

The shout made Clara jump even though she had been expecting it. The words were indistinguishable, but the urgency was plain. O'Harris threw open the door and they charged into the barn. At the main doors the same procedure was happening, except that the doors proved to be barred from the inside and that had brought Tommy and Chase to a halt. It also meant a quick escape through them was impossible for the woman stood in the middle of the barn.

She was dressed in pale brown trousers and a loose man's shirt which was tucked into the waistband. She had long dark hair which flew wildly about her shoulders. Clara had been picturing a slighter older version of the girl in the photograph when she imagined what Elizabeth would look like. She had not expected her to look so old. She must only be in her late twenties, but she could easily have been mistaken for someone in their forties. Her hair was streaked with grey and looked unkempt, her eyes were bloodshot, the pupils small pinpricks despite the darkness of the barn. Clara guessed she was taking some kind of drug, certainly the way she flicked about her head suggested she was out of her head on something. She had been looking up to where Jones had shouted; he was still in the loft, leaning over the edge. When O'Harris burst in through the door with Clara behind, she had turned her attention on them and roared in fury.

"Leave me alone!" She yelled. "Get out!"

From behind a pile of old hay a second female voice called out urgently.

"Help me! I am a prisoner!"

"Be quiet!" Elizabeth yelled at the speaker. She now drew a knife out of her waistband. "Do you want money? Hah! You won't get any! I'll kill every single one of you, do you think I won't!"

"Elizabeth, we are here to rescue your sister Elaine," Clara said calmly. "And to hand you over to the authorities."

"You!" Elizabeth stuttered out the word and then laughed heartily. "You cannot do anything to me. You are all weak fools, whereas I am strong, stronger than all of you!"

She glanced back up at Jones and growled. It was a horrible, animalistic sound that made Clara shudder. The woman's sanity was no longer apparent. Whether it was the drugs she had taken that had tipped her over, or the heady rush of the freedom to do as she pleased, she was no longer even attempting to pretend to be normal.

"Get down from there! Where I can see you!" She was wagging the knife at Jones.

"Stay put Jones!" O'Harris called out.

"Yes, Sir!" Jones responded, having not budged an

inch.

"You!" Elizabeth pointed the knife at O'Harris. "S...stop countering my instructions. I'll cut out your tongue, yes I will!"

Clara was creeping to the side, trying to see where Elaine was. Behind them she could hear Tommy and Captain Chase hurrying through the back door, having given up on the barred main entrance. Clara felt somewhat better knowing they were all there, but she was worried about the knife Elizabeth held. She was certain the woman would have no qualms about stabbing any of them with it.

"Elaine!" Chase called out to his wife.

"Dylan!" Elaine sobbed. "I am down here!"

"Do not touch her!" Elizabeth raced forward as Captain Chase started to run to his wife. She waved the knife and he halted a few feet from her. "She is my sister, understand? Mine!"

Chase was stunned by the creature before him and for a moment did not know what to say. Clara was not sure there was anything that could be said to bring sanity back to Elizabeth's mind.

"We are going to rescue Elaine," she told Elizabeth. "You will not stop us."

"N...n...no! She is my sister, I told you that!" Elizabeth swung the knife in Clara's direction. Chase started to step forward and she swung it back at him.

There were now four of them crowded around Elizabeth, keeping a distance from her knife but still ready to strike and catch hold of her. Elizabeth unconsciously took a pace away from them. She was surrounded, but could still do a lot of damage if she wished.

"Stay back!" She snarled at them.

"It is over, Elizabeth," Clara said patiently. "You cannot escape, not this time. Did you really think you could hold your sister prisoner?"

"I had to," Elizabeth's face fell, maybe some ray of

rationality coming back to her mind. "She was going to tell the police what I was doing. Elaine doesn't understand. That's not her fault, but I had to prevent her from telling anyone. I haven't hurt her, I never would."

Clara did not believe this last statement at all. Elizabeth sounded almost sincere, but there was a sense she was playacting, saying the words she thought people wanted to hear.

"Just put down the knife," O'Harris spoke steadily. "No one ought to get hurt."

Up in the loft above, Jones had drawn his revolver and had it ready in his hand. He shuffled and the gun rapped on the wooden beams that formed the loft floor catching Elizabeth's attention. She glanced up and in that moment Captain Chase flew at her and grabbed her around the middle.

"Get the knife!" Clara cried out, seeing that Elizabeth was still free to strike with the blade.

O'Harris raced forward and clasped her knife arm; in that same moment Elizabeth bit Captain Chase on the neck and he yelled out in pain, trying to fling himself away. The crazed woman then tried to sink her fingers into his eye sockets. Tommy and Clara were running forward to help, but the woman had turned into a monster and Chase was forced to withdraw to save himself from having his eyes put out. He had scratch marks across his cheeks from Elizabeth's savage fingers. He jumped backwards, trying to swing away from the woman and collided with O'Harris in the process.

Elizabeth was free once again and started to run towards the far door. Clara dived in front of her, knowing it was far from a wise thing to do, but having to do something. Elizabeth didn't stop her charge, she ran at Clara raising up the knife to strike. Clara did not know which way to move, she felt that whatever she did Elizabeth would attack her, and she was terrified of ending up on the floor and vulnerable to the woman's wrath.

"Clara, move!" Tommy yelled out.

They were all trying to reach her, but Elizabeth would get there first. Clara finally turned and began to run.

"Clara, Clara!" Elizabeth repeated her name as she chased her. Thoughts of escape had left the woman's mind, replaced with a blood-thirst for revenge against anyone who was handy. "Clara, Clara! Pretty Clara!"

Clara was nearly at the open door when the old farmer appeared through it.

"What's going on?" He asked.

Clara could not stop herself in time and collided with him, causing them to both tumble to the floor. Clara gave out a cry as she realised Elizabeth was right behind her and lunging down with the knife.

"Clara, Clara!"

The noise of the revolver seemed to break the spell of terror hanging over everyone. Elizabeth's headlong dash was halted instantly. She went limp almost at once and fell face forward onto Clara and the old farmer, the knife falling from her hand and wedging itself into the floor, point down into the wood. Elizabeth gave a slight moan as she landed on top of Clara, her face against Clara's shoulder.

Clara was not going to risk any chance of the woman still being intent on revenge. She shoved her away brutally and Elizabeth rolled onto the floor, now face up. She was making gurgling sounds and reddish bubbles were issuing from her mouth.

There were two bullet holes in her chest and blood was seeping out fast. Clara was smeared in it and the old farmer was burbling about a dead woman in his barn. The others came hurrying over and O'Harris crouched by Clara.

"I'm fine," she told him before he could ask. "This is all her blood."

"This is murder!" The old farmer bleated. "I'm calling the police!"

"Please do," Clara said to him coolly. "Ask that

Inspector Park-Coombs comes over personally and say that we have found Elaine Chase."

While she was saying this, Captain Chase was making his way to his wife. She had been hidden behind piles of hay, her hands tied behind her back. She was hungry and scared, but otherwise unhurt. She had been lucky; Elizabeth had wanted to reminiscence about their childhood and could not bring herself to dispatch the sister who had been the best part of that time. Elaine had nursed those feelings, hoping someone would come for her, and yet each day she was imprisoned growing more certain they would not. She burst into tears when her husband released her and flung her arms around him. Captain Chase was trembling with emotion too.

Tommy walked over to Elizabeth Denis. He knelt beside her and felt her pulse. Her eyes were dimming and her breathing had turned into pained rasps. Her hand fluttered, it seemed she was reaching out to Tommy. He took it and held it. Kindly he spoke to her.

"It's all right. Let it go now. Let it go."

Elizabeth tried to take a deep breath and failed. Her chest fell and her eyes drifted closed. Her hand that had clutched Tommy's tightly for a moment, now went limp. She was gone.

"Who shot her?" Clara asked.

"That would be me, miss," Jones had finally extracted himself from the loft. "Didn't think I had an option, miss."

"Thank you," Clara said.

Jones smiled.

"Couldn't let her hurt you, miss."

The party slowly regrouped. The old farmer had disappeared, though not very fast, and soon the police would arrive. There would be explaining to do, but Clara doubted Park-Coombs would waste much time over it. The situation had always seemed to have an inevitable outcome. Elizabeth was not the sort of woman who would let herself be captured alive and her ferocity made her too dangerous to allow her to escape.

Captain Chase helped his wife walk towards them. She had been only supplied with limited food and water for a fortnight and she looked weak and thin. Her ankles had often been tied up like her wrists and they were swollen. But her eyes were bright and she looked elated, as if a miracle had occurred that she could hardly of hoped for.

"Miss Fitzgerald, I owe you the greatest of thanks," Captain Chase stood before Clara, holding his wife tight to him. "Without you, I don't think we would have found my wife. You never gave up even when things looked at their worst. Especially the other night…"

He tailed off, not wanting to say more about his suicide attempt. Clara needed to hear no more.

"You are most welcome, Captain Chase," she told him. "And you Mrs Chase. I have heard much about you and to meet you in person is most gratifying."

"Thank you, from the bottom of my heart, thank you," Elaine smiled and then burst into tears, still not quite believing her ordeal was over.

"Let's get out of this barn," O'Harris suggested to them all. "The sun is shining and I think we could all do with the fresh air."

They found an old log outside that was wide enough to allow Captain Chase and his wife to sit side-by-side on. The others rested on the grass. The sun was indeed soothing and the trauma of the last few moments slowly lifted. Jones said he would walk to the farmhouse and see if he could persuade the farmer to supply them with some food and drink. Elaine did not yet feel up to walking and the others felt they should stay and await the police. Jones walked away down the hill.

"What happened Elaine?" Chase asked his wife. "How did this all start?"

Elaine looked abashed.

"My sister was confined to an asylum when I was a girl. We were very close, and I didn't understand. I thought my parents had been mean to her. I was told I could not speak of her to anyone, she was a secret, but that did not stop me finding out the address of the asylum and sending birthday cards and Christmas cards to my sister. I wrote letters too, but the asylum wrote back and said they would not pass them on. It was their rule," Elaine sighed. "The years passed, and it became more of a habit than anything to send the cards. Sometimes Elizabeth would send a card back. When we moved into the cottage I included our new address in the card, so she would know where to send hers. I never gave it a thought.

"Then, a few weeks ago, she turned up on the doorstep. I was so surprised. Elizabeth asked had I not received the letter from the asylum and I said I had not. She laughed and said it must have got lost in the post, how typical! I laughed too and then we hugged, and I cried. I was so pleased to see her."

Elaine fell silent as she recalled what had happened next. How she had realised her sister was up to no good and felt a fool for believing in her. How she had hoped to convince her sister to behave by telling her she would go to the police, and how that had resulted in her being kidnapped off the road.

"That day, Elizabeth had planned to snatch me when I walked home from the Players, but when I got in Miss Erskine's car she had to alter her plans. She ran out in the road in front of us to drive Miss Erskine off the road!"

Elaine shuddered with the horror of it all. No one knew what to say. Clara's gaze drifted down the hill. A figure was walking up. She recognised him.

"Here comes the inspector," she rose to her feet and smiled at Elaine. "He will understand. Explain it all to him."

Elaine gave her a weak smile.

Then they all turned to await the inspector's arrival.

Chapter Thirty-one

The inspector did understand. Clara escorted him to the body of Elizabeth Denis and explained what had happened. She was trying not to think too hard about how close the woman had stood to her with a knife in her hand. Inspector Park-Coombs was solemn, as a policeman must be when his suspect has been shot dead by a member of the public. The situation did not take a great deal of elaborating; Park-Coombs said he would contact Greenviews to confirm what they had told Clara about Elizabeth, purely as part of procedure. He did not doubt Clara's statement that the woman was dangerous and unstable. The fact she had held her sister prisoner in a barn was evidence enough of that.

Clara told Park-Coombs about Dickie and they both concurred that rounding him up would do little good.

"Easily led, that one," Park-Coombs nodded. "Not really bad. In any case, don't want people thinking you'll turn them into the police the second they speak to you."

"That would be awkward," Clara agreed.

Les Martin was another matter. Park-Coombs' face clouded as he heard the name.

"He wouldn't let us search his farm," he said. "I imagine that would be because we would have found stuff we shouldn't have there."

Elizabeth had not been hiding her stolen goods in the same place as her sister, enough sense in her head to know that it was best to keep her operations separate. No stolen goods were to be found in the barn.

"I'll deal with Les Martin," Park-Coombs said. "You and the others get along home."

When Clara stepped back outside, she saw that two police constables were bringing a makeshift stretcher up the hill for Elaine. Jones had clearly organised this, as he was walking behind them looking like a very cocky sheepdog herding his charges forward. O'Harris grinned at Clara.

"Always was a little big for his boots," he whispered to her.

"On this occasion, I am glad for it," she replied.

Slowly the party descended down the hill. Elaine looked exhausted and close to unconsciousness. Jones promised that an ambulance had been summoned and would arrive soon. The farm did not have a telephone, but another constable had been sent off with instructions to find one. They could have taken Elaine in the car, but it was agreed that an ambulance would be better as she could remain on the stretcher. Captain Chase fussed over his wife until the clatter of horses' hooves indicated the arrival of the ambulance. Then she was loaded carefully inside and they disappeared.

All that was left was for the others to drive home. Tommy glanced at his watch as he climbed into the Bentley.

"Gosh! Nearly time to collect Annie!"

"She is coming home today?" O'Harris queried, receiving an affirmative answer from both Clara and Tommy. "You best take the car then. Jones can drop me near the house and then take you to the hospital."

"You really don't have to, we would have managed," Clara protested mildly.

"Nonsense!" Jones declared from the front seat. "What

am I here for if I don't drive people about?"

"Shooting dangerous criminals, old boy," O'Harris said dryly.

No one knew whether to laugh or grimace at that.

Annie was picked up on time and deposited along with Clara and Tommy safely at home. She looked tired just from the journey and walked stiffly. She glanced up the stairs, knowing she would have to mount them to reach her bedroom and her weariness increased.

"Don't worry," Tommy told her, "We have made up a bed in the downstairs morning room. Where I used to have my bedroom."

Annie's look of relief said it all. Clara was a little hurt that her friend had not expected them to automatically make such a consideration for her. Maybe Annie didn't give them enough credit.

"There is something else I have arranged for you," Tommy told Annie. "But it will wait until you have recovered."

"Go settle in your room," Clara informed her, feeling somewhat empowered to be back acting as a nurse. "I have made a shepherd's pie for dinner and plum duff for pudding."

"Oh," Annie said, looking mildly worried.

Clara rolled her eyes at her.

"Have some faith!"

Tommy helped Annie to her temporary bedroom and Clara chuckled to herself as she headed into the kitchen. Annie's expectations of Clara's domestic abilities were really low, that was obvious enough. She would aim to improve upon that in the coming weeks. The private detective business was going to be temporarily on hold while she restored her friend to full health. It was the least she could do for Annie.

~~~*~~~

A fortnight later Clara took tea with Captain O'Harris at

the Convalescence Home. They sat on the terrace overlooking the gardens where several of the patients were getting a cricket lesson from Tommy. He had been a star bowler before the war and there had been tentative talk of getting him back on the team. He might have a limp, but he still had a sound bowling arm and he could run almost as fast as he used to. Annie was sitting in a deck chair in the shade of a tree, watching proceedings. Clara gave a sigh of contentment as she found herself surrounded by the people she loved so dearly.

"Happy?" O'Harris asked her.

"Very," Clara replied.

"Have you heard anything more about the Chase case?"

"Elaine is doing well. She was even up to walking the boards as Lady Macbeth," Clara smiled.

"Much to the chagrin of certain people!"

"And to the delight of others," Clara laughed. "Greenviews have been informed of what happened and I believe a full review of their security procedures is being implemented. Elizabeth was buried quietly and privately, without her family attending. It as an unmarked grave, I believe."

O'Harris was silent a moment. Clara took a sip of tea.

"I wonder if she would have cared?" He said at last.

"From an emotional point of view, I doubt it. From the context of her ego, yes, she would have cared very much. She was the sort of person who expected the world to go to town for her, who thought she was the most important person around and no one else mattered," Clara tilted her head. "Thank goodness she was mistaken."

"And Les Martin?"

"The farmer who betrayed his neighbours? Oh, the police raided his yard and found all the stolen goods in his various outbuildings. He attempted to say he was not involved, that someone had asked to store the stuff there, but no one believed him," Clara explained. "He will be in court next month I believe for his first hearing. And that brings to a conclusion the farm robberies scare."

"Well, now I've asked about the grim stuff, let's talk about cheerful news. I want to hear all about that baking contest."

Clara burst out laughing and then pressed a hand over her mouth.

"Oh, I shouldn't, but it was so extraordinary," Clara glanced over to Annie who was absorbed in watching the cricket practice. "Tommy set up a camp bed in the kitchen, where Annie could recline and call out instructions as he endeavoured to bake a perfect Victoria Sponge. They were at it every day for a full week. Annie started off so patiently, but every attempt made her more frustrated. Apparently, his elbow action was shocking."

"Elbow action?" O'Harris looked baffled.

"For beating together the butter and sugar. There is a knack. It is rather all in the wrist, but the elbow must act as a stabiliser. Tommy was prone to using too much elbow and too little wrist."

"You learn something new every day," O'Harris raised his eyebrows, making Clara chuckle more.

"Honestly, I tasted cake after cake and thought they were all delightful, but what do I know?" Clara winked.

"Annie was not convinced the stratagem would work, but it was the best of a bad situation and on Saturday there was a perfectly lovely sponge ready to be taken to the competition. Annie felt bad putting her name to it, as she had not been 'hands-on' in the making, but after much debate it was agreed that only with her input could such a fine cake have been made. She said her name could be on the entry card, as long as Tommy put his name too, as it was a joint effort."

"A worthy compromise," O'Harris said.

"And so the cake went off to the show. We all attended, Annie in Tommy's old wheelchair as she is still limited to how much walking she can do. It was a delightful day."

"And the outcome of the contest?"

Clara lowered her voice.

"Second."

"Not beaten by the detested Jane Jenkins?" O'Harris asked in mock horror.

"No, actually, that was the quite the event of the day. Jane Jenkins proudly presented her cake which was the only one out of them all to be filled with fresh cream instead of butter icing. This naturally made it stand out and there was a little uncertainty if that would seal her as the winner. She was crowing before the judges had even applied the taste test."

"Sounds like a recipe for disaster," O'Harris nodded wisely.

"It was," Clara had to resist smiling, as that rather seemed like gloating. "Jane had acquired her cream a couple of days before, and the weather had been remarkably warm. By the time she whipped it up for her cake I think it was safe to say it was 'on the turn'. The cakes were sat in a tent on the green, a very warm tent, and the cream did not stand up to the conditions so well. It looked very nice, but the first bite told all. I can still remember the appalled looks on the judges' faces as they tasted the cream and then had to find some way of spitting it out politely.

"Needless to say, the cake was hastily removed from the competition and dispatched into the nearest rubbish bin. Jane was mortified and fled the contest, heartily embarrassed. I believe I heard Annie tutting to herself about the difficulties of using fresh cream."

"Then, if Jane did not win, and Annie came second, who makes the finest cake in town?"

Clara grinned with amusement.

"That would be little Robbie Buttress, son of Henry Buttress the butcher. Robbie is all of ten and a keen baker. He wants to run his own cake shop when he grows up. I believe it will be a fine success and even Annie could not be disappointed at losing to him. He had worked his heart out on that cake. You know poor Robbie's mother died in the 'flu epidemic?"

"I did not, though I know of Buttress Butchery."

"Robbie learned to bake from his grandmother. He cooked that sponge all by himself, even the jam was made by him. His father was so proud. I saw him discreetly wipe away a tear from his eye. There could have been no worthier winner and Annie was quite happy to come second to him."

"Then this baking war between her and Jane Jenkins is at an end?" O'Harris asked.

"I doubt that," Clara smirked. "Those two will be at war until the day they die, but at least Annie has the upper hand when it comes to sponges."

"We all have our pride and our envy," Captain O'Harris noted. "It is learning to tame them that is the hardest part."

"Not everyone does," Clara's mind had turned back to Elizabeth Denis, who was consumed by both her pride in herself and her envy of others. A recipe for disaster, for sure.

"Tommy really should play for the county team again," O'Harris noted as Tommy demonstrated an over-arm bowl. "I think I shall try to persuade him."

"Why not?" Clara replied, settling a little more into her chair.

Her contentment returned. Everything in that precise moment was right with the world. Annie was recovering nicely, Tommy and O'Harris were enjoying life and putting their war demons behind them. And then there was Clara. She was quite happy to just sit and bask in the glow of other's wellbeing, that made her feel good.

What a shame Elizabeth Denis could not have been like that. How much better her life and the life of her family would have been. Clara shut that thought away. Today was not about Elizabeth Denis. Today was about Clara and her friends.

Let this moment last forever, Clara thought to herself. She could live a lifetime on this moment.

Printed in Great Britain
by Amazon